She Died a Lady

JOHN DICKSON CARR

writing as

CARTER DICKSON

Polygon

First published in 1943 by Penguin Books.
This edition published in Great Britain in 2019 by Polygon,
an imprint of Birlinn Ltd.

West Newington House
10 Newington Road
Edinburgh
EH9 1QS

www.polygonbooks.co.uk

1

ISBN 978 1 84697 493 9
eBook ISBN 978 1 78885 207 4

British Library Cataloguing in Publication Data
A catalogue record for this book is available on request
from the British Library.

Typeset by 3btype.com

1

Rita Wainright was an attractive woman, and only thirty-eight. Alec, her husband, must have been twenty years older. At that dangerous phase of Rita's mental and emotional life, she met Barry Sullivan.

As for me, I regret to say I was the very last person who noticed what was going on.

The family doctor is in a position at once privileged and difficult. He knows nearly everything. He can preach all kinds of sermons. But he can do this only if people come to him for advice. And he can't discuss the matter with anybody else. A gossiping doctor is one abomination which even this age hasn't yet inflicted on us.

Of course, I am not very active nowadays. My son Tom – he is Dr Tom where I am Dr Luke – has taken over most of the practice. I can't, any longer, get up in the middle of the night and drive a dozen miles over bad North Devon roads, as it is Tom's pride and joy to do. He is the born country G.P.; he loves his work as I loved it. When Tom goes to see a patient, he gets wrapped up in the case and tells the patient all the imposing medical terms for what's wrong with him. This impresses and pleases the patient; it inspires confidence to start with.

'I'm very much afraid,' Tom will say, in that grave way of his, 'that we have here . . .' And then out reels the Latin, yards of it at a time.

True, a few of them insist on sticking to me. This is merely because there are still a lot of people who would rather have an indifferent elderly doctor than a good young one. When I was a young fellow, nobody would trust a doctor who didn't have a beard. And something of that idea still exists in little communities like ours.

Lyncombe, on the North Devon coast, is a village which has since come into terrible notoriety. It shocks and jars me to write about this even yet, but it has to be done. Lynmouth (which you probably know) is the seaside resort. Then you climb the steep hill, or take the funicular, up to Lynton on the cliffs. Farther still up the slope is Lynbridge; and then, where the road straightens out before it crosses the wastes of Exmoor, is Lyncombe.

Alec and Rita Wainright lived in a large bungalow some distance farther on. They were isolated, four miles from anybody or anything. But Rita had a car, and didn't seem to mind. It was a beautiful spot, if a little damp and windy: the back garden of 'Mon Repos' stretched to the very edge of the cliffs. Here there was a romantic promontory called Lovers' Leap. Seventy feet below, the sea foamed in over rocks; there were strong currents and deep, evil tides.

I liked Rita Wainright, and still like her. Under those artistic poses of hers, she was genuinely kind-hearted. Servants worshipped her. She might have been flighty and unstable, but you could feel her vitality wherever she went. And nobody could deny that she was a fine figure of a woman: glossy black hair, tawny skin, bold eyes, and a nervous intensity of manner. She wrote verses, and should have had a younger husband.

Alec Wainright was more of a puzzle, though I knew him well and used to go out there on Saturday nights to play cards.

At sixty, Alec had a fine brain going a little to seed like his habits and manners. He was well-to-do in his own right; he had been a professor of mathematics, and married Rita out in Canada eight years before when he had been teaching at McGill University. Shortish and thick-set, with a gentle voice and a preoccupied manner, he seemed to the younger people an odd choice for Rita. But he had – at least, before the situation grew desperate – a real twinkle of humour. He could talk entertainingly when he chose. And he was very fond of Rita; he had a passion for hanging her with diamonds.

The trouble was that, even before all this, Alec had been drinking too much. I don't mean that his drinking was loud or in any way objectionable. On the contrary, you hardly noticed it. Each evening he would quietly put down half a bottle of whisky, and then go quietly to bed. He drew still further into his shell; he seemed to fold together like a hedgehog. Then came the shock of the war.

You remember that warm Sunday morning, with the September sunshine over everything, when the announcement came over the radio: I was alone in the house, in my dressing-gown. The voice, saying, 'We are at war,' seemed to fill every part of the house. My first thought was: 'Well, here it is again,' in a kind of blankness; and then: 'Will Tom have to go?'

For a while I sat and looked at my shoes. Laura, Tom's mother, died while I was in the last one. They played 'If You Were The Only Girl In The World', and it makes my eyes sting sometimes when I hear that tune.

I got up, put on my coat, and went out to the High Street. There was a fine show of asters in our front garden, with the chrysanthemums just budding. Harry Pierce, at the Coach and Horses over the way, was just opening up his bar; you could hear the door scrape and bump against quiet. You could also hear the noise of a motor car coming slowly along the street.

Rita Wainright was driving her S.S. Jaguar, which glittered with highlights under the sun. Rita wore some close-fitting flowered stuff, which set off her figure. She seemed to stretch lithely, like a cat, as she let in clutch and brake to stop the car. Beside her sat Alec, looking shapeless and shabby in an old suit and Panama hat. It startled me a little: he seemed old and deathly even then, though his gentle expression remained.

'Well,' Alec said flatly, 'it's happened.'

I admitted it had. 'Did you hear the speech?'

'No,' answered Rita, who seemed under a suppressed excitement of some kind. 'Mrs Parker ran out into the road to tell us.' The brown eyes, with their very luminous whites, were bewildered. 'It doesn't seem *possible*, does it?'

'I am sick,' said Alec gently, 'of the stupidity of mankind.'

'But it isn't *our* stupidity, dear.'

'How do you know it isn't?' asked Alec.

Some yards down the road, a gate creaked. Molly Grange came out, with a young man I had never seen before.

Molly is one of my favourites. At this time she was a straightforward, sensible, pretty girl in her middle twenties. She had the fair hair and blue eyes of her mother, with her father's practicality. But most of us, certainly Rita at least, glanced first at the stranger.

I must admit he was a fine-looking young man. His appearance struck me as vaguely familiar until I placed it: he looked like a film star, but not offensively so. He was tall and well-built and he had a pleasant laugh. His thick hair, parted on one side, was as black and glossy as Rita's. His features were handsome, and he had light, quizzical eyes. He was about Molly's own age. In contrast to the drabness of our own clothes, he wore a cream-white suit which fitted him loosely, and a somewhat startling tie.

That must have been when the spark touched the powder-train.

Rita called: 'Hell-*o*, Molly! Heard the news?' Molly hesitated, and it was easy to guess why. Rita had recently had a violent row with Molly's father, the Wainrights' solicitor. But both of them ignored that.

'Yes,' said Molly. Her forehead wrinkled. 'Pretty dreadful, isn't it? May I present . . . Mrs Wainright, Professor Wainright. Mr Sullivan.'

'Barry Sullivan,' explained the newcomer. 'Very glad to meet you.'

'Mr Sullivan,' said Molly, somewhat unnecessarily, 'is an American.'

'Are you really?' cried Rita. 'I'm from Canada myself.'

'Is that so? What part of Canada?'

'Montreal.'

'Know it well!' declared Mr Sullivan, leaning on the door of the car. But his hand slipped, and he stepped back again. Both he and Rita seemed suddenly a little rattled. Rita's matured beauty – at thirty-eight, the best of all ages – came up like a blown flame. This boy of twenty-five annoyed me.

All of us, perhaps, might have noticed more if we had not been so preoccupied. For myself, I completely forgot young Sullivan. Certainly it was months before I saw him again, though he spent a good deal of time with the Wainrights during the fortnight he was there.

He was, it appeared, an actor of some promise. He lived in London, and was staying at Lyncombe on holiday. He went in bathing with Rita – both of them were fine swimmers – he played tennis with Rita; he photographed and was photographed by Rita; he walked to the Valley of Rocks with Rita. Alec liked him, or at least came partly out of torpor in the young man's presence. I suppose there must have been gossip, especially when he came down once or twice during the winter to visit them. But I never heard any gossip.

We were all, for our sins, rather cheerful during that winter of '39 to '40. When bad weather put an end to my visits to the Wainrights, I lost touch with them. Tom bounded about the roads in his Ford, doing five men's work. I sat by the fire, saw an occasional patient, and tried to take my retirement seriously. When you have a bad heart, you can't play the jumping-jack at sixty-five. But I heard that Alec Wainright was taking the war badly.

'He's become a news-fiend,' somebody told me. 'And his booze bill at Spence and Minstead's –'

'How do you mean, news-fiend?'

'Turns on the radio at eight o'clock. Hears the same news-bulletin at one, again at six, back at nine, and sees he doesn't miss it again at midnight. Sits crouched up over that radio like a paralytic. What the devil's wrong with him? What's he got to worry about?'

On the tenth of May, 1940, we found out.

Those were bewildered days. Nazi tanks were loose like blackbeetles across a map. You could almost smell the smoke of destruction from the other side. We puzzled our wits as to what was wrong; in a daze we saw the fall of Paris and the collapse of all ordered things. It was as though you found that the very school-books of your youth had been telling you lies. I need not describe those times. But on the twenty-second of May, with the French Channel ports already menaced, Rita Wainright rang me up.

'Dr Luke,' the pleasant contralto voice said, 'I want to see you. Badly.'

'Of course. Let's have a hand of cards one evening, shall we?'

'I mean – I want to see you professionally.'

'But you're Tom's patient, my dear.'

'I don't care. I want to see *you*.'

(Tom, I knew, never liked Rita much. It is true that she tended to dramatise everything, which is anathema to a medical man trying to discover what is wrong. Tom never allowed for this, and said that the damned woman would drive him scatty.)

'*Can* I come and see you? Now?'

'Very well, if you insist. Come by the side door to the surgery.'

I hadn't an idea what was wrong. When she entered, shutting the door with a firmness that made its glass panel rattle, her air was one of defiance underlaid by hysteria. Yet in a way she had never looked handsomer. There was a bloom and richness about her, a sparkle of eye and a flush of natural colour, which made Rita seem twenty-eight instead of thirty-eight. She wore white; her finger-nails were scarlet. She sat down in the old armchair, crossed her knees, and said unexpectedly:

'I've quarrelled with my solicitor. No clergyman would do it, naturally. And I don't know any J.P.s. You've got to . . .'

Then Rita stopped. Her eyes seemed to shift and change as though she could not reach the proper determination. She pressed her lips together, showing mental indecision like a physical pain.

'Got to what, my dear?'

'You've got to give me something to make me sleep.' She had changed her mind; no doubt about that. This was not her original request. But her voice rose. 'I mean it, Dr Luke! I'll go off my head if you don't!'

'What seems to be the trouble?'

'I can't sleep!'

'Yes, but why not go to Tom?'

'Tom's a slowcoach. And he'd only lecture me.'

'Whereas I wouldn't?'

Rita smiled a little. It was a smile which would have turned my head thirty years ago. But it was more than that. It erased the fine lines from the corners of her brown eyes; it showed the charm and the muddle-headed good nature behind all those emotions. Then the smile faded.

'Dr Luke,' she said, 'I'm terribly, horribly in love with Barry Sullivan. I've – I've slept with him.'

'That's no news, my dear, from the look of you.'

This took her aback.

'You mean you can *tell*?'

'In a way. But never mind that. Go on.'

'I suppose it shocks you.'

'It doesn't exactly shock me, Rita, but it worries me like the very devil. How long has this been going on? What the lawyers call intimacy, I mean.'

'The – the last time was last night. Barry's staying at our house. He came into my room.'

No doubt about it, to say I was worried would be putting it mildly. I felt that cardiac twinge which is a bad danger-sign, so I shut my eyes and waited for a moment.

'What about Alec?'

'He doesn't know,' Rita returned promptly. Again her eyes shifted. 'He doesn't seem to notice anything much, nowadays. And, anyway, I doubt whether he would mind if he did now.'

(More danger-signs.)

'People notice much more than you think they do, Rita. As regards being fair to Alec . . .'

'Do you think I don't know that?' she cried out. It was hitting on the nerve. 'I'm fond of Alec. It's not a lie or a pretence: I really am fond of Alec, and I wouldn't hurt him for the world. If he would mind, I couldn't face it. But you don't understand. This isn't just an infatuation or a – a carnal thing.'

(That, my dear, is the very reverse of true. But you probably believe you are telling the truth, so let's leave it at that.)

'It's the real thing. It's my whole being and my whole life. I know what you're going to say. You're going to say Barry is a little younger than I am. That's true, but *he* doesn't mind.'

'Yes. What does Mr Sullivan say to all this?'

'Please don't talk about him like that.'

'Like what?'

'"Mr Sullivan",' Rita mimicked. 'Like a judge. He wants to go and tell Alec.'

'With what end? Divorce?'

Rita drew a deep breath. She shook herself impatiently.

She stared round the little surgery as though it were a prison. I think, too, that she felt it as a prison. This was no acting or self-dramatisation. A poised and reasonably intelligent woman had begun to talk, even to think, like a girl of eighteen. Rita's fingers twisted a white handbag all the time her eyes roved.

'Alec's a Catholic,' she said. 'Didn't you know that?'

'As a matter of fact, I didn't.'

The strained eyes fastened on me.

'He wouldn't divorce me even if I wanted him to. But, don't you see, that isn't the point. It's the thought of *wounding* Alec. It's the thought of how he'd look, maybe, if I did tell him. He's been so terribly good to me. He's old and he hasn't got anybody to turn to.'

'Yes. There's that.'

'So I can't just run away and leave him, divorce or no divorce. But I can't give up Barry, either. I can't! You don't know what it's like, Dr Luke! Barry hates this clandestine business as much as I do. He won't wait for ever; and, if I put him off much longer, there's no telling what might happen. It's all such a *mess*.' She looked at a corner of the ceiling. 'If only Alec would die, or something like that . . .'

A certain thought, which entered unbidden, turned me cold.

'What,' I asked, 'are you intending to do?'

'But that's just it! I don't know!'

'Rita, how long have you been married?'

'Eight years.'

'Has this sort of thing ever happened before?'

Round swung her eyes, grown guileless and imploring in their intensity. 'It hasn't, Dr Luke! I swear it hasn't! That's why I'm sure this is the real – well, grand passion. I've read about it and even written about it, but I never knew what it was like.'

'Suppose you did run away with this fellow . . .'

'I won't *do* that, I tell you!'

'Never mind. Suppose it. How would you live? Has he got any money?'

'Not much, I'm afraid. But –' Again Rita hesitated, on the brink of telling me something; and again, miserably, she decided against it. Her teeth fastened in her full under-lip. 'I'm not saying it isn't a practical consideration. But why bother about it at a time like this? It's Alec I'm worried about. Always Alec, Alec, Alec, Alec!'

Then she became literary. The dangerous thing about this high-flown talk was that she meant every word of it.

'His face is a kind of ghost that keeps coming between me and Barry all the time. I want him to be happy and yet neither of us can be happy.'

'Tell me, Rita. Were you ever in love with Alec?'

'Yes, I was. In a way. He was perfectly charming when I first knew him. He used to call me Dolores. After Swinburne's Dolores, you know.'

'And now?'

'Well? He doesn't beat me, or anything like that. But –'

'How long has it been since you've had physical relations with Alec?'

Her face grew tragic.

'I keep telling you, Dr Luke, it isn't like that at all! This affair with Barry is something entirely different. It's a kind of spiritual rebirth. Now don't rub your hand over your forehead, and sit there looking at me over your spectacles and down your nose!'

'I was only . . .'

'It's something I can't describe. I can help Barry in his art, and he can help me in mine. He's going to be a great actor one day. He laughs at me when I say that; but it's true, and I can help him. All the same, that doesn't solve my particular problem. I'm nearly going crazy under it. I want your advice, of course, though I know what it'll be beforehand. But what I want most of all is something that will make me sleep for just one night. Can't you *please* give me something that will make me *sleep?*'

Fifteen minutes later, Rita left. I stood and watched her go down the side path between the laurel hedges. Once, before reaching the gate, she looked into her handbag as though to make sure something was there. She had been on the edge of hysteria while telling her story. But hysteria was gone now. In the way she touched and smoothed her hair, in the very set of her shoulders, you could see a dreaminess as well as a defiance. She was eager to get back home to 'Mon Repos' and to Barry Sullivan.

2

On the evening of Saturday, the thirtieth of June, I went out to the Wainrights' house to play cards.

It was thick, thundery weather. Matters were straining towards a breaking-point in more respects than one. France had capitulated; the Führer was in Paris; a disorganised weaponless British army had crawled back, exhausted, to dry its wounds on the beaches where it might presently have to fight. But we were still reasonably cheerful, with myself as complacent as the rest. 'We're all together now,' we said; 'it'll be better' – God knows why.

Even in our little world of Lyncombe there was impending tragedy as clearly to be heard as a knocking at a door. I learned more about the Wainright-Sullivan business when I talked to Tom on the day after Rita's visit.

'*May* cause scandal?' echoed Tom, who was fastening his bag preparatory to the morning round of calls. '*May* cause scandal? It's a flaming scandal already.'

'You mean it's being talked about in the village?'

'It's being talked about all over North Devon. If it weren't for this war situation, you'd hear nothing else.'

'Then why wasn't *I* told about it?'

'My dear governor,' said Tom, in that irritatingly kindly way of his, 'you can't even see what's under your own nose. And nobody ever tells you gossip anyway. You just wouldn't be interested. Let me help you into a chair.'

'Confound it, sir, I'm not as doddering as all that!'

'No, but you've got to be careful of that heart,' said my serious-minded son. 'All the same,' he added, whacking shut the catch of his medicine-case, 'it beats me how people can carry on like that and think they're not noticed. That woman has completely lost her head.'

'What's . . . being said?'

'Oh, that Mrs Wainright is an evil woman leading on an innocent young man.' Tom shook his head, drew himself up, and prepared to lecture. 'That's medically and biologically unsound, by the way. You see –'

'I am sufficiently acquainted with the facts of life, young man. Your presence in this world testifies to that. So *he* gets all the sympathy, then?'

'If you could call it sympathy, yes.'

'What's this Barry Sullivan like? Do you know?'

'I haven't met him, but they say he's a decent sort. Free spender; typical Yank; that kind of thing. All the same, it wouldn't surprise me if he and Mrs Wainright got together and murdered the old man.'

Tom delivered this statement with a wise and portentous air. He didn't believe it himself; it was just his way of airing knowledge, or fancied knowledge; but it struck so sharply and unpleasantly in line with my own thoughts that I reacted as fathers will.

'Nonsense!' I said.

Tom teetered back on his heels.

'You think so?' he said grandly. 'Look at Thompson and Bywaters. Look at Rattenbury and Stoner. Look at . . . well, there must be a lot of them. A married woman approaching middle age falls for a mere youngster.'

'Who are you to be talking about mere youngsters? You're only thirty-five yourself.'

'And what do they do?' inquired Tom. 'They don't do anything sensible, like getting a divorce. No. They go scatty and kill the husband. It happens in nine cases out of ten; but don't ask me *why* it happens.'

(Talk to one of them, my lad; see the nerves shake and the brain dither and the self-control dissolve; then perhaps you'll understand.)

'But I can't stand here gassing,' pursued Tom, stamping his feet on the floor, and picking up the medicine-case. He is large and broad and sandy-haired, as I was at his age. 'Got an interesting case out Exmoor way.'

'It must be something special, if you call it interesting.'

Tom grinned.

'It's not the case. It's the personality. Old boy named Merrivale, Sir Henry Merrivale. He's staying with Paul Ferrars at Ridd Farm.'

'What's wrong with him?'

'He fractured his big toe. He was up to some shenanigans – can't imagine what – and he fractured his big toe. It's worth going out there just to hear his language. I'm going to keep him in a wheelchair for six weeks. But if you *are* interested in Mrs Wainright's latest escapade . . .'

'I am.'

'Right. I'll see if I can pump Paul Ferrars. Discreetly, of course. He must know her pretty well; he painted her picture a year or so ago.'

But I forbade this as unethical, and preached Tom quite a lecture about it. So I waited for over a month, while the world continued to clatter round our ears and people talked of little but Adolf Hitler. Barry Sullivan, I learned, had gone back to London.

I drove out once to see Rita and Alec, but the maid said they were at Minehead. Then, on that overcast Saturday morning, I met Alec.

Anybody would have been shocked at the change in him. I met him on the cliff-road, between Lyncombe and 'Mon Repos'. He was stumping along slowly and aimlessly, his hands clasped behind his back; even at a distance you could see him shaking his head from side to side. He wore no hat; the wind ruffled his sparse greyish hair and flapped back his old alpaca coat.

Though shortish in figure, Alec Wainright used to have a thick breadth of shoulder. Now he seemed to have shrunk. His square, blunt-featured face, with the kindly expression and grey eyes under tufted eyebrows, had become blurred. It was not that the face had degenerated, or even changed in any definable way: it had merely lost its expression, heightened by a slight twitching of the eyelid.

Alec was not drunk, but he was in a dream. I had to call out to him.

'Dr Croxley!' he said, and cleared his throat. His eyes lighted up a little. To Alec I was not Dr Luke or even plain Luke; I had the formal title. 'It's good to see you,' he continued, and kept on clearing his throat. 'I've been wanting to see you. Intending to see you. But –'

He made a vague gesture, as though he could not at the moment recall the reason.

'Come over here,' he urged. 'This bench. Sit down.'

There was a stiff breeze blowing, and I said I wished Alec had a hat. Vaguely fussed, he fished an old cloth cap out of his pocket and crammed it on. Then he sat down beside me on the bench. Still he kept shaking his head from side to side in a depressed way.

'They don't realise,' he said in his gentle voice. 'They don't *realise!*'

This made me turn round, until I saw what he meant.

'He's coming. He'll be here any day now,' said Alec. 'He's got the planes; he's got troops; he's got everything. But when I tell them at the pub, they say, "Oh, for God's sake shut up! Haven't we got enough to depress us without that?"'

Alec sat back, folding his stumpy arms.

'And, do you know, in a way they're quite right. But they don't *realise*. Look here!' This time he fished a crumpled newspaper out of his pocket. 'See this item?'

'Which item?'

'Never mind. The liner *Washington* is coming to Galway to pick up Americans who want to get back to the States. The American Embassy says it's their last chance. What does that mean? Invasion. Don't they realise that?'

His fretful voice trailed away. But, at the words, no friend of Alec's could fail to see a sudden hope.

'Speaking of Americans . . .' I began.

'Yes. I knew there was something I wanted to tell you.' Alec rubbed his forehead. 'It's about young Sullivan. Barry Sullivan, you know. Nice lad. I don't know if you've met him?'

'Is *he* going back by the *Washington*?'

Alec blinked at me and made fussed gestures.

'No, no, no! I never said that. Barry's not going back to America. On the contrary, he's come down to visit us again. Arrived last night.'

This, I think, was where I became most conscious of the conviction that we were heading for disaster.

'Here's what I wondered,' pursued Alec, with a meagre attempt at heartiness in his voice. 'What about coming out to the house tonight for some cards. Like the old days. Eh?'

'With the greatest of pleasure. But –'

'I'd thought of inviting Molly Grange,' said Alec. 'You know: the solicitor's little girl. Young Barry seems rather keen on her, and I've had her out there for him several times.' Alec smiled a rumpled smile; he was really anxious to please. 'I had even thought of inviting Paul Ferrars, that artist chap at Ridd Farm, and a guest he's got, and perhaps Agnes Doyle. Then we could have two tables.'

'Whatever you say.'

'But Molly, it seems, isn't coming home from Barnstaple this weekend. And, anyway, Rita thinks it would be more cosy and intimate if we just had the four of us. This is the maid's night off, and a bigger crowd is awkward.'

'Of course.'

Alec looked out to sea, a wrinkle between his eyebrows. His determination to please, his evident concentration on it despite other matters that racked his mind, was dogged and somewhat pathetic.

'We ought to entertain more, you know. Yes. We really ought to entertain more. Have young people about us. I realise it's dull for Rita. And she says it's bad for me. Thinks I'm getting morbid.'

'You are. And, frankly, if you don't stop this drinking –'

'My dear fellow!' breathed Alec, in a tone of hollow and injured astonishment. 'Are you trying to tell me I'm drunk?'

'No. Not now. But you polish off a pint of whisky every night before you go to bed, and if you don't stop it –'

Once more Alec looked out to sea. Folding his hands, he smoothed the baggy skin across the backs of them. He kept clearing his throat. But his tone changed: he sounded less hazy and muddled.

'It hasn't been easy, you know,' he said. 'It hasn't been easy.'

'What hasn't been easy?'

'Things,' answered Alec. He struggled with himself. 'Financial things. Among others. I had a lot of French securities. Never mind. We can't put the clock back to . . .' Here Alec sat up, galvanised. 'I almost forgot. Watch: I've left my watch back home. Do you happen to know what time it is?'

'It can't be much past twelve.'

'Twelve! Good lord, I've got to get back! The news, you know. One o'clock news. Mustn't miss the news.'

His anxiety was so infectious that my own fingers shook when I took my watch out of my pocket.

'But, man, it's only five minutes past noon! You've got all the time in the world!'

Alec shook his head.

'Mustn't risk missing the news,' he insisted. 'I've got my car, of course. Left it down the road a way when I came for a stroll. But I have to walk at a snail's pace to get to the car. Stiff joints. Look here, you won't forget about tonight?' Getting up from the bench, he wrung my hand and looked at me earnestly out of the once-sharp grey eyes. 'I'm not very entertaining company, I'm afraid. But I'll try. Maybe we'll do some puzzles. Both Rita and Barry are fond of puzzles. Tonight. Eight o'clock. Don't forget.'

I tried to hold him back.

'Just a minute! Does Rita know about this financial trouble of yours?'

'No, no, no!' Alec was shocked. 'I wouldn't worry a woman about a thing like that. You mustn't mention it to her. I haven't told anybody but you. In fact, Dr Croxley, you're just about the only friend I've got.'

And he stumped away.

I walked back to the village, feeling a little heavier weight of trouble on my shoulders. I wished the rain would fall and get it over with. The sky was lead-coloured; the water dark blue; the headlands, at bare patches in their green, like the colours of a child's modelling-clay run together.

In the High Street I noticed Molly Grange. Alec had said she wouldn't be coming back from Barnstaple that weekend – Molly owns and manages a typewriting bureau there – but presumably Rita had been mistaken. Molly smiled at me over her shoulder as she turned in at her father's gate.

It wasn't a pleasant day. Tom dashed in for a very late tea just after six. He was doing a post-mortem for the police at Lynton on a somewhat messy suicide; he gave me all the details as he wolfed down bread and butter and jam, and hardly heard what I had to tell him. It had gone eight o'clock, and the sky was darkening, when I drove out the four miles to 'Mon Repos'.

It would not be blackout time until past nine o'clock. Yet no lights showed in the house. That in itself inspired a feeling of disquiet.

'Mon Repos' had originally been a handsome bungalow, large and low-built, with a slanting tiled roof and leaded-paned windows against mellow red brick. Most trees won't thrive in sea air, and the grass of the lawn was sparse. But a tall yew hedge screened it from the road. There were two sanded drives, one to the front door and one to the garage at the left. Beside the garage was a tennis court. A creeper-hung summer-house stood on the lawn at the right.

Now, however, the whole place had gone faintly to seed. Nothing very noticeable, nothing greatly to remark. The hedge was just beginning to need trimming. Somebody had left bright-coloured beach chairs out in the rain. One of the shutters had a loose hinge, which the handyman – if there was a handyman – had not bothered to repair. It was present less in tangible details than in an atmosphere of subtle decay.

You became conscious of the place's isolation, of its God-forsaken loneliness after dark. Anything could happen here; and who the wiser?

The light had grown so bad that I was compelled to switch on my head-lamps when I drove in. The tyres of the car crunched on sand. Nothing else stirred. Hardly a breeze from the sea ruffled that muggy heat. Behind the bungalow, beyond a long stretch of damp reddish soil, you could dimly make out the line of the cliffs which fell seventy feet to rocks and water below.

The light of the head-lamps, hooded, ran ahead dimly to the open doors of the garage. It was a double garage, with Rita's Jaguar inside. As I slowed down, a figure appeared round the side of the house and wandered towards me.

'Is that you, Doctor?' Alec called.

'Yes. I'd better run the car into the garage, in case it rains. Be with you in half a tick.'

But Alec didn't wait. He blundered over into the glow of the head-lamps, and I had to stop altogether. Putting his hand on the door of the car, he peered up and down the drive.

'Look here,' he said. 'Who cut the telephone-wires?'

3

The engine of the car had stalled, and I started it again. Alec was not even angry; he sounded merely puzzled and troubled. Though you could smell whisky about him, he was quite sober.

'Cut the telephone-wires?'

'It was that damned Johnson, I expect,' Alec declared without rancour. 'The gardener, you know. He wasn't doing his work. Or at least Rita says he wasn't. So I had to sack him. Or at least Rita sacked him. I hate trouble with people.'

'But . . .'

'He did it to spite me. He *knows* I always ring up Anderson at the *Gazette* office every evening to see if they've got any news that isn't released to the B.B.C. The phone wouldn't work. Then, when I lifted it higher, the wires came loose from the little box. They'd been cut and stuck back in again.'

For a second, there, I thought Alec was going to cry.

'It was a low trick, a damned unsportsmanlike trick,' he added. 'Why won't people let you alone?'

'Where are Rita and Mr Sullivan?'

Alec blinked.

'Come to think of it, I don't know. They must be somewhere

about.' He craned his neck round. 'They're not in the house. At least, I don't think they are.'

'Hadn't I better go and round them up, if we're going to play cards?'

'Yes. Do that. I'll go and get us something to drink. But we won't play cards just yet, if you don't mind. There's a very fine radio programme going on at eight-thirty.'

'What is it?'

'I'm not sure. *Romeo and Juliet*, I think. Rita particularly wants to hear it. Excuse me.'

He moved across the sparse-grown lawn in the twilight, and stumbled over something. As though instantly conscious that I might think he wasn't sober, he glanced round, tried to look dignified, and sauntered on.

I ran the car into the garage. A nerve was switching in the calf of my leg when I got out. It was not that I was so anxious to find Rita and young Sullivan: I wanted a chance to think.

First I walked round to the back of the house. The breeze was colder here, smoothing down coarse grass on the edge of the cliff; the stretch of damp red soil was deserted. Hardly seeing anything, deaf and blind with preoccupation about those cut telephone-wires, I circled the bungalow and passed the summer-house.

They must have heard me. From inside the summer-house there was a stifled, startled exclamation. I glanced round – the light was just good enough to see inside – and then I walked on very quickly.

Rita Wainright was half sitting, half lying across a mat on the grubby wooden floor of the summer-house. Her head had been bent back, and her arms were round Sullivan's shoulders just before he sprang away. Both faces turned towards me. The open mouths, the peculiar guilty shine of the eyes, the frightened spasmodic reaction of heightened senses: I saw these things only in a flash, a sliding past the eye, before I hurried on.

But I saw them.

Perhaps you think that an old duffer like myself shouldn't have been embarrassed. But I was, badly. Probably more so than those two. It wasn't the actual fact: which was, after all, only a good-looking woman being kissed. It was the rawness, the grimy floor of the summer-house, the sense of forces now released and beyond control.

Look out: danger, something kept saying. *Look out: danger. Look out: danger* . . .

Behind me a husky voice called: 'Dr Luke!'

If Rita hadn't called out, I shouldn't have stopped. I was pretending not to have seen them. They should have played up to this, but their consciences wouldn't let them.

I turned round. My head felt light and my voice was thick, partly from shock and partly from wrath. It wasn't as bad as Rita's voice or Sullivan's, but it was noticeable.

'Hullo, there!' I found myself saying, in such a tone of hypocritical surprise that I could have kicked myself. 'Is there somebody inside?'

Rita stepped out. Her dusky skin now had a colour, especially under the eyes, which showed the rate at which her heart must have been beating. She drew her breath with difficulty. Her light tweed suit and white blouse were rumpled; she brushed surreptitiously at the skirt. Behind her in the doorway lurked Sullivan, clearing his throat.

'We – we were in the summer-house,' cried Rita.

'We were talking,' said her companion.

'We intended to come in straightaway.'

'But we got to talking. You know how it is.'

Barry Sullivan coughed abruptly as his voice grew husky. I had not remembered him as looking quite as callow or young. He was a handsome fellow beyond any doubt, straightforward of eye if somewhat weak of jaw. But all the confident self-assurance of a year ago had gone: unless I much misread the signs, he was as badly gone on Rita as she was gone on him, and ready for anything.

A breeze stirred in the vines of the summer-house. The emotional temperature between those two was so strong that it surrounded them like a fog; they could not get rid of it. A drop of rain fell, and then another.

'I'm – I'm not sure if you've met Barry?' Rita went on, in a voice as though she were calling on tiptoe over a fence. 'I think you were there when we first met, though? Dr Luke Croxley.'

'How do you do, sir?' muttered Sullivan, and shuffled his feet.

'I remember Mr Sullivan very well. I believe' – it was impossible to keep acid out of this – 'I believe he's one of our most promising West End actors?'

Sullivan's handsome forehead wrinkled.

'*Me?*' he exclaimed, and tapped himself on the chest.

'You are, too!' cried Rita. 'Or you will be!'

The boy looked even more uncomfortable. 'I don't want to sail under any false colours, sir,' he said.

'I'm sure you don't, Mr Sullivan. I'm sure you don't.'

'He means . . .' cried Rita.

'He means what, my dear?'

'Look. I've never played in the West End,' said Sullivan. 'Just a couple of provincial engagements, and not very good ones at that. For the past two years I've been selling automobiles for Lowther and Son.' His dark eyes, with the hollows drawn slantwise under them, moved to Rita. 'I'm not *worthy* . . .'

'You are too,' said Rita. 'Don't say things like that!'

They were in such a state of mind that they might have poured out the whole story (or so I thought then), if Barry Sullivan had not suddenly noticed it was beginning to rain. He looked up at the sky. He looked at his immaculate sports coat and grey flannels, with the silk scarf knotted and thrust into the neck of the shirt. All his confused frustration rushed out in some form of activity.

'I've got to get those beach chairs in,' he shouted. 'They've been rained on before. Excuse me.'

'Darling, you'll get *wet!*' cried Rita, with such passionate naïveté that it would have been funny if matters had not reached a point where something had to happen, one way or the other.

I walked with Rita to the front door of the bungalow. She pressed her hands together and twisted the fingers. Also, she had been drinking: you realised that when you got close to her.

'I can't stand this,' she said flatly. 'I'd rather be dead.'

'Don't talk nonsense!'

'Are you so sure it's nonsense, Dr Luke? I don't think you are.'

'Never mind that, my dear. Just tell me: what games have you been up to?'

'So you did see us back there in the summer-house. I thought you did. Well, *I* don't care.'

'I wasn't talking about the summer-house. I want to know who cut the telephone-wires.'

Rita stopped short, drawing together her thin eyebrows. Her expression was so bewildered that I could not help believing it was genuine.

'What on earth are you talking about? I didn't cut any telephone-wires. I don't know anything about them.' A curious look flashed through her eyes. '*Are* they cut? In our house? What do you think it means?'

Giving me no chance to answer, she opened the front door and hurried in.

The big sitting-room of the bungalow was lighted. So was the dining-room behind it. Furnished in blue and in white satin, with a soft glow of yellow-shaded lamps, the sitting-room showed little trace of seediness or neglect. Over the fireplace hung Rita's portrait, by Paul Ferrars. The brass andirons glistened, the rugs were thick, a bottle and syphon stood on a side table.

Alec Wainright sat by the radio, with a whisky and soda in his hand.

'Er – hello, my dear,' murmured Alec. He lifted his glass and drank. It seemed to warm and brighten him. 'We've been looking for you.'

Rita spoke in a muffled voice.

'Barry and I were over at the tennis court.'

'Ah. Have a good time?'

'It was all right. Have you done the blackout? This is Martha's night out, remember.'

'All done, my dear,' replied Alec, sweeping his glass. 'All done by our little hubby. We're going to have a lot of fun tonight.'

Rita looked like a tragedy-queen. You could almost see her gritting her teeth. She seemed torn between a very genuine tenderness for Alec, who was making obvious efforts to come out of his daze, and an equally genuine desire to throw something at him. The former feeling conquered. Rita spoke with an effort at brightness and even coyness.

'What's all this Dr Luke is telling me about somebody cutting the telephone-wires?'

Alec's face clouded.

'It was that damned Johnson,' he said. 'Sneaked in here and cut 'em. Did it just to spite me. It's not serious. But if we had to phone the fire-department or the police or somebody like that . . .'

'I want a drink,' said Rita. 'Why in heaven's name doesn't somebody give me a *drink*?'

'There on the table, my sweet. Help yourself. We won't let the doctor scare us tonight. This is a special night.'

'I want a drink with ice in it,' Rita almost screamed at him.

Her voice went up with shattering effect before she controlled herself. Though she tried to smile at me, indicating that everything was all right, her hands were shaking nevertheless. Rita walked across this room into the dining-room. The little wooden heels of her sandals clacked on the hardwood floors. At the door of the kitchen she paused and turned round again.

'I'd rather be *dead*,' she cried through the two rooms: not loudly, but with extraordinary intensity. Then she slapped open the swing door, and disappeared into the kitchen.

Alec only looked mildly surprised. Seen sideways under a lamp, his broad blunt-featured face was less shrunken and dead-looking. The broad mouth quivered occasionally, but not often. He had washed his face, brushing the scanty grey hair carefully.

'A bit off-colour, I imagine,' he said. 'Too much exercise in this heat. That's what I always tell her – Ah, my boy, come in! Sit down! Pour yourself something to drink!'

We could hear the rain pattering on the roof of the bungalow. Barry Sullivan came in from the hall, dusting his hands on a handkerchief. The instant defensiveness of his manner, the way in which he seemed mentally to shy back, should have been as plain as print to Alec. This young man was suffering from a guilty conscience far worse than Rita's.

'Thanks, sir,' said Barry, and picked up the bottle from the table. 'I'd like a shot, if you don't mind. I don't use it ordinarily. But tonight –'

'Tonight's a special occasion. Eh?'

The glass slipped out of Barry's fingers, clattered on the table, and rolled off to the floor. But it landed on a rug, and did not break. The tall young man was down after it in an instant, falling on his knees like a collapsing clothes-horse. He did not look at Alec when he got up.

'I must be the clumsiest ox in the world!' he declared, gesturing with such violence that this time he nearly broke the glass against the bottle. 'I can't imagine what made me do that. It slipped. Look! It slipped just like this.'

Alec chuckled. The nerve twitched faintly at his eyelid.

'My dear boy! Don't mention it! So long as you didn't break the bottle!' (Alec was so pleased with this that his chuckle became a whinny of mirth.) 'Now sit down. At eighty-thirty we're going to turn on the radio –'

'Radio?'

'For a play Rita wants to hear.' He looked at me. 'It *is* the *Romeo and Juliet* one. I looked it up in the *Radio Times*. Then we'll be just right for the news at nine. By George, you know, I'm rather sorry I didn't invite Paul Ferrars and that guest of his.'

The swing door to the kitchen creaked open. Rita, carrying a gin-and-lemon combination in a tumbler which tinkled with ice, walked through the dining-room on rapping heels.

'What's that about Paul Ferrars?' she asked rather sharply. And instinctively, as she lifted the glass to her lips, her eyes moved to her own portrait above the mantelpiece.

Whether or not Paul Ferrars can paint may be a matter for debate among the critics. All I can say is that the picture here seemed extraordinarily good to me. It was a half-length. Ferrars had painted her in an evening gown, with a diamond necklace at her throat and diamond bracelets on her wrists. This last touch had seemed bad taste to Rita; but it was Alec's suggestion and he was extremely pleased with it.

Yet a touch of parody showed in that portrait. Though it was undeniably Rita and emphasised her beauty, there were touches about her half-smile which might not have pleased Alec if he had been able to understand them. Rita in the flesh regarded it with distaste; and then, for some reason, quickly looked away.

'What's that about Paul Ferrars?' she repeated.

'He's got a guest, my dear. Isn't the guest a patient of yours, Doctor?'

'No. He's a patient of Tom's,' I said. 'Tom confined him to a wheelchair, and now he's got a motor wheelchair – latest type of thing – sent down from London.'

'Merrivale, the fellow's name is,' explained Alec. 'He's a detective.'

Barry Sullivan poured himself a stiff whisky, added very little soda, and swallowed it.

'That's not true!' cried Rita. 'He's from the War Office. Mrs Parker told me.'

'He's not an official detective, no. But he's been tangled up in all kinds of murder cases. Fact!' Alec nodded rapidly. 'Thought we might get him started on his reminiscences. Something like that. Interesting stuff, probably. Always was interested in crime myself.'

Rita and young Sullivan exchanged a glance over Alec's head. As clearly as though he had spoken, the boy's look said: 'Do we act tonight?' and Rita's glance, with the full strength of her nature egging him on, answered: 'Yes.' I confess, myself, to a touch of panic at that moment. Barry poured himself another whisky, added even less soda, and swallowed it; his eyes were scared but determined. Rita went over to smooth her husband's scanty hair.

And Alec turned on the radio.

4

'*You have been listening to Shakespeare's* Romeo and Juliet, *adapted for broadcasting by Kenneth MacVane. The cast was as follows.*'

The rain had momentarily ceased. Nothing could be heard in that sitting-room but the poised voice repeating a list of names. Emotions had been strung to so high a pitch that I nearly started out of my skin when the heavy, quivering gong-notes of Big Ben banged with tinny reverberation out of that loud-speaker, and slowly struck nine.

'*This is the B.B.C. Home Service. Here is the news, and this is Bruce Belfrage reading it.*'

Alec, who had been sitting in a semi-stupor with his chin sunk on his chest, roused up. Edging his chair closer to the radio – its castors squeaked sharply – he bent his head forward for real attention.

'*Very slight enemy air activity was reported this afternoon when a single enemy reconnaissance plane flew over the –*'

In a wing chair not far from me, Rita Wainright sat bolt upright, so straight that her back seemed to be arched. An empty glass trailed from the fingers of one hand. She saw nothing. Her eyes were smeary with tears, which suddenly overflowed and trickled down her cheeks; but she did not blink or make any move to wipe them away.

The blackout had made this room very hot. And Sullivan had been smoking cigarettes incessantly. The smoke lay in rifts round the golden lamps, getting into your throat and eyes. Rita moved a little. Beginning in her back, an uncontrollable trembling began to shake up through her whole body. She swallowed hard. The glass dropped from her fingers and fell softly on a rug; but she retrieved it by groping like a blind woman. Then, suddenly, she got to her feet.

'Rita!' said Barry Sullivan. 'No!'

'Yes,' said Rita. 'We agreed.'

Alec whipped round from the radio almost with a snarl.

'*S-h-h!*' he hissed at them, and instantly fell somnolent with his ear against the loud-speaker.

'*– assured his audience that if France were ever again to assume her rightful place and prestige on the Continent –*'

Standing rigid, Rita turned her head and dabbed with the heel of her hand at her brimming eyes. It lifted the eyelid, giving a grotesque touch to her face as she moved her head from side to side. Becoming conscious of the glass in her hand, she blinked at it and spoke.

'Get ice for drink,' she muttered in a thick voice. Turning round, she marched into the dining-room. She might have been marching to a gallows, though of course any thought like that was nonsense. The noise of her shoe-heels clacked above the unruffled common-sense voice from the loudspeaker. The kitchen door squeaked, and then she had gone.

'*Colonel Lindbergh added that the United States, in his opinion, had no conceivable interest in any trans-Atlantic quarrels which –*'

'I'd better go and help her,' said Barry Sullivan.

For the third time Alec twitched round, rolling up his eyes and pleading for silence.

The young man did not seem to hear him. Putting his own

glass carefully on the table, Sullivan kept his face averted from me as he moved after Rita. But, as a consideration for Alec, he walked very softly. Even the kitchen door hardly creaked as he went through. There was a light under that door.

What I expected when those two reappeared, I am not sure I can tell. So strong can grow the power of suggestion, so poisoned can grow the nerves, that there would have been no surprise in hearing Rita invite Alec out to that homely kitchen, and the boy lurking near with something sharp in his hand. They surely wouldn't attack Alec with a witness on the premises? But why not? Bywaters did it. Stoner did it. Both Rita and Sullivan were half drunk. What *does* a murderer look like, when he comes softly up behind his victim?

When those two came back . . .

But they did not come back.

The voice on that radio seemed to have been speaking for ever. I had heard all the items at six o'clock, and came to dread the length of each one when I recognised it. Alec, comatose except when he would nod his head at a telling point, never once stirred. Still the kitchen door did not creak; still there was no sound.

'*That is the end of the news. It is now eighteen and a half minutes past nine o'clock. At twenty minutes past you will hear . . .*'

Alec switched off.

Rousing himself, he raised his head and peered across at me. He must have noticed my expression. An odd, sly little smile twisted round his lips.

'My dear doctor,' he observed gently, 'did you think I didn't know?'

'Didn't know what?'

Alec nodded in the direction of the kitchen.

'How those two have been carrying on behind my back,' he said.

The creepiest part of this was that it seemed to be the old

Alec Wainright who spoke. The stocky little figure had relaxed. His expression was no longer so blurred. Humour, tolerance, had crept back into their house as his eyelid ceased to twitch; even his tone of voice and choice of words were subtly altered. Sitting back in the big chair, he folded his hands over his stomach.

'Yes,' he agreed, following my glance to the bottle on the table. 'I've drunk myself into a peaceful state of mind. I'm even beginning to forget,' he touched the radio, 'this.'

'And I'm to sit by and see you drink yourself to death to achieve peace of mind?'

'That,' he said cheerfully, 'just about sums up the situation.'

He *was* the old Alec Wainright, except for a heightened colour and a protuberant vein in his temple.

'Speaking of Rita . . .' he went on.

'How long have you known about her and young Sullivan?'

'Oh, since the beginning.'

'And what are you going to do about it?'

'Well,' said Alec, hunching his shoulders into the chair for a more comfortable position, 'what would *you* do about it? Cut up a row and make myself look foolish? The cuckolded husband has always been a figure of fun. Don't you know that?'

'Then you don't mind?'

Alec closed his eyes.

'No,' he answered reflectively, 'I can't say I do. Why should I mind? I'm past that sort of thing myself. I'm very fond of Rita, but not in that way. And I hate fuss. This isn't the first time she's fallen, you know.'

'She swore to me in my office –'

'Aha,' said Alec, opening his eyes, 'so she's been talking to you?' He laughed. 'But then I can see why she wouldn't tell. I'm rather proud of her prowess in that direction, to tell you the truth. No. Barry Sullivan's a nice lad. She might go farther and fare worse. No. I've found it much better to pretend I don't notice anything.'

'You think that's better?'

'It's the least I can do for her.'

'Have you any idea how those two are taking this?'

'Oh, they'll stew a little.'

'Stew a little? Then you haven't realised I've been sitting here all evening on something a good deal worse than pins and needles, wondering whether they were planning to kill you?'

Despite the padding of whisky, Alec was honestly startled. His face writhed up. He didn't like this intrusion into his dream-world, and started to laugh at it: only to become serious again.

'My dear doctor, don't talk such rubbish! Kill me! I can see you don't know my wife. No, but let's face it. They aren't planning to kill me. But I can tell you what they are planning to do. They're . . .' He broke off. 'Where the devil is that draught coming from?'

There was, in fact, a very palpable draught creeping round our ankles from the direction of the dining-room. The swing door to the kitchen creaked sharply, but nobody came in.

'I hope they haven't gone out and left the back door open,' fretted Alec, 'with a light on in the kitchen. Any light on this cliff can be seen for miles out at sea. The wardens will be having a fit.'

I wasn't thinking of the wardens.

It must have taken me only five or six seconds, laboriously as I have to move, to reach that creaking door.

The kitchen, large and white-tiled, was empty. On the white-enamelled table-top, held down by Rita's empty glass, lay a tiny piece of paper hastily torn from the kitchen memorandum-pad. A damp breeze blew straight in my face from the back door, which stood wide open, pouring a blaze of light outside.

To seal up rooms, to close doors and draw curtains, becomes a nervous instinct always lying at the back of your mind like a phobia. Lights are more than an offence; they are a shouting crime. But, though I reached that door in considerable haste, I did not immediately close it.

Though past blackout time, it was not quite dark outside. Outlines swam in dimness. Nothing could be grown or cultivated here close to the cliff, but that large expanse of damp dark-red soil had not been left entirely bare. A few geometrical designs – Alec's mathematical soul showed here – had been laid down in tiny white-painted pebbles. And, in the centre, the outline of a path some four feet wide had been indicated by the pebbles. That path led straight out in dimness to the cliff edge known as Lovers' Leap.

Lovers' Leap.

There was an electric torch, hooded in tissue-paper, on top of the refrigerator. My bad heart threatened some ugly things when I took the torch, closed the back door behind me, and stumbled down the two wooden steps.

It was just light enough, under a wet and smoky sky, to see the two lines of footprints even without the aid of the torch.

Those footprints began where the sparse grass died. Always damp, the soil had grown softer yet with rain. Out ran the ghostly lines of pebbles, out ran the footprints – one set firm and steady, the other lagging behind with slower steps. I started to plunge out over them. But you don't forget, even in this state, thirty years of acting as an occasional police surgeon. Your instinct pushes you, as it pushed me now; pushed me to one side, fiercely, to avoid those footprints.

I walked down beside the path to the edge of the cliff. Rita's face went before me.

I haven't a head for heights. They make me turn dizzy, and I want to jump. So I hadn't the nerve actually to walk to the brink and peer over, as most people in this district so casually do. Dirt or no dirt, mud or no mud, I got down on my hands and knees. I crawled out to the hump of scrub-grass beside the place where the footprints ended, and put my head over.

The tide in these parts begins to go out about four o'clock in the afternoon. So it was coming in again now, barely covering the rock-fangs seventy feet below. I couldn't see much except dim white flickers. But I heard its hiss and drag among the rocks. Damp and sea-air blew at me, feeling over my face and flattening down my eyelids.

Then I just lay there in the dirt, a heavy old man feeling useless and ill. Even now, lying safely on the ground, it scared me to look over. My fingers opened and I dropped the electric torch. I saw it turn over, a brief firefly light winking and dwindling, until it disappeared without sound or trace in the place where two human beings had gone.

Presently I crawled back like a crab. It was easier when you didn't have that light-headed feeling of looking over a precipice, of being swung as though on cobwebs over nothing. The cliff was a sheer face of ribbed stone, as bare as your face. Their bodies wouldn't have struck against anything until they landed. And, when they landed . . .

I got up and walked back to the house.

Alec was still in the living-room, standing by the table and pouring himself more whisky. He looked dreamy and vaguely pleased.

'Did they leave the door open?' he asked. And then: 'Look here, what's the matter with you? Where did you get all that dirt on you?'

'You'd better have it straight,' I told him. 'They've gone crazy and thrown themselves over the cliff.'

Silence.

It took Alec some time to assimilate this. They used to bring children to me and say: 'Now, foolish, don't make such a fuss. You know Dr Luke won't hurt you.' And, because the child trusted me, it knew Dr Luke wouldn't hurt. But sometimes you can't help hurting, no matter how much you try; then you would see the child's lower lip go down, and the startled way it looked at you in reproach just before the tears. And Alec Wainright, a drunken man past his best years, regarded me exactly like that.

'No!' he said, when he had finally realised the meaning of the words. 'No, no, no!'

'I'm sorry. There it is.'

'I don't believe it,' Alec almost screamed. He put down the glass, and it spun across the polished top of the table. 'How do you know?'

'Go out and look at the footprints. His footprints and hers. They go out to the edge of Lovers' Leap, and they don't come back. There's a note on the kitchen table, but I didn't read it.'

'It's not true,' said Alec. 'It's a . . . Wait a minute!'

Alec turned round, lurching a little in his stiff joints. Steadying himself against the table, he made for the door to the main hall. I heard him going as fast as he could up the stairs. I heard him moving about in the upstairs rooms, opening and shutting doors or drawers.

Meantime, I went out to the kitchen, where I ran hot water to wash my hands. A brush was hanging up on a hook beside the stove; it was actually a shoe-brush, though I never noticed that at the time, and I tried to clean up my clothes with it. I was still at this work, patiently brushing, when Alec returned.

'Her clothes are still there,' he said through cracked lips. 'But –'

Here he held up a key, making waggling gestures which conveyed nothing. It was an odd sort of key, on the Yale pattern but much smaller; on its chromium head you could see the tiny engraved word *Margarita*, with a true-love knot.

'Don't go out there!' I said, as Alec started unsteadily for the back door.

'Why not?'

'You mustn't mess up the tracks. Alec, we'll have to get the police.'

'Police,' repeated Alec, not certain of the word. He lowered himself into a white chair by the kitchen table. 'Police.' He tasted the word again; and then, as is usual in such cases, became frantic. 'But we've got to *do* something! Can't we . . . you know: go down there?'

'How? Nobody could climb down that cliff. Besides, the tide's coming in. It'll have to wait until morning.'

'Wait,' whispered Alec. 'Wait. But we can't just sit here!' He focused his wits. 'You're right. The police will know what to do. Ring up the police. Or I'll do it.'

'How can we ring up the police? Somebody's cut the telephone-wires.'

Stayed by the recollection of this, he put up a hand to his forehead. His complexion, between whisky and emotion, had a mottled look very unpleasing to anybody's eye: especially the medical.

'But we've got a car,' he pointed out. 'We've got two cars. We could drive in and –'

'That's exacdy what we're going to do, if you feel strong enough.'

Startlingly, the electric refrigerator began to hum in that sedate kitchen. Alec, as he swung round to find the cause of the noise, noticed for the first time that little slip torn from the kitchen memorandum pad, scribbled on with a pencil, and left under the glass on the table. He removed the glass and picked up the paper.

'I'm all right,' he said. 'I still can't believe this. It's all . . .' But his eyes filled with tears nevertheless.

I had to get him his hat – he is as helpless as a child in these matters – and a raincoat in case the rain started again. He insisted on going out to look at the footprints with the aid of another electric torch. But there was nothing to see except the footprints, and only images of Rita crowding back on both of us.

He seemed to be holding up well, despite his physical condition. It was not until we were out in the front hall, on our way to the car, that he collapsed beside the hat-stand in a dead faint. The little key, engraved with the name *Margarita* and the true-love knot, dropped out of his hand and fell on the hardwood floor. I had never guessed how very much he loved Rita, but I guessed then. I picked up the little key and put it in my waistcoat pocket. Then I set about the task of getting Alec upstairs.

The bodies of Rita Wainright and Barry Sullivan were recovered two days later. They were washed up on a shingle beach a few miles down the coast, and some small boys ran to fetch the police. But it wasn't until the post-mortem that we learned how they had really died.

5

That was the day I first met Sir Henry Merrivale, under circumstances that will long be remembered in Lyncombe.

War or no war, the village could talk of little but the suicide pact of Rita Wainright and Barry Sullivan. It angered me. Very little sympathy was expressed for either of them, especially Rita. The general trend of it was: 'Wouldn't you know she *would* do a damn silly theatrical thing like that?'

On the other hand, Alec got no great shakes of sympathy himself.

''E ought to 'ave walloped 'er,' said Harry Pierce at the Coach and Horses. 'Then she wouldn't 'a' done it.'

I failed to see the logic of this. Besides, too much talk of walloping wives is done by those who would never have the nerve to utter a large-sized boo to their own particular spouses: as, for example, Mr and Mrs Pierce. It was all the more irritating because Alec's collapse had been rather more serious than I had feared. A trained nurse was with him day and night, and Tom went out to see him twice a day.

On Monday morning before lunch, having been confined to the premises by strict orders of Tom, I was taking the sun in our back garden when Molly Grange came round to see me. She walked down the path between the tall blue delphiniums, to the open space under the tree where the wicker chairs stand.

'How are you feeling, Dr Luke?'

'I'm perfectly fit, thanks. What has that idiotic son of mine been telling you?'

'That you've been – exerting yourself.'

'Nonsense!'

Molly sat down in a wicker chair opposite me.

'Dr Luke. It's a dreadful business, isn't it?'

'Of course!' I said. 'You knew Barry Sullivan, didn't you? In fact, you were the one who introduced him to . . .'

I bit my tongue, hoping there were no unpleasant memories. But Molly did not seem to mind. People at first glance seldom realised how attractive Molly was. Like most fair-haired, blue-eyed girls who do not apply make-up so that their faces may be known, like ships, by their markings, Molly seemed ordinary.

'I didn't know him very well. Only slightly,' she said. She lifted one slim hand and examined the fingers. 'But it's a horrible affair just the same. Dr Luke – you don't mind talking about it?'

'No, not at all.'

'Well,' said Molly, sitting up straight, 'what *happened*?'

'Didn't Tom tell you?'

'Tom's not an awfully good story-teller. Then he just says: "Hell, woman, don't you understand plain English?"' She smiled, but her face grew grave again. 'So far as I can gather, you and Mr Wainright were starting out towards the car, to go for the police, when Mr Wainright collapsed.'

'That's right.'

'You dragged him upstairs and put him to bed . . .'

'That didn't hurt me.'

'Tom says it might have. Anyway, what I can't understand is this. Tom says you *walked* from "Mon Repos" to here. You walked four miles and more in the dark –'

'It wasn't completely dark. The stars came out when the rain cleared.'

Molly waved this aside.

'And came back here,' she said, 'to telephone the police at Lynton. You didn't get back until half past eleven or going on for twelve. But there must have been two cars at least out there. Why didn't you come in a car?'

'Because,' I said, 'there wasn't any petrol for the cars.'

Molly looked bewildered. The memory of going out to that garage, and finding what awaited me there, had no soothing effect on the temper.

'My dear Molly, somebody had turned the tap of the petrol-tanks and let it all run out. Both Alec's car and mine. Even apart from the question of how scarce the stuff is, I can't see the particular fun of a practical joke like that. Don't ask me why anybody did it! Or why the telephone-wires were cut. But it was done. And I was stranded. What's more, I left the house carrying a little souvenir-key that Alec sets great store by for some reason, and had to give it to Tom to take back to him. I left him very ill, but I had to get help somehow. Barring radio or carrier-pigeons . . .'

'It was a silly thing to do,' Molly admitted. 'And at a time like *that*. You've no idea who did it?'

'The diabolical Johnson could have done it. Anybody could have done it.'

'Johnson?'

'A gardener Alec sacked. But where was the sense?'

'They haven't found the – they haven't found Rita and Mr Sullivan?'

'No. Everything's out of joint. Including you, now I come to think of it. Why aren't you in Barnstaple this morning? How's the typewriting bureau getting on?'

Molly pressed her lips together. She brushed her fingertips against her temple, seeming for the first time uncertain. Her ankles were set exactly together, as precise as a ledger in her workroom.

'The typewriting bureau,' she informed me, 'will just have to take care of itself for a day or two. I'm feeling a bit under the weather myself. Not ill. Just –' She dropped her hand. 'Dr Luke, I'm worried. I didn't really like Rita Wainright, you know.'

'Not you too?'

'Please wait. I'm honestly trying to be fair. And I want to submit something to your judgement rather than argue a case.' Molly hesitated. 'Do you think you could come down to our house for a few minutes? Now? I've got something there I think you ought to see.'

I looked back towards our own house. Tom had finished surgery at eleven, and was on his morning round. It seemed probable that I could sneak out and sneak back again without being caught. When Molly and I emerged into the front garden, the High Street lay serene. The High Street – by courtesy – is in fact the main road, a good surface of asphalt, which runs for some distance on a very slight rise until it disappears round the turning at what used to be Miller's Forge. Lined with small houses and shops, it dozed in the sunshine to a subdued murmur of voices coming from the open doors of the Coach and Horses over the way. Mr Frost the postman was on his round. Mrs Pinafore, Licensed to Sell Tobacco and Sweets, was sweeping her doorstep.

But it did not remain peaceful. Molly turned to stare.

'My word!' she said.

From far up the street, at the Miller's Forge end, issued the steady *pop-pop-pop* of a motor vehicle in motion. Squarely in the middle of the road, proceeding with steadiness and intensity, came a wheelchair.

Seated majestically in the wheelchair, hands gripping the handle of the rod which communicated with a small front wheel and served as steering-gear, was a very broad and stout man in a white linen suit. His bald head glistened in the sun. The spectacles were pulled down on his broad nose. A shawl was draped, invalid-fashion, round his shoulders. Even at a distance you could discern on his face an expression of almost inhuman malignancy. He bent forward tensely, with absorbed concentration, while the motor accelerated to a louder *pop-pop-pop*.

Round the corner of Miller's Forge, running hard and breathless in pursuit, came Paul Ferrars the painter.

After him galloped my son Tom.

After them both came a policeman.

'Slow down!' Ferrars was bellowing, in a choking voice which made heads appear at windows. 'That's a steeper grade than it looks! For the love of Mike slow . . .'

Upon the face of the man in the wheelchair was now a lordly sneer. As though conscious of his prowess, he made the chair swerve left and right in graceful fashion like a master of the art of skating. Even then, Tom maintains, things would have been all right if it had not been for the dogs.

Our dogs in Lyncombe, as a rule, are a mild-mannered lot. Motor cars they understand. Wagons and bicycles they understand. But the spectacle of a joy-riding invalid, in a chair apparently equipped with a supercharger, was beyond comprehension and therefore maddening to the canine soul. As though conjured by magic, they came pouring over fences into the foray.

The din of their barking rose deafeningly above the *pop-pop-pop* of the chair. The Andersons' Scotch terrier Willie was so excited that he turned a complete somersault, landing on his back. The Lanes' Airedale made a daring dash under the wheels. Roused from his scientific absorption, the man in the chair attempted reprisals. He leaned out and made a face at them. It was, indeed, a face so terrifying that the more timorous shied back again, barking frantically; but a so-called Manchester terrier sprang on the front of the chair and attempted to get his teeth in the steering-apparatus.

The invalid replied in spirited fashion by picking up a crutch and aiming a vicious swipe with it. This was good as terrorism but bad as tactics. The steering of the chair was already under dispute. Now proceeding at a pace truly alarming, it sailed gracefully up Hicks's driveway to the pavement; swept along the pavement at a time when – I regret to say – Mrs McGonigle, our esteemed laundress, was coming backwards out of her gate with the week's washing; and returned to the road again by way of Pinafore's drive.

'Cut off your *motor!*' Ferrars was screaming from behind. 'For the love of Mike cut off your *motor!*'

This was good advice, which the invalid either could not or would not heed. Surrounded by dogs, the speeding wheelchair swept past Molly and me as we stood at the gate. The invalid's malignant expression never changed as his chair lurched over a crown in the road, described a sweeping arc in front of the Coach and Horses, and disappeared, majestically, through the open doors of the saloon-bar.

In went the dogs, in went Ferrars in pursuit, in went Tom, and in went the constable already taking out his notebook.

'My word!' Molly said again.

'Gentleman seems in a hurry to get a drink,' observed the postman.

From the pub, it is true, issued sounds suggesting that this dipsomaniac was already climbing over the counter to get at the bottles behind the bar. The crashing of glassware, the thudding of chairs, the barking of dogs, mingled above all with the profane protests of men whose beer has been spilled as they lift it to their lips.

The ensuing fifteen minutes were perhaps the most lively ever spent in Harry Pierce's bar. One by one the dogs were shot out. Though peace was restored by liberal largesse, one powerful voice – that of the man in the wheelchair – thundered above everything. When he reappeared, wearing a look of savage martyrdom, Ferrars was pushing his chair.

'Now listen, test-pilot,' Ferrars was saying. 'This thing is a wheelchair.'

'All right, all right!'

'It's for helpless people to ride in. You're not supposed to treat it like a new Spitfire. Do you realise we could never have squared that charge of driving a motor vehicle to the public danger, if you hadn't been a friend of Superintendent Craft?'

An expression of hopeless and passionate misunderstanding went over the face of the malignant gentleman.

'Looky here,' he said. 'Burn it all, all I was tryin' to do was see what she'd do flat out on an open road. And what happened?'

'You nearly wrecked the damn village, that's what happened.'

'Do you realise I might 'a' been killed?' howled his companion. 'I come along peacefully, not botherin' anybody. And all of a sudden about fifty vicious mongrels come chargin' out and set their teeth in me . . .'

'Where did they set their teeth in you?'

The other glowered.

'Never you mind where they set their teeth in me,' he said darkly. 'If I get hydrophobia, you'll find out soon enough. I been condemned to a lonely life, laid up with a serious injury to my toe. It's a fine thing if I can't get a little good fresh air in my wheelchair, all nice and quiet, without every ruddy dog in the neighbourhood wantin' to chew me up.'

This could be no other than the great and dignified H.M., of whom we had already heard so much. Molly and I attracted his attention almost at once. But we attracted it in an unfortunate way.

During his royal progress through the village, we had been too startled to do anything but keep a straight face. Now, however, Molly found it too difficult to keep her gravity. She suddenly made a strangled noise through her pretty nose, turned away, and held on to the bars of the gate.

Sitting in his wheelchair outside the pub, Sir Henry Merrivale directed one glance at us through his spectacles. He lifted a malevolent finger and pointed.

'That's what I mean,' he said.

'Sh-h-h!' urged Ferrars under his breath.

'Why don't *I* ever get any sympathy?' demanded H.M., addressing the air. 'What makes such a pariah of *me*? If it happens to anybody else – lord love a duck, it's tragic. It's all coos and clucks o' sympathy. But, if it happens to the old man, it's just funny. When they come to bury me, son, I expect the parson won't be able to speak for laughin', and he'll have the whole funeral-party rollin' in the aisles before he's said ten words.'

'They're friends of mine,' said Ferrars. 'Come over and meet them.'

'I'm goin' to turn on my motor?' offered H.M. hopefully.

'You are *not*. I'll push you. Sit still.'

The High Street was now quietening down, except for a few dogs which still lurked bristling at corners and eyed the stationary wheelchair with the deepest suspicion. Tom, who had left his car beyond Miller's Forge to join in the chase, took his leave for another call before lunch. And the great man, trying to assume an idle and graceful posture with one hand on the handle of the steering-gear, was bumped across to join us.

The first movement of the chair was greeted by a violent chorus of barking. Several of the enemy shot out of hiding, and had to be chased away.

'You've guessed who this is,' said Ferrars, as H.M. ceased flourishing his crutch. 'That's Dr Luke Croxley, Tom's father. And the young lady who laughed is Miss Grange.'

Paul Ferrars, I must admit, showed up today in a much more human light than usual. He is – or was – a sardonic sort of fellow, thirtyish and lean, with a long nose and a didactic manner. He wears paint-stained flannels and old sweaters, and yells if people try to talk about chiaroscuro.

'I'm terribly sorry, Sir Henry.' Molly spoke with real apology.

'I didn't mean to laugh at you, and it was dreadfully rude of me. How's your toe?'

'Awful,' said the great man, indicating a right foot still bandaged. His sour expression softened a little. 'I'm glad *somebody's* had the decency to ask that question.'

'We were all very sorry to hear about it. How did you come to do it, by the way?'

H.M. looked as though he hadn't heard the question.

'He was showing us,' Ferrars explained instantly, 'how he played rugger for Cambridge in '91.'

'And I still think there was dirty work. If I can prove it on this feller behind me . . .' H.M. paused, with a deep sniff, and then spoke to Molly with that shattering directness I was to learn about in the future. 'You got a boyfriend?' he asked.

Molly stiffened.

'Really –' she began.

'You're too pretty not to have a boyfriend,' said the great man, who was merely paying her a compliment in return for her consideration in inquiring after his toe. 'You must have lots of 'em. I mean to say, a sympathetic gal like you must find 'em swarmin' up the ivy practically every night.'

And then, idiot that I am in dealing with young people, I must put in *my* oar.

'Steve Grange,' I said, 'believes Molly is a little too young to be thinking about marriage just yet. Though we'd always rather hoped that she and Tom . . .'

Molly was breathless and very much on her own dignity.

'Let Tom speak for himself, then,' she said rather sharply. 'And I really don't know how we came to be discussing my affairs all of a sudden.'

'You're wasting your time, Molly,' observed Ferrars, with a flash of his faint catlike quality. 'Tom is one of nature's bachelors. Anything in skirts, to him, is something to be put on the table, and – dissected. Could you possibly be interested in anyone else?'

Molly regarded him curiously.

'That would depend,' she answered, 'on his experience.'

'Experience?' mocked Ferrars. 'From *you*?'

His faint smile flashed under the long nose. He lounged with the weight on one hip, his hands thrust into the pockets of paint-stained trousers and his lean elbows sticking out like wings.

'But maybe you're right,' he added, and his face clouded over. 'This isn't exactly the time to be discussing the matter of love affairs, present or projected. One love affair had too sticky a finish on Saturday night for my taste. Has anybody heard any more about that business, by the way?'

Perhaps Ferrars' question was less casual than it had sounded, for he must have seen – as we all saw – the police car coming along the High Street from the direction of Lynton. The car slowed down, idled, and came to a stop near my gate. Superintendent Craft climbed out from behind the wheel. Craft, whom I have known for many years, is a tall, long-faced man with one glass eye and a slow-speaking bass voice.

The fixity of that glass eye gives him a sinister air which is belied by his character. Craft is modestly sociable, and likes his pint as well as the next man. His office is at Barnstaple, where he lives, and he has studied every police manual on earth.

He walked straight up to H.M.

'I wonder if I could have a word in private, sir?' he requested, in that rolling voice. Then he paused, hesitated, and turned the dead eye on the rest of us as he added deliberately: 'We've recovered the bodies.'

6

All of us remained very quiet in the warm street. Propping his crutch against the side of the chair, H.M. peered up without enthusiasm.

'You mean,' he grunted, 'those two who chucked 'emselves off the cliff Saturday night?'

'That's right.'

'Then what do you want to see me about? They're dead, ain't they?'

'Yes, sir, they're very much dead. But there's some little doubt about the evidence just the same.' Superintendent Craft looked at me. 'I'd also like to have a word with you, Doctor, if I may.' His good eye indicated the others meaningly. 'Is there anywhere we could go to talk?'

'Why not come into the house? Or, better still, the back garden?'

'That's fine for me, Doctor, if it'd suit Sir Henry?'

H.M. merely grunted. Ferrars, who had taken out a pipe and was filling it from an oilskin pouch, watched them with frank curiosity.

'Other company excluded, I suppose?' Ferrars said.

'Sorry, Mr –' Craft didn't know Ferrars' name and presumably didn't want to know it. 'Sorry, sir. Official business.'

Ferrars was unabashed. 'Then, if you don't mind, I'll just push the Big Shot into the back garden and return for him in half an hour. If he insists on starting that infernal motor, I can't stop him. But I'm walking back to Ridd Farm with him, in case he tries to break his neck again. Where did you find the bodies, if that's not a secret?'

The superintendent hesitated. 'Washed up on the beach at Happy Hollow early this morning. Now, sir!'

Molly Grange turned round and walked away without a word. I seemed to remember that there was something she had wanted to show me; but this, evidently, could wait.

Not without squawks, Sir Henry Merrivale was impelled round the tangled paths to the back garden. The sun was a little warm for his invalid's shawl, so he stuffed it behind him. Then he and Superintendent Craft and I sat under the apple-tree while Craft produced a notebook.

'See here,' H.M. growled, with surprising meekness. 'I got a confession to make.'

'Yes, sir?'

'The old man's bored,' said H.M. 'I've been sitting on my behind for what seems like years. They don't want me in London' – the corners of his mouth drew down – 'and they don't seem to want me anywhere, and I'm sort of lost and at a loose end.'

(I wondered why, since somebody had said he occupied a very important position at the War Office.)

'So if you've got anything of a stimulatin' nature to ask me, I'm all for it. There's only one question I'd like to ask you at the beginning, son. And be awful careful about the answer.'

'Yes, sir?' Craft prompted.

Opening the pocket of his linen suit, to display a considerable corporation ornamented with a large gold watch-chain, H.M. fished out a case full of what proved to be vile black cigars. He lit one of these, and drew in a long sniff as though he found the smoke unpleasant: which, in fact, it definitely was. His small sharp eyes fastened on Craft.

'Was there any jiggery-pokery about those footprints?' he asked.

'I don't quite follow that. Jiggery-pokery how?'

H.M. regarded him dismally.

'Oh, my son! I've got a nasty suspicious mind.'

'Well, sir?'

'You see two lines of footprints, a large set made by a man's shoes and a small set made by a woman's shoes, leadin' out through soft soil to a full stop. No other prints at all. Now, to the mind of radiant innocence that means a man and a woman have gone out to the high-jump. Hey? But to this sink of low tricks here' – H.M. tapped his forehead – 'it may mean the whole thing's a fake.'

Superintendent Craft frowned, spreading out his notebook on his knee.

'A fake how?'

'Well, suppose, for some reason or other, these two only want to *seem* dead. All right. The woman stands on the steps outside the back door. She walks out, alone, across the soft soil to a little patch of scrub grass on the edge of the cliff. In her hand she's holdin' a pair of the man's shoes. Got that?'

'Yes, sir.'

'There she takes off her own shoes, and puts on the man's shoes. In these she just walks backwards, beside the first line of tracks, until she reaches the steps again.' H.M. made a mesmeric pass with his cigar. 'And there, d'ye see, you've got two sets of footprints to fulfil the conditions. It's an awful simple dodge, son.'

He broke off, beginning to simmer and glare, because Superintendent Craft was laughing.

It was a soft sound, deep and hardly audible, a laughter of genuine appreciation. It lit up Craft's gloomy face, in contrast to the fixity of his glass eye, and made his chin fold out over his collar.

'You see anything so funny about that?' demanded H.M.

'No, sir. It's rather good. And it would be all very well in the story-books. The only thing I can tell you is that it didn't happen.'

Then Craft grew very serious.

'You see, sir, it's like this. I don't want to talk fancy, but footprints are a very well-studied branch of criminology. Gross has a whole chapter on them. Contrary to what people believe, footprints are harder to fake than almost anything else. In fact, it's almost impossible to fake them, and certainly impossible in the way you're talking about. This "walking backwards" business has been tried before. It can always be spotted a mile off.

'A person walking backwards can't help leaving traces of it. The steps are shorter; the heel is turned inwards; the weight's distributed in a totally different way, slanting from toe to heel. Then there's the question of the two persons' weights.

'I'd like you to see some plaster casts of those prints we took on Saturday night. They're honest prints. No jiggery-pokery about them. The man was five feet eleven inches tall, weighed eleven stone ten, and wore number nine shoe. The woman was five feet six inches tall, weighed nine stone four, and wore number five shoe. If there's one thing we can be certain about in the business, it's this: *Mrs Wainright and Mr Sullivan walked out to the edge of that cliff, and they didn't come back.*'

Craft paused, clearing his throat.

And, as I can see now, what he said was quite true.

'Oh, ah,' grunted H.M., eyeing him from behind the oily smoke of the cigar. 'You take your scientific criminology pretty seriously in these parts, don't you?'

'*I* do,' the superintendent assured him. 'Though I don't often get a chance to apply it.'

'Meanin' that you think you can apply it here?'

'Let me tell you what happened, sir.' Craft glanced round, raked the garden with his sinister eye, and lowered his voice. 'As I told you, the bodies were washed up at Happy Hollow very early this morning. They'd been dead and in the water since early Saturday night – I needn't give all the gruesome details – and you'd naturally have thought they died of fractures or drowning. But they hadn't died of fractures or drowning.'

A very curious look had come into H.M.'s eye.

'Hadn't died of . . . ?'

'No, sir. Both of them had been shot through the heart at very close range, body-range, with some small-calibre weapon.'

It was so quiet in the garden that we could hear somebody talking over a back fence two houses away.

'Well?' growled H.M., though he seemed annoyed by some inner suspicion which made him puff very violently at the cigar. 'If you're goin' to be so ruddy scientific and technical, *I* can tell you there's nothing very unusual or surprisin' in that. Plenty of suicides, especially suicide pacts, do just that. They make double-sure of flyin' to glory. They stand on the edge of a river; the man shoots the girl; over she goes; he shoots himself, and over *he* goes. Finish.'

Craft nodded solemnly.

'That's true,' he agreed. 'What's more, the wounds were characteristic suicide-wounds. Naturally, I couldn't verify anything until we had a post-mortem report. But the coroner phoned Dr Hankins, and Dr Hankins did a post-mortem for us this morning.

'Each victim had been killed by a .32 bullet. Fired, as I told you, at body-range. The clothes were powder-burned. There was burning, blackening, and tattooing of the wounds. That's to say' – Craft held up a well-sharpened pencil and sighted along it – 'unconsumed bits of the propellent were embedded in the skin. Showing for certain sure the shots were fired at body-range. Double suicide.'

'Well, then,' said H.M., 'what's bitin' you? Why have you got such a funny look on that dial of yours? There's your evidence.'

Again Craft nodded solemnly.

'Yes, sir, there's my evidence.' He paused. 'Only, you see, it wasn't a double suicide. It was a double murder.'

Now, you who read this record have been expecting it. You have been waiting for that word 'murder', and perhaps wondering when it would first occur. To you it is only the preparation for a battle of wits. But to me – having the thing flung in my face like this – every word Craft said came with a cold shock better left to your imagination.

The talk of shot-wounds, '*unconsumed bits of the propellent were embedded in the skin*', was bad enough when this applied to Rita Wainright. As we sat in the garden under the apple-tree, Rita had become no more than a heap of flesh on a morgue-slab. But any talk of murder, of someone feeling a hate violent enough to kill both Rita and Barry Sullivan, was completely incredible.

H.M., his mouth open, regarded Craft with something like awe. But he did not comment.

'Now, let's take the weapon,' pursued the superintendent. 'To be exact, a .32 Browning automatic. If Mr Sullivan shot the lady, and then shot himself – or the other way round, if you prefer – then you'd expect the gun to fall into the sea along with 'em. Wouldn't you?'

H.M. eyed him. 'I don't expect anything, son. You're tellin' the story. You go ahead.'

'Or else,' argued Craft, 'you'd expect to find it on the cliff somewhere near the place where they went over. But you wouldn't' – here he lifted the pencil and raised his shaggy eyebrows for emphasis – 'you wouldn't expect to find it lying in the main road a very long distance from the sea, and fully half a mile away from the Wainrights' house?'

'So?' said H.M.

'I'd better explain that. Is anybody here acquainted with Mr Stephen Grange? He's a solicitor at Barnstaple, but he lives here at Lyncombe.'

'Very much so,' I answered, as H.M. shook his head. 'That was his daughter out there in the street with us a while ago.'

Craft digested this.

'On Saturday night,' he went on, 'or, rather, about one-thirty o'clock on Sunday morning, Mr Grange was driving back home in his car from a visit to Minehead. He passed the Wainrights' bungalow. We – I mean the police – were there at the time, but naturally Mr Grange didn't know there was anything wrong.

'He was driving very slowly and carefully, as all people ought to do nowadays. About half a mile further on in the direction of Lyncombe, his lights picked up something bright and shiny lying at the side of the road. Mr Grange is a careful and methodical sort of gentleman, so he got out to investigate.'

(Just like Steve Grange.)

'It was a .32 Browning automatic, bright polished steel except for the hard-rubber grip. Mind you, Mr Grange hadn't any reason to think anything was wrong. It was just a gun. But, as I say, he's a careful and methodical sort of fellow who's been no end of help to us. He picked it up in his finger-tips' – Craft illustrated – 'and he could tell by smelling the barrel that it had been fired some hours before.

'He took it home with him that night. Next day he turned it in at the police station at Lynton. It was sent on to me at Barnstaple. In fact, it arrived early this morning: just after I'd got the news about two drowned bodies that weren't drowned, but had bullet-holes in 'em. Two bullets had been fired from this gun; and it'd been wiped clean of fingerprints. I turned everything over to Major Selden, the ballistics man. I've just come from him. The bullet that killed Mrs Wainright and the bullet that killed Mr Sullivan were both fired from that Browning automatic.'

Superintendent Craft paused.

H.M. opened one eye.

'Uh-huh,' he murmured drowsily. 'D'ye know, son, I've been rather expecting that, somehow.'

'But that's not all the major was able to say. If we hadn't found the automatic, we'd have thought for certain it was suicide. Perfect crime, as you might call it. But this particular gun has got a distinct "back-fire", as some of them have. That's to say, in non-technical language, you can't possibly fire it without a back-fire of unburnt powder-grains that get embedded in your hand –'

H.M. was no longer drowsy. He had sat up straight.

'– like a trade-mark. Neither Mrs Wainright's hand nor Mr Sullivan's hand had the marks. So it wasn't suicide, sir. It was murder.'

'There's no doubt about that, son?'

'You just talk to Major Selden. He'll convince you.'

'Oh, my eye!' muttered H.M. 'Oh, lord love a duck!'

Craft turned round to me. He was apologetic but determined. His good eye smiled while the other remained lifeless.

'Now, Doctor, we've already had *your* testimony.'

'You have. But this is the most fantastic –'

'Yes,' admitted Craft, 'that's just the trouble. Now let's see.'

He leafed back through his notebook.

'At nine o'clock on Saturday night, fixed by the news on the radio, Mrs Wainright ran out of the house. Mr Sullivan followed her. Mrs Wainright, or somebody, left a note on the kitchen table saying she was going to do herself in. Am I correct there?'

'Yes, that's right.'

Craft, I knew, was speaking to H.M. rather than to me.

'Two sets of footprints, one of Mrs Wainright's and one of Mr Sullivan's, lead out to the edge of the cliff. There's absolutely no fake or trickery – we establish this – about those prints.

'*But*,' said Craft, 'between nine o'clock and nine-thirty, somebody shot both the victims. The shooting was done at body-range. The murderer must have been standing in front of them, close enough to touch them. And yet there are no footprints anywhere else, except Dr Croxley's.

'At half past nine Dr Croxley got alarmed and went out to see what had happened to them. He saw the tracks leading to the cliff-edge. He went out there, looked over, and came back to the bungalow.' Here Craft grew heavily whimsical. 'I don't suppose you shot those two yourself, did you, Doctor?'

'Great Scott, no!'

Craft smiled in that un-funny way of his.

'Don't worry,' he advised. 'I've been a good many years in this district. I can't think of anybody less likely to do murder than Luke Croxley.'

'Thanks.'

'But there's good evidence to show you didn't do it,' Craft went on, 'even if we were mugs enough to suspect you.' He turned to H.M. 'Dr Croxley hasn't been a police surgeon for nothing. He remembered to keep away from those footprints and not mess them up.'

'I was just wonderin' about that, son.'

'In fact, he stayed a good six feet away all the distance out. Those tracks run, all of them, in straight parallel lines. He couldn't very well have stood six feet away from the nearest victim, facing the same direction and never even turning sideways, while he shot 'em both at body-range. No: his testimony's all right. We'll accept it.'

This time I put even more acid into my thanks.

Craft ignored it. 'But you see where that puts us, Sir Henry. I won't ask you to come and look at the bodies, because they were pretty badly smashed up by the fall and by knocking along the coast all this time . . .'

'They weren't,' I said, 'unrecognisable?'

Craft grinned: a sickly sort of grin, as even he seemed to realise.

'Oh, no. No funny business about *that*. They're the bodies of

Mrs Wainright and Mr Sullivan, all right. All the same you ought to be glad you didn't have to do the post-mortem.'

(Rita, Rita, Rita!)

'But as I was saying to Sir Henry, I'm going to have a packet of trouble on my hands with this case. I want to try my hand at it. And if there's any advice you could give me, I'd appreciate it a very great deal.

'You see how it stands. Two persons were shot as they stood on the very edge of a cliff. The murderer couldn't have climbed up or down that cliff. Presumably he couldn't fly. Yet he approached them and got away without leaving a footprint on that whole expanse of soil. If we hadn't found the weapon later, it would have been a perfect crime passing as a double suicide. It may be a perfect crime even yet. I'd be interested to hear what you think about it.'

7

H.M.'s cigar had gone out. He blinked at it in a displeased way, and turned the stump round in his fingers.

'Y'know,' he observed. 'I once told Masters –'

'Chief Inspector Masters?'

'That's right. I once told Masters he had a habit of getting tangled up in the goddamnedest cases I ever heard tell of. It seems to me the Devon County Constabulary can qualify for nearly as high marks. And yet I dunno. There's reason in this. Cold reason.' He brooded. 'What I want is facts; *all* the facts. So far all I've had is a sketchy account from Paul Ferrars, when we thought it was suicide. What's the rest of the story?'

'Will you tell him about it, Dr Croxley? You've followed it from the beginning.'

I was only too glad.

If Rita had been murdered, I felt towards her murderer a black hatred – a personal vindictiveness – beyond anything Christian charity allows. I was thinking, too, of Alec collapsed and fainting in the hall. So I started at the beginning, and told the story pretty much as I have outlined it in this narrative.

Though it was a long recital, they did not seem to find it

tedious. We were interrupted only twice. The first time was when Paul Ferrars arrived to claim his guest. He was chased away by H.M. with more lurid language than a man usually employs towards his host; but Ferrars only grinned and retired. On the second occasion, Mrs Harping, my housekeeper, came bowling down the path with a hand-bell to say that lunch was ready.

Mrs Harping is indispensable. She bosses us and doses us – there is something odd about the spectacle of two doctors meekly swallowing home-remedies – and washes our shirts and cooks our meals. It required some firmness to say I wanted two extra plates added for lunch, the meal to be served here under the apple-tree, at a time when food was just beginning to get scarce. But I got my way, and finished telling the story after the cloth was cleared.

'Well, sir?' prompted Craft 'Does anything strike you?'

H.M., who had been occupied with the steering-handle of the wheelchair, turned his sharp little eyes sideways.

'Oh, my son! Lots of things. The first point – but we'll let that go, for the moment. There's other points almost as interesting.'

He sat silent for a moment, ruffling his hands across his big bald head.

'*Imprimis*, gents, why did somebody have to let the petrol out of the cars as well as cuttin' the telephone-wires?'

'Assuming,' I said, 'that the person who did it was the murderer?'

'Assuming it was anybody you like. What was the purpose of it? Was he tryin' to prevent discovery of a crime which nobody was supposed to spot as a crime? But how? You weren't at the North Pole. You were less than half a dozen miles from a police station. Discovery couldn't have been prevented. Why call attention to the possibility of hokey-pokey in a perfectly straightforward suicide pact?'

'It might have been done by Johnson.'

'Sure. But I'll lay you ducats to an old shoe it wasn't.'

'And the next point?'

'That's a part of the same foolishness. As our friend Craft says, this murderer has got away with a practically perfect crime. Then the silly dummy goes and chucks the gun down in a public road where it'll probably be found. Unless –'

'Unless what?'

H.M. brooded.

'I could bear to hear a lot more about that gun. For instance.' He blinked at me. 'When you found the petrol let out of the cars, you set out and foot-slogged to Lyncombe after a telephone. You must have walked by that very same road where Mr Grange later found the automatic. Did you notice it?'

'No, but that's not surprising. I'd dropped and lost the Wainrights' electric torch. That road was pretty dark.'

H.M. attacked Craft.

'Well, then!' he persisted. 'You went out there with a squad of coppers, in a car. You must have had lights. You got there, you've been tellin' me, about a quarter to one. Still some time before the thing was found. Did *you* see the ruddy gun?'

'No. Nothing odd in that either, sir. We were driving in the opposite direction, on the other side of the road.'

'Phooey!' said H.M., puffing out his cheeks in a richly sinister way, and sitting back to contemplate us fishily. He folded his hands across his corporation and twiddled his thumbs. 'I don't say there's anything rummy in it, you understand. All I want, burn me, is information! Next, that alleged suicide-note. Have you got it?'

From between the leaves of his notebook Craft took out the paper. It was only, as I have said, a little slip torn from the kitchen memorandum-pad and scrawled on with the pencil that went with it. It said:

Juliet died a lady. No recriminations. No putting it off. I love everybody. Goodbye.

H.M. read the words aloud, and I had to put up a hand to shade my eyes. He regarded me sombrely.

'Dr Croxley, have you seen this?'

'Yes.'

'Is it in Mrs Wainright's handwriting?'

'It is and it isn't. I should say yes: that it's her handwriting under very strong emotion.'

'Looky here, Doctor.' H.M. was powerfully embarrassed. 'I can see you were fond of this gal. I'm not askin' these things out of idle curiosity. Do you think Mrs Wainright meant to kill herself?'

'Yes.'

'If you'll excuse me, sir,' burst out Superintendent Craft, whacking his fist down on his knee, 'that's just it. That's the real puzzler. That's what gets me. If those two were going to kill themselves anyway, why murder 'em?'

This was a point I had been trying to put clearly myself. But H.M. shook his head.

'Nothing much to that, son. Not necessarily, I mean. They could have meant to kill themselves, and lost their nerve. The same thing has happened lots of times. Then a certain person, who's determined to see 'em both dead, steps in and shoots. Only . . .'

He continued to scowl, ticking his thumb and second finger against the note, as some obscure thought bothered him like dyspepsia.

'Let's face it,' he said. 'This is what is humorously known to the press as a crime of passion. There's no need to go star-gazin' after motives. Somebody either (a) hated Mrs Wainright so much because she was carrying on with Sullivan, or (b) hated Sullivan so much because he was carrying on with Mrs Wainright, that both of 'em had to be knocked off.'

'Looks like it, sir,' agreed Craft.

'Therefore we got to rake up scandal whether we like it or not. Speakin' personally,' observed H.M., with great candour, 'I got a low mind and a great taste for scandal myself. According to what the doctor tells us, this Alec Wainright believed his wife had been carrying on with somebody long before she met the late lamented Sullivan.'

'She swore to me –' I began.

H.M. was apologetic.

'Sure. I know. All the same, I'd like a bit of testimony that's not quite so dewy-eyed and prejudiced as hers. When can we have a word with the husband?'

'You'll have to ask Tom about that. Not immediately, I should say, and possibly not for some time.'

'In the meantime, did you ever hear anything about swoonin' love affairs?'

'Never.'

H.M. blinked at Craft. 'What about you, son?'

'That's not much in my line.' The superintendent hesitated. 'But I'm bound to admit I never heard anything against the lady. And things do get about, you know, in little places like this.'

"What we want,' said H.M., handing the suicide-note back to Craft, 'is a woman's touch in this, and a woman's fine serene unconsciousness of the laws of slander. It'd interest me strangely to have a word with that gal there.' He nodded his head in the direction of Molly Grange's house. 'She strikes me as bein' a sensible bit of goods, with her eyes open. What's more, a little *causerie* with her father –'

'We could go over there now,' Craft suggested. He consulted his watch. 'It's pretty late in the afternoon, and Mr Grange ought to be home before long.'

H.M. fumbled at the side of the wheelchair. The whir of the motor throbbed out against stillness, growing to its steady *pop-pop-pop* which carried as far as the High Street. It had an instant response. Ears were on the alert, tails quivered, bodies grew tense. A distant din of barking rose in challenge. H.M. squinted round evilly.

'Grr, you little blighters!' he said. Then his sense of grievance bubbled up. 'Looky here, son: I got a protest to make. Can't you for the flamin' love of Esau do something about those ruddy DOGS?'

It was evident that Superintendent Craft found the great man sometimes difficult to deal with.

'You'll be all right, sir, if you just take it slowly! I told you yesterday, when you were cutting figure-eights on Mr Ferrars' lawn –'

'I'm a mild-mannered bloke,' said H.M., 'known far and wide for the urbanity of my temper and the ease of my bearing. I love animals like St Francis of Assisi, blast their ears. But fair's fair and enough's enough. Those faithful friends of man out there nearly made me break my neck this morning. If I got to go through this business like a Russian grand duke in a sleigh pursued by wolves, I say it's a goddamned persecution.'

'I'll go ahead of you, and keep them off.'

'Then there's another thing,' said H.M. very quietly. 'When we see the gal down there' – again he nodded towards Molly's – 'what are we going to tell her? People still think the thing was a suicide pact. Do we let on it's murder yet, or do we keep it up our sleeves?'

Craft rubbed his chin.

'I don't very well see how we can keep it back,' he decided. 'There'll be the inquest on Wednesday anyway. And if we want to learn anything beforehand –'

'Let her have it straight, then?'

'I should say so, yes.'

H.M. bumped up the garden path like a man on a pogo-stick, and navigated the distance pretty well. The Granges – father, mother, and daughter – live in a modest house, very trim and tidy. The long bay windows of the sitting-room stood open; somebody was playing a piano inside.

When we had hoisted H.M. up the front step, a trim maid admitted us to the hall and then the sitting-room. The furnishing of that white room showed means and taste. In Steve Grange's house, nothing was ever untidy or out of place. Molly, looking surprised to see us, got up from the grand piano in the bay window.

All three of us, I think, were a little uncertain and inclined to clear our throats. Eventually, I was the goat who spoke.

'Molly,' I said, 'you told me this morning you had some ideas about this unfortunate business. Rita Wainright and Barry Sullivan, I mean. You had something you wanted to show me.'

'Oh, that!' said Molly, without interest. She reached down with one finger and plinked at a treble key on the piano. 'I was wrong about that, Dr Luke. I – I'm rather glad I was wrong. It was beastly.'

'But what was it you wanted to show me?'

'Nothing,' replied Molly. 'Only an old puzzle-book.'

'Wow!' said H.M., with such lively interest that we all turned towards him. Molly flashed him a quick glance, and then fell to tapping at the piano keys again. 'I wonder if we were thinking of the same puzzle? But it won't work, my gal. It's too easy. Burn me, if only it *were* as easy as that!' H.M. groaned and shook his fist. 'All the same, I wonder if we were thinking of the same puzzle?'

Somewhere at the back of my mind, hazy and tantalising, drifted a recollection that someone else in this affair had once mentioned puzzles in some way. I could not place it.

'I wonder too,' smiled Molly. 'But please sit down! I'll go and call mother. She's only in the garden.'

'We'd rather you didn't do that, miss,' said Superintendent Craft in a sepulchral voice. 'Our business is with you alone.'

Molly laughed a little.

'Well!' she said rather breathlessly, and plumped down on the piano-bench. 'Do sit down anyway! What was it you wanted?'

'Do you mind if I close the doors, miss?'

'No, not at all. What on earth . . . ?'

Craft performed the ritual. When he did take a chair, balancing his long body on the edge of it, he spoke with the same sepulchral earnestness.

'Miss, I want you to prepare yourself for a good bit of a shock.'

'Yes?'

'Mrs Wainright and Mr Sullivan didn't commit suicide. They weren't even drowned. They were both deliberately murdered.'

Silence. A clock on the mantelpiece ticked faintly.

It was more than a shock to the girl: you could see that. Her lips opened. Her hands fell, without sound, on the piano keys. The blue eyes moved towards me for confirmation, and I nodded my head. When Molly spoke, it was in a low and husky voice.

'Where?' she asked.

'On the edge of the cliff.'

'They were *murdered*,' Molly repeated incredulously, 'on the edge of the *cliff*?'

As she said the word 'murdered', Molly craned round to glance at the net-curtained windows, as though afraid she might be overheard in the street.

'That's right, miss.'

'But that's impossible! They were alone. There weren't any footprints except theirs. Or at least that's what I was told.'

Craft remained patient. 'We know that right enough, miss. But it's true. They were killed by somebody who seems to be able to float in the air. I'll ask you to keep that strictly private and confidential for the moment. Still, there it is. And we thought you might be able to help us.'

'How were they – killed?'

'They were shot. Didn't you hear about the .32 automatic that . . . ?'

H.M. intervened here by clearing his throat with a hideous violence and thrust of the head which suggested a dragon in a Disney film. It startled Molly into jangling a discord from the piano keys.

'As the superintendent says,' H.M. remarked more mildly, 'we've got a beauty of an impossible situation. There's a friend of mine in London, named Masters. If *he* was here, he'd be havin' a fit. I'm glad the local people take it more sensibly.'

'But how do you *know* they were murdered?' persisted Molly. 'Isn't that an impossible assumption in itself?'

'It's a long story, my wench, and it can wait. Since we're getting no further with the mechanics, we thought we'd have a look at another side of it. Now tell me. You knew Mrs Wainright fairly well?'

'Yes. Fairly well.'

'Did you like her?'

Molly smiled wryly at me.

'No. Not very much. Please don't misunderstand me. I didn't *dislike* her. I thought some of her poses were rather silly. I thought she made eyes at the men too much –'

'And you disapproved of that?'

'I have better ways of employing my time,' said Molly primly.

'So?'

Molly spoke hastily. 'Please don't misunderstand that either. I didn't in the least disapprove of Rita. It just seemed silly to be thinking about it *all* the time.'

'Thinkin' about what all the time?'

Molly's face slowly turned pink. 'Love affairs, of course. What on earth else could I mean?'

'Oh, I dunno. People have different words for different shades of what they mean. But what I was really getting at was this. Did she ever have a serious extramarital affair before Sullivan? We're not askin' out of idle curiosity.'

For a long time Molly considered this, ruffling the back of her hand along the piano keyboard.

'I suppose you want an honest answer to that?' she asked in a troubled voice. Then she looked up. 'The honest answer is: I don't know. You see, when I say she made eyes at the men I don't mean she ran after them. She didn't. And there's a difference. I always thought she was perfectly faithful to Mr Wainright. What exactly are you looking for?'

Craft intervened.

'We're looking for a motive, miss. We're wondering if there was anybody who cared enough about Mrs Wainright to go off his rocker and kill both of 'em when she fell for somebody else.'

Molly stared at us.

'But surely,' she burst out, 'surely you're not thinking anything about poor Mr Wainright?'

Up to this time, I can honestly say, the thought of Alec's being in any way connected with the affair had never once entered my head. Such is your blindness when you are so close to a person that you can't see him. However logical, any such conception remains hidden behind the screen of your preconceived ideas. But, after one glance at the superintendent and H.M., it became clear that they had never suffered from this form of blindness.

Superintendent Craft smiled rather like Hamlet's father's ghost.

'Well, no,' he answered. 'We don't think anything like that, miss. Because we can't. That's the trouble.'

'I don't understand.'

'When a wife gets herself killed, especially in a business like this,' Craft went on, 'naturally, the first person you want to hear all about is the husband.'

'*That* nice little man?' cried Molly.

'Any husband,' said Craft, comprising the tribe within the sweep of his arm. 'But, according to Dr Croxley – and we believe him – Mr Wainright was in Dr Croxley's presence every second of the time between nine and nine-thirty on Saturday night.

'And even supposing,' Craft added, turning the faraway grin towards me, 'there'd been any funny business after nine-thirty. Concealing evidence, or cleaning up, or the like. Still Dr Croxley was with him, until he collapsed. After he collapsed, if the doctor's given us a correct account of his condition, he couldn't very well have left his bed for anything at all.'

'He certainly couldn't have left his bed,' I agreed. 'I'll take my Bible oath on that.'

'You see how it is,' Craft explained. 'We've got to look in another direction. This wasn't a crime for money, or anything of that sort. We've got to find somebody who hated them both enough to want to kill them *together*. That's a private thing, a personal thing. And as we see it, miss, the answer will be somewhere in Mrs Wainright's affairs.

'You said a while ago that you always "thought" she was faithful to her husband, but as though you weren't quite sure yourself. If there's anything you can tell us, miss, I might remind you it's your plain duty to go ahead and speak out. Can you tell us anything?'

Molly made a face of distaste. Looking down in front of her, she touched a few chords on the piano; but very lightly, as though she were half afraid to touch them. Hesitation, uneasiness, and doubt were all to be seen in her expression.

Then she drew a deep breath and looked up.

'Yes,' she replied, 'I'm afraid I can.'

8

'I don't like to tell it,' Molly complained, lifting one shoulder higher than the other, 'because it sounds uncomfortably like sneaking. But it wasn't. I couldn't help it. And you can repeat it if you like.'

'Yes, miss?'

'It happened in the spring. April or thereabouts: I'm not sure. It was on a Sunday, and I was out walking. Do you know the little lane that leads off the main road to Baker's Bridge three miles or more from here?'

Superintendent Craft opened his mouth to comment, and shut it again. He merely nodded.

'I'd turned into that lane, intending to walk as far as Baker's Bridge and return to Lyncombe by the back way. I was walking rather fast, because it was getting towards twilight. It was a damp day, with the trees just turning green. About two hundred yards along that lane, there's a little stone house: a kind of studio. Some artist or other used it years ago, but it's been vacant for a long time. Do you know the one I mean?'

'Yes, miss.'

'When I was maybe thirty yards from the house, first I noticed a car pulled in beside it. An S.S. Jaguar: Rita's car, though I didn't identify it at the time. The house had gone to rack and ruin; what used to be the glass roof of the studio was all broken and messy. Two persons were standing in the doorway, partly in and partly out. One was a woman in a bright red jumper – that was the only reason I noticed her at all, against the dusk. The other was a man. I can't tell you who he was or even what he looked like; he was back in the doorway.

'The woman had her arms round him. I can't help it, but that's what I saw.' Molly looked defiant and angry. 'The woman tore away from him. Even then I couldn't tell who she was. She hurried out through the mud to the car, and got in. The car started up with a whir among the dead leaves. It swung round and came towards me. That was when I recognised Rita at the wheel.

'She didn't see me. I doubt if she noticed anything. She looked . . . well, all tousled and mad, with a martyred expression, as though she hadn't been enjoying herself at all. The car went tearing past me, before I could call out to her. Not that I should have called out anyway. I wondered whether to walk on or turn back, but I decided it would look conspicuous if I didn't go on. I didn't see anything more of the man.

'And that's all I can tell you. It isn't much. I doubt if it proves anything. But you asked me whether there was somebody in her life whom we haven't heard about. There is – or was.'

Craft took out his notebook, which seemed to disturb Molly, and wrote half a dozen words in it.

'I see, miss.' He spoke in a colourless voice. 'That was on the Baker's Bridge road, you say? About half a mile, maybe, from the Wainrights' own house?'

'That's right.'

'You couldn't describe the man, by any chance?'

'No. He was only a shape and a pair of hands.'

'Tall or short? Young or old? Fat or thin? Anything like that?'

'I'm sorry,' said Molly. 'That's all I can tell you.'

'You never heard – yes, maybe we've got to go as far as this. You never heard any gossip connecting Mrs Wainright with anyone in this neighbourhood?'

Molly shook her head. 'No, I never did.'

For several minutes H.M. had sat motionless, his eyes closed and an expression of Gargantuan sourness turning down the corners of his mouth.

'Looky here,' he said. 'We've heard a lot about Mrs Wainright. Could you tell us anything about Sullivan? Could you tell us, for instance, what his real name was?'

This time he succeeded in startling Craft and me as much as he startled Molly.

'His real name?' repeated Molly. 'His real name is Barry Sullivan, isn't it?'

'The theatrical ignorance of this generation,' said H.M., 'would be enough to turn my hair grey if I had any. Oh, my wench! What would you think of an actor nowadays who had the nerve to call himself David Garrick or Edmund Kean?'

'I should think,' Molly answered very thoughtfully, 'it was a stage-name.'

'Uh-huh. And the real Barry Sullivan was one of the best-known romantic actors of the nineteenth century. Mind: it *may* be a coincidence. There may be a real Mrs Sullivan who called her handsome son Barry. But, takin' it in connection with the stage, it's interestin' enough to be investigated.'

H.M. brooded.

'If you think there's anything in it,' he went on, 'you could always find out through the American Consulate in London. Or through the Actors' Equity, maybe. Or even through the place where he worked sellin' motor cars.'

Craft nodded.

'I've already wired the C.I.D. there,' he replied. 'Tell you about that part of it later.' To my surprise, Craft's normally calm face was suffused with blood, and he kept clearing his throat. He did not even seem interested in the subject of Barry Sullivan.

'Tell me, miss. You're sure it was the Baker's Bridge road?'

Molly opened her eyes. 'Good heavens, of course I'm sure! I've lived here all my life.'

'Didn't your father say anything to you yesterday or today?'

Molly blinked at him. 'My father?' she repeated.

'Didn't he tell you it was on the main road, not ten feet from the entrance to the Baker's Bridge road, that he found an automatic pistol late Saturday night?'

This time it was Craft's surprise to all of us. H.M. used words of violence and obscenity, which I am old-fashioned enough to think should not be used in front of a girl like Molly. But Molly hardly heard him. She was clearly so astonished that Craft went on to explain.

'No, he certainly didn't say anything here at home. But then – I don't suppose he would. He never tells much to Mother and me.'

'He'd no reason to suppose there was anything wrong, miss,' the superintendent pointed out. 'We didn't know ourselves, until late this morning, it was the gun that killed those two.'

'Father's going to be awfully cross about this,' Molly burst out.

'Cross? Why should he be?'

'Because he hates being mixed up in anything like this, even as The Man Who Found the Gun,' she retorted. 'He says there's practically nothing that isn't bad for a solicitor's practice. And when he learns I've been talking about poor Rita, even after she's dead . . .'

The trim maid tapped at the door and put her head in.

'Shall I serve tea, Miss Molly?' she inquired. 'Mr Grange has just come home.'

Steve Grange was – I suppose I should say *is*, but let the tense remain – a lean, wiry man in his middle fifties. Very straight in the back, very springy in his walk, he had precision and a dry assurance of manner. His bony facial structure, of the sort called clean-cut, was not unhandsome; his black hair was just turning grey against rather withered skin; and he had a narrow line of greyish moustache; and he was always well-dressed to the point of dandyism. He came in carrying the evening paper, and Craft let him have the news straight in the face.

'Good God!' he said. 'Good God!'

He stood for a time staring at us, his dark grey eyes incredulous, and he kept slapping the folded newspaper into the palm of his left hand.

Then he turned briskly to Molly.

'Where's your mother, my dear?'

'In the back garden. She . . .'

'You'd better go and join her, then. Tell Gladys not to serve tea just yet.'

'If you don't mind, Daddy, I'd rather . . .'

'Better go and join her, my dear. I want to talk to these gentlemen.'

Molly's face showed no mutiny when she left. Steve continued to slap the newspaper against the palm of his left hand, a wiry and vital figure with sharply intelligent eyes. He took a turn up and down the room before he sat down, with decision, in a chair opposite us. A frown gathered between his eyebrows.

'This is an awkward business,' he declared. His bony hand made a slight outward gesture. 'Unpleasant, yes. But awkward as well. It's a wonder you ever found the bodies.'

Craft nodded.

'I've been thinking the same thing, sir. What with the currents along this coast, and all. But we did find the bodies, and we did find the gun. Thanks to you.'

Steve's frown deepened.

'Yes. Frankly,' he said with energy, 'if I had had any idea what it was, I'm not sure I should have turned it over to you. That may be bad citizenship; but there it is.'

He drummed with his well-manicured fingers on the padded arm of the chair.

'Trouble!' he added. 'Trouble, trouble for everybody now.'

'I was just wondering, sir. You can't tell us anything about that pistol, can you?'

'See here, Superintendent,' observed Steve. His dry tone had its usual effect. 'You don't imagine *I'm* mixed up in this affair, do you?'

'No, no, sir! I only –'

'Glad to hear it. Very glad to hear it.' Steve even achieved a wintry sort of smile. 'You recovered the bodies. Well! Without any firearm, you would still have believed it a suicide pact. You only found differently when you got your hands on a gun with a distinctive backfire. If *I* had had anything to do with killing those two, do you think I should helpfully have handed over the gun to you?'

Craft chuckled.

'Not exactly. What I meant was that you're the local head of the L.D.V.' – this was what we then called the Home Guard – 'and you might have seen it somewhere before.'

'I can't say. Not to identify it, certainly. You noticed that the registration number was filed off?'

'Yes, sir.'

'Frankly, Superintendent, and speaking subject to correction: I doubt if you'll ever trace that gun. In the old days, when anybody who bought ammunition had to show his firearms licence, it must have been easy to check up. But nowadays? With ammunition being issued to nearly anybody who wants it?'

Steve's disapproval grew. He set his elbows on the arms of the chair, put his finger-tips together, and half closed his eyes. I have always thought of this as a conscious mannerism, designed to impress; but Steve has done it for so long that he forgets how pompous it looks.

'Army officers, I notice, have a deplorable habit,' he said.

'When they go into restaurants or clubs or theatres, they very often take off their holster-belts and leave them hanging openly in cloak-rooms or anywhere else. Nowadays officers carry what pattern and calibre they like. Why more guns aren't stolen . . .'

'You think that may have happened?'

'I don't know. I only threw out the idea.' Steve turned his head slightly. 'And this, I believe,' he added in an agreeable tone, 'is the famous Sir Henry Merrivale?'

'Uh-huh,' agreed H.M., who was staring in a singularly cross-eyed fashion at the crutch propped up in front of him.

'Happy to have you in my home, Sir Henry. I've heard a great deal about you from a mutual friend of ours.'

'Oh? Who's that?'

'Lord Blacklock. A client of mine.' Steve said this not without self-consciousness.

'Old Blackie?' said H.M. with interest. 'How is he these days?'

Steve settled back for a cosy chat about the great.

'Not in very good health, I'm afraid. No.'

'I'll bet he ain't,' agreed H.M., warming to the human touch. 'He's never been the same since he went out to New York and started drinkin' Sterno out of alcohol lamps.'

'Indeed?' said Steve, after a slight pause. 'I can't say I've ever seen him exactly – well! the worse for liquor.'

'It's his wife,' volunteered H.M., and explained this to Craft and me. 'She's the worst old bitch west of the Bristol Channel, but she really does keep Blackie under control.'

Steve looked as though he wished he hadn't brought the subject up.

'Anyway,' he said manfully, 'Lord Blacklock seems very much annoyed with you.'

'Old Blackie annoyed with me? Why?'

Steve smiled. 'I believe he invited you to spend a part of the summer at his country seat. And instead, he says, you chose to go and stay with this fellow . . . what's his name?'

(Steve knew perfectly well what it was, though he snapped his fingers casually and pretended he didn't.)

'Paul Ferrars?'

'That's it,' said Steve. 'The artist.'

'I don't see why in blazes I shouldn't go to see the young feller,' said H.M. 'He's paintin' my picture.'

In the silence that followed this, a deep suspicion seemed to strike H.M. Adjusting his spectacles, he peered slowly round our group, studying each face in turn with a concentrated effort to find any lack of gravity there.

'Is there anybody here,' he rumbled challengingly, 'who can tell me any reason why I *shouldn't* have my picture painted? Is there any reason why I *oughtn't* to get my picture painted? Hey?'

(I could think of one reason, an aesthetic one, but it seemed more tactful not to mention this.)

'That young feller,' pursued H.M., 'is a friend of my younger daughter. He wrote me just about the most insulting letter I've ever had, and I've had plenty. He said I had the funniest face he'd ever run across, even including his student days in Paris, and would I come down here so he could preserve it for posterity? It was so insultin', gents, that I came down out of curiosity.'

'And stayed?'

'Sure. I will say this for the bloke: he's doing me justice. It's a fine picture, and I'm going to buy it. It's not quite finished, because some low-hearted hound made me do this.' H.M. thrust out his foot under the rug. 'And I wanted to pose standing up, and I'm only allowed a short time each day on my feet.' H.M. sniffed, and added modestly: 'He's paintin' me as a Roman Senator.'

Even Superintendent Craft was jarred by this.

'As a *what*, sir?'

'As a Roman Senator,' repeated H.M. After looking at Craft very suspiciously for a moment, he illustrated by drawing himself up with immense dignity and throwing the end of an imaginary toga over his shoulder.

'I see.' Steve Grange spoke without inflection. 'Mr Ferrars has had some success, I believe.'

'You don't like him, do you?'

'I'm afraid, Sir Henry, I don't know him well enough either to like or dislike him. I may be an old-fashioned family man, but I dislike what used to be known as Bohemian ways. That's all.'

'How did you feel about Mrs Wainright?'

Steve got up from his chair. He walked across to the bay-window behind the piano, held back one of the lace curtains, and looked out into the street. On the way, I noticed, he eyed his reflection in a mirror on the wall; for Steve, like most of us, had his own share of human vanity.

'Mrs Wainright and I,' he answered, 'had a rather serious quarrel more than a year ago. Anybody will tell you that. We haven't spoken since.'

Then he turned round from the window and spoke decisively.

'The nature of that quarrel must remain a secret. Mrs Wainright wanted me to do something for her, in a professional way, which I considered unethical. That's as much explanation as I can give you.

'I've discouraged Molly from going out there as much as possible. Understand me: Molly is her own mistress. She makes her own living and is entitled, within reason, to her own life. But the Wainright set, and the Bohemian set, don't appeal particularly to me. I'm very careful about the people who come here to see Molly. And I tell her so.'

This was where I felt called on to register a protest.

'Now look here,' I said with some vehemence. 'What exactly do you mean by the "Wainright set"? You don't call playing bridge or hearts on Saturday night a very Bohemian sort of life, do you? Damn it all, I do that myself!'

Steve smiled.

'By the "Wainright set", Dr Luke, I meant Mrs Wainright herself and any of her younger male admirers.'

Superintendent Craft coughed. 'That's just it, sir. We're looking for the man in the case. The man that your daughter saw with Mrs Wainright out at the old stone studio on the Baker's Bridge road.'

The skin tightened across Steve's cheeks and jaws, as though the high-boned ascetic framework of the face had hardened inside. But he spoke mildly.

'Molly should never have told you that. It was indiscreet and perhaps even actionable.'

'You don't doubt your daughter's word?'

'Not at all. Though I often think she's too imaginative.' Steve rubbed the side of his jaw. 'As for this studio business, maybe some more or less innocent flirtation . . . !'

'Leadin' to murder?' inquired H.M.

'Speaking as a lawyer, gentlemen, let me tell you something.'

Returning to his chair, Steve sat down comfortably.

'You'll never prove there was any man in the case,' he stated, tapping his finger-tips together. 'I'll tell you something more. You're wasting your time in trying to show it was murder. It was a suicide pact, and any coroner's jury is certain to bring it in as such.'

Though Craft started to protest, Steve silenced him with a lifted hand. There was a slight smile under Steve's thin edge of moustache, but it did not extend up to his eyes. His face was serious, earnest, and thoughtful. I could have sworn he believed every word he said.

'The more I think it over, gentlemen, the more *I'm* convinced it was a suicide pact,' he affirmed. 'On what evidence do you base your assumption of murder? On two things. First, the absence of powder-speckling on the hand of either victim. Second, the finding of the gun some distance away. Yes?'

'Yes, sir. And that's good enough for me.'

'Well, let's see.' Steve leaned his head against the back of the chair. 'Let's state a hypothetical case. Mrs Wainright and Mr Sullivan decide to kill themselves. Sullivan procures an automatic.

They walk out to the edge of the cliff. Sullivan first shoots her and then himself. On his right hand he's wearing . . . what? A glove?'

It was very quiet in the white sitting-room, except for the ticking of the clock.

I started to say: 'A glove on his own hand to shoot himself?' But, at the very moment I said it, certain cases in medical jurisprudence as well as in my own experience returned with unnerving distinctness. Steve Grange continued:

'Let's remember the habits of suicides. A suicide will take the most elaborate precautions not to "hurt" or "pain" himself. If he hangs himself, he'll often pad the rope. He seldom or never shoots himself through the eye, though that's the one certain method. He puts a cushion in the gas-oven to make his head comfortable.

'Now this particular gun had a bad backfire. Backfire means a very painful powder-speckling; perhaps a bad burn. Sullivan has to shoot Mrs Wainright even before he shoots himself. Isn't it natural . . . in fact, isn't it inevitable . . . that he'll wear a glove?'

Neither H.M. nor Craft said anything, though I could detect a startled look on the latter's face and he gave a barely perceptible nod.

Steve Grange nodded towards a wall of books at the back of the room.

'We're great crime-readers here,' he told us with faint apology. 'So I'll go on. Isn't it true, Superintendent, that bodies washed up out of water always have some of their clothing – and sometimes nearly all of it – torn away?'

Craft grunted.

His glass eye had acquired, if possible, an even more unnatural appearance. He peered up and down from his notebook.

'It's true enough,' the superintendent admitted. 'I've known one or two of 'em washed up stark naked except for their shoes. Shoes never go, because the leather shrinks. Mrs Wainright and

Mr Sullivan were pretty fully clothed, though most of it was rags. But what you mean is – the first thing to go would be an open glove?'

'That's exactly what I mean.'

Here Steve hesitated, trying to gnaw at the edges of his small moustache.

'Excuse me,' he said in his dry voice. 'The next part isn't pleasant for me. It's going to offend an old friend. But I can't help it.'

He looked straight at me, and spoke gently.

'Dr Luke, let's be fair. Yours were the only other footprints there. We all know how much you liked Mrs Wainright. You'd have hated (admit this!), you'd have hated the idea of having it known she committed suicide because she couldn't be faithful to her husband.

'The gun must have fallen on that tiny little semi-circular patch of scrub grass on the edge of Lovers' Leap. While you were lying at full length, looking over the edge, you could have reached out with a cane and hooked the gun towards you. Confound it, you *must* have! Then you took it back with you, and dropped it in the road on your way home to get the police.'

Again Steve gave me an earnest look, of disapproval mingled with commiseration, before turning to the others. He was bending forward, palms upturned, and forehead furrowed with apologetic horizontal wrinkles.

'Say what you like, gentlemen. That's the only possible explanation,' he declared.

(Here H.M. looked at him very curiously.)

'It's the only one a coroner's jury will accept. You see that? Also, it's the true one. The suicide-note confirms it. The facts confirm it. We all like Dr Luke –'

Craft grunted.

'– And we appreciate his good intentions. But the danger of it!' said Steve. 'The unfairness of it! A whole mess of scandal and unpleasantness, a whole trial and badgering of perfectly innocent people, can be avoided if Dr Luke will just admit he told a white lie.'

Once more there was a silence. Craft unfolded his long length from the chair and peered down at me. All three of them were looking at me with a significance and speculation it was impossible to mistake.

'BUT I DIDN'T DO THAT!' I found myself shouting at them.

How to explain? How to explain that I only wished it had been like that? That I should cheerfully have lied if any good purpose could be gained by it? But that this was murder, the murder of a friend, and such things are to be avenged.

'No, sir?' intoned Superintendent Craft, in a very odd tone.

'No!'

'Luke, my dear old chap!' remonstrated Steve. 'Remember the state of your health!'

'Damn and blast the state of my health! I hope I may drop dead this minute' – here Steve put out a protesting hand – 'if every word I've told you hasn't been the gospel truth. I don't want to hound anybody. I don't want to rake up scandal; I hate scandal. But truth is truth, and we can't tamper with it.'

Craft touched my shoulder.

'All right, Doctor,' he said in a friendly voice which sounded even more ominous. 'If you say so, that's that. Let's just go outside and talk it over, shall we?'

'I tell you –'

'Unless Mr Grange has got anything more to tell us?'

'No, I'm afraid not.' Steve got up. 'You'll stay to tea?'

But, when we declined this invitation, he was clearly relieved.

"Well, perhaps you're right. I do think the doctor here ought to go over and lie down. When is the inquest?'

'Day after tomorrow,' said Craft, 'at Lynton.'

'Ah!' Steve nodded and consulted his watch. 'I'll have a word with Mr Raikes. He's the coroner, isn't he? A great friend of mine.

I'll tell him one or two of our ideas, and I'm sure he can persuade the jury to see the truth. Good afternoon, gentlemen; a very good afternoon. There'll be a great load off my mind this night.'

And he stood in the front door, almost jauntily, his hands in his pockets and a breeze smoothing his hair, as we pushed H.M. down the path to the street.

9

'For the fiftieth and last time, Superintendent Craft, I did *not*.'

'But you heard what Mr Grange said, Doctor. That's the only way it could have happened!'

'You thought it was murder, this morning.'

'Ah! Because I wasn't smart enough to think of that explanation. See here, now.'

Craft's patience, undoubtedly, was wearing thin. He and I were sitting in the front seat of the big police car, bowling out along the main road towards the Wainrights' bungalow.

We had piled H.M. and H.M.'s wheelchair into the tonneau: the chair placed sideways, H.M. himself on the back seat. His thick arms were folded across his barrel chest; and, with the top down, the wind blew up like horns the two tiny tufts of hair on each side of his bald head. For two miles or more he had not said a word. Superintendent Craft was doing the talking.

'It works, don't you see?' he persisted, his good eye rolling towards me. 'There's not a single objection to it. Here are three lines of footprints' – he illustrated – 'going out to the edge of the cliff –'

'Keep your hands on the wheel!'

'Right. Theirs end on a little bit of coarse grass, maybe four feet across: the only grass on that cliff. Yours end in a kind of splosh where you crawled out on your stomach. The tracks are parallel, it's true. Yours are six feet away from theirs, it's also true.'

'Good!'

'But,' Craft pointed out, 'you heard what Mr Grange said. When the gun fell on the grass, you could have stuck out your arm with a cane . . .'

'What cane? I don't carry a cane. Ask anybody. What do you think I am: a desiccated old fossil tottering to the edge of the grave?'

Here I thought I heard from the back seat a distinct sniff and snort of approval. But Craft was occupied with other matters. He was intently regarding the road ahead.

'By the way, Doctor. I've just remembered.' Craft cleared his throat. 'When our little one was so ill last January, you were in to see him for three weeks on end, nearly every night. And you never sent in a bill. What might we owe you, now? Roughly?'

This rather bewildering change of subject made me blink. I could think of nothing which interested me less in the broad world.

'My good Craft, how the devil should I know? I haven't time to bother with things like that. Ask Tom. Maybe he knows.'

'Or maybe not,' said Craft. 'For all the way he goes on, he's just as foggy and loony as you. *He* seldom sends in a bill either; and then, mostly, he sends 'em to the wrong people. I'm trying to do the best I can for you!'

'Look here: I don't need any money.'

Craft gripped the steering-wheel more tightly.

'Maybe not; but damned if you don't need a lot of help. This inquest – you know that – is on Wednesday. And you're under oath when you testify. You also know that?'

'Certainly.'

'Are you going to tell the same story at the inquest that you've been telling us?'

'Why not? I tell you it's true!'

'Listen,' said Craft. 'The jury will almost certainly bring in a verdict for a suicide pact. He shoots her; then shoots himself. In that case, they're bound to add a rider saying you tampered with the evidence. And in that case (*now* have you got it?) we shall have to arrest you for perjury.'

This was a beautiful thought, which I confess had not previously occurred to me.

I am not at a time of life where one enjoys being chucked into the cooler for telling truths. To younger men there seems something noble about this, though I have never quite understood why. Like Galileo, I am willing to go down on my knees and deny that the earth moves, if peace can be brought to the home thereby. But this was a personal matter.

'You mean,' I said, 'that you won't want to arrest anybody to whom you owe money?'

'That's about the size of it,' Craft acknowledged. 'If you'd only save us all a lot of trouble by telling the truth!'

'I promise, so help me, to tell the truth, the whole truth, and nothing but the truth.'

Craft contemplated me very suspiciously. You could see he was more or less bewildered and at a dead end, because he knew I wasn't in the habit of lying and yet here were the apparent facts to prove it. I don't blame him. If I had been in his place, I shouldn't have believed myself. He craned round towards the back seat.

'What do *you* make of it, sir?' he asked. 'As Mr Grange said, it's the only way the thing could have been done.'

'Well . . . now,' growled H.M. 'It's those very words "only way" which make me distrust the whole business.'

'You distrust it because it *is* the only way?'

'Yes,' said H.M. simply. 'I wish Masters could hear you sayin' that.'

'But did you ever hear of a murderer who could float in the air?'

'Oh, my son! You don't know my history. I've seen a feller who was dead, and yet who wasn't dead. I've seen a man make two different sets of finger-prints with the same hands. I've seen a poisoner get atropine into a clean glass that nobody touched.' He sniffed. 'As for a murderer floating in the air, I'm expectin' to meet one any day. It would just round out my cycle before the old man goes into the dustbin.'

'What dustbin?'

'Never mind,' glowered H.M. He looked at me. 'See here, Doctor. Let's assume for the moment you're telling the truth.'

'Thanks.'

'When you went out to the edge of that cliff on Saturday night, did you notice any gun lyin' there?'

'No.'

'Suppose there'd been one, though. Would you have noticed it?'

'I don't know.' Images rose again in their vividness and pain. 'I was too upset to notice anything much. My impression is that there wasn't a gun there, but I couldn't swear to it.'

'Well, take something else.' Unfolding his arms, H.M. pointed at Craft. 'An automatic ejects its spent cartridge-cases. Did the coppers find any spent cartridge-cases there?'

'No. But, you see –'

'I know, I know! Another lesson in elementary criminology. Spent shells don't just roll out of the magazine when they're fired. They're thrown out with a snap, high and to the right. They'd probably have popped over into the sea. Did you have a look at the foot of the cliff?'

'No, sir. It was high tide when we got there, thirty feet up, and I knew the bodies would have been washed away. As for finding two little brass cartridge-cases . . .'

'All the same, did you *look*?'

'No, sir.' Craft hesitated. 'Speaking of elementary criminology, what did you make of the Granges?'

'I like the gal quite a lot. Though, d'ye see, I generally distrust these wenches who fire up and say they've got no interest at all in the opposite sex. It generally means they've got a whole lot of interest tucked away somewhere. Just as –'

H.M. shut his eyes briefly. The corners of his mouth turned down. Folding his thick arms again, he sat back in the tonneau and fixed his eyes on the road ahead. When he spoke again, it was more mildly.

'I say, son. Are we anywhere near this Baker's Bridge road? I've got an awful yen to have a look at that studio where Mrs Wainright was carryin' on.'

Craft was surprised.

'It's only a little way ahead,' he replied. 'We can easily stop by there if you'd like to.'

'Then do it. Mind!' H.M.'s voice was querulous. 'I haven't got the ghostiest idea what we're goin' to find there, or see there, or do there. Probably nothing. But the urge remains.'

The road to Baker's Bridge, which winds across country to join the main Barnstaple road by a short-cut, is little more than a narrow lane. From here, too, you can take another track out towards the wastes of Exmoor. It was six o'clock in the afternoon when we turned into the lane, on a dirt track between highish banks. The tall, thin trunks of the trees, patched with moss, stood up against filtered sunshine which made a hazy and softened light. The road swallowed us up. Something ran with a scurry across dead leaves. And some fifty yards along the winding lane, Craft braked the car abruptly.

'Ho?' he muttered.

A little elderly man was coming towards us under the arching trees. He wore a broad-brimmed hat and a rusty suit; a grimy shirt was fastened, without necktie, at his throat. His white moustache, luxuriant and drooping, had turned partly brown as though singed with the tar of cigarettes. It stood out against his complexion. As he plodded along, he appeared to be addressing some lengthy if inaudible speech to the trees.

'Very good customer to meet,' said Craft. 'That's Willie Johnson.'

'Oh? You mean the gardener that the Wainrights sacked? Better stop him, son, and have a word.'

This was unnecessary. Mr Johnson stopped, saw us, and stood transfixed. Then he came towards us with dignity, swinging – as a mark of the gentleman and even the dandy – a malacca stick. Also, he was full of beer. Not drunk: just thoroughly and oozily full of beer, which appeared to flow along his veins and get out at his eyes. He drew up his thin neck out of the collar and addressed Craft.

'I 'ave a complaint to make, I 'ave,' he said.

Craft was patient but weary.

'Now listen, Willie. The sergeant at Lynton says he's getting tired of your complaints.'

'Not of this one, 'e won't. It's' – Mr Johnson searched his mind – 'it's larceny. Yes, sir. Larceny. 'E stole it.'

'He stole what?'

'Ah!' breathed Mr Johnson, as though this were the most darkly sinister part of the business. He lifted the stick and attempted to tap his nose with it: an unsuccessful move, which annoyed him. 'Four feet long it were, and 'e stole it. That gentleman'll find out, 'e will!'

'Who will?'

'That Mr Wainright, that's lost as nice a lady as you'd ever want to see. Some people pities 'im. But I say no. I say 'e's got a nasty sly look about 'im, when 'e thinks you don't see it.'

'You're drunk, Willie. Come round and see me when you get sober. I want to ask you some questions.'

Mr Johnson protested vehemently that he was not drunk. It was H.M. who intervened.

'Look here, son. You must have lived a pretty long time in this district?'

Our informant's local pride was touched. He announced that he had lived here first twenty, then thirty, then fifty years.

'You know the studio a little way on along this road? Uh-huh. Who does that place belong to?'

'Belonged to old Mr Jim Wetherstone,' Mr Johnson replied promptly, 'that died eight, ten years ago. '*E* let it to an artist-chap that killed hisself there, like they do.'

'Yes, but who does it belong to now?'

'Estate's got it, lawyers and all. 'Oo'd live there, anyway? When there's no drains and an artist killed 'isself and all?' Mr Johnson spat into the road. 'Cost an 'undred pound to put that place in repair, and 'oo'd live there anyway?'

H.M. fished in his pockets for silver as largesse; but he could find only a ten-shilling note. And this, to the dismay of Craft and the incredulous astonishment of Johnson, he tossed over.

'You can buy a lot of beer with ten bob, Willie,' Craft said warningly.

'Beer?' inquired the other, with real dignity. 'I'm a-going to the pictures.' (We had a film down at Lynton once a week.) ''Tis a educational film, about the Romans that burnt Christians to a stake and all. And the girls 'adn't got no clothes on,' he added. He was so grateful that the beer came out of his eyes. 'Good day, Mr Craft. And a very good day to *you*, sir. I 'ope your stay in our district will be both long and pleasant.'

'You be careful!' Craft shouted after him. 'One of these days you'll be seeing pink rabbits; and then watch out!' Willie did not deign to turn round. 'He'll be all right,' the superintendent said, 'when he's dried out a little. I wish you hadn't given him that money, though. The studio isn't much further on.'

It stood, in fact, about two hundred yards from the entrance to the main road. Though this lane is not much used, I had passed the house on many occasions at one time or another, and it had seemed dismal enough. But it had never seemed more dismal than now, at the first vague onset of twilight.

There was no wall round it. It stood a short distance back from the road, a barnlike stone place once whitewashed, but now a dirty grey. A peaked, sloping roof had a north side once made of glass-panes; but few of these had been left, amid splinters and gapings, and those which remained were so dirty as to seem blacked out.

Heavy double-doors, almost big enough to drive a lorry through, faced the road. Round at the side there was a little door, with two steps leading up to it from a rank-grown path. This must have been where Molly had seen Rita Wainright, in a red sweater, standing with her arms round somebody while the spring dusk deepened.

There were no downstairs windows. And the two upstairs windows – at least, on the sides we could see – were boarded up. At the right, beyond us, was a heavy stone chimney. Behind this studio rose up the pine trees, of that sombre green which seems black. If you were fanciful, you might have thought Rita's ghost was here. Near the double doors facing the road, I remember, there was a little patch of bluebells.

Craft raced the motor and then cut it off, so that damp warm stillness crept in around us.

And that was when we heard a woman screaming.

They were not loud screams. That, in a way, was what made them frightening; from physical exhaustion, or terror draining the nerves, they could barely be forced through a dry throat. They gave the old studio no pleasant voice in that dusk. They wrung pain out of it, and fear certainly. They were accompanied by a weak, faint, despairing hammering at what we identified as one of the boarded-up windows upstairs: the left as you faced the studio.

We had to leave H.M. behind, despite his bellowings. There was no time to move him. Craft waited only long enough to get an electric torch out of the side pocket of his car.

'Front doors,' he said over his shoulder. 'Unlocked, I think.'

And we went for them.

The front doors, of rather handsome seasoned oak, *were*

unlocked. Though some vandal had fastened hasps and a padlock to the outside of them, the lock hung loose. We pushed them open – they were set flush with the ground – and went in.

The place was damp and mouldy. But, owing to the big skylight, we could see pretty well; and the plan of the house emerged out of shadows. It consisted of one big room, the studio, with kitchen and storeroom built out at the rear. Over the front doors had been built a kind of gallery inside, for the floor of a room within a room. Thus there was no proper upstairs, but only this partitioned room against the front wall, hung over our heads. A (once) white-painted staircase along the right-hand wall led up to its closed door.

A faint moaning or whimpering came from up there.

'That's it,' Craft said.

He switched on the electric torch and swung it round before we hurried up those stairs. The studio had a brick-paved floor like a farmhouse. The black throat of a big fireplace gaped against the right-hand wall. A few bits of broken furniture were scattered across the floor.

'It's all right!' Craft shouted. 'We're coming!'

At the head of the stairs, the door was locked. But there was a (new) key in the door, and Craft turned it. That door opened without any squeaking. As it did so, we heard a moan of alarm from inside, and a rustle across the floor.

'Who's there?' called a woman's voice.

'It's all right,' Craft repeated. 'It's all right, miss. I'm a police officer.'

He sent the beam of his light inside. The transformation scene beyond made you blink. Between Craft's torch and the clunks and glimmers of light through boarded windows, you could see that the room was not only furnished, but richly furnished.

Then the beam of the torch moved across and rested on the woman – or girl, rather – who was trying to shrink away from us by pressing against the wall round the corner of a Japanese cabinet. The lacquer-and-gilt-and-pearl design of the cabinet winked back at us. As the light rose to her face, the girl put her arms over her eyes and cried out.

Everything about her spoke of the town rather than the country. Her delicate high-heeled shoes, now crusted with grey dried mud. Her tan silk stockings, badly laddered. Her white-slashed green frock, also mud-spotted. She was very small, not more than five feet tall; but she had one of the most beautiful figures, on the plumpish side, it has been my good fortune to see. The phrase 'pocket Venus' occurred to me, but I put it away in remembrance of the state she was in.

What made her tremble so much, and as steadily as though it were convulsions, was not fear alone. It was physical weakness. Craft took a step forward, and she shrank away again. Putting up a hand to shade her eyes, she tried to peer at us.

'Now steady!' insisted Craft, who was getting rattled himself. 'I tell you I'm a police officer! You're perfectly safe; do you understand that? Who – who are you?'

The girl started to cry.

'I'm Mrs Barry Sullivan,' she answered.

10

If this took Craft aback, he gave no sign of it.

'How long have you been locked up in this place?'

'I don't know.' She had a pleasant voice, with an American accent, now rendered into gulps by her trembling. 'Las' night, maybe. Mor'ing. For God's sake ge' me out of here!'

'You're all right now, miss. Come along with us, and nothing's going to hurt you. Just take my arm.'

She edged round the corner of the cabinet, took two steps, and went down flat on her knees. I picked her up and steadied her.

'How long has it been,' I asked, 'since you've had anything to eat?'

She searched her mind. 'Yes'erday morning. On the train. Where's my husband? Where's Barry?'

Craft and I exchanged a glance. I led her over and sat her down on an overcushioned ottoman.

'She's in no shape to walk just yet, Superintendent. Can't we get any real light in here?'

'Oil-lamps,' said the girl. 'Burnt out. No oil.'

I suggested to Craft that the only thing to do was to knock the boards off the windows. He declined firmly, with a true

English horror of violating property rights. So I, always the goat, had a shot at it. It became clear why the girl had been unable to get out for herself; the window I attacked was as solidly nailed as a coffin. I finally managed it by getting up on a chair and kicking. It made some clatter; pieces and fragments of wood flew wide. As I emerged, I found myself looking down into the evilly-squinting face of Sir Henry Merrivale. He showed not the least surprise, but sat in the car and simply looked at me.

I said: 'Got any brandy?'

It seemed to me, even at that distance, he turned slightly purple. But still without saying anything, he reached into his hip pocket and took out an enormous silver flask, which he waggled slowly in the air like bait. When I went down to get it, signs of an explosion were as palpable as heatwaves.

'There's a girl upstairs,' I said, 'hysterical with fright and half dead from hunger. Somebody locked her in. She says she's Mrs Barry Sullivan.'

All signs of an explosion died away.

'Oh, lord love a duck!' he muttered. 'Does she know about . . . ?'

'No. Apparently not.'

H.M. handed me the flask. 'Then for the love of Esau get back up there before Craft tells her. Hop to it!'

Exertion is supposed to be bad, but I made it in a very short time. Twilight entered the garish room through one window. She was still sitting on the ottoman, in her stained clothes, with Craft showing surprising delicacy and tact. Though she still shook convulsively, she was now making some attempt to laugh at it.

Despite a drawn face, despite disarranged hair, despite the ravages of tears to make-up and eyebrow-pencil, she was a very pretty girl. This pocket Venus had dark brown hair done into the little curls which I believe were fashionable then. She had a small mouth, and large, grey, shining eyes just now blurred and puffed. Even looking as she did, she managed to retain some of that sleekness in which every accent is put on sex-appeal.

She started to laugh again – showing fine teeth – when she saw the flask.

'Boy,' she said, 'could I use a shot!'

I poured the flask-cup full. Though her hand shook, she drained it without winking, coughed, and held it out for more.

'No. That'll do for the moment.'

'Maybe you're right. I don't want it to make me cock-eyed. Sorry to be such a softie. Has anybody got a cigarette?'

Craft produced a packet, and lit one for her. Her hand trembled so much that several times she missed her mouth altogether, but the brandy was taking hold. What disturbed me most was the glaze of fright in her eyes.

'Look,' she began. 'What is this? What's going on here?'

'That's what we hoped you could tell us,' said Craft, 'Miss . . . Mrs . . .'

'Sullivan. Belle Sullivan. Look. Are you really a cop? No kidding?'

Craft produced his warrant-card.

'And who's the other guy?'

'That's Dr Croxley, from Lyncombe.'

'Oh. A doctor. That's all right, then.' The hand with the cigarette wavered. 'I want to tell you just about the most horrible –'

'If you'd rather not talk now, Mrs Sullivan,' I said, 'we've got a car outside to take you to some place more comfortable.'

Craft looked stern. '*I* think, sir, it might be better to tell it now.'

'Yes. I think so too.' She shuddered again. 'Look. My husband is a fellow named Sullivan, Barry Sullivan. I don't suppose you know him.'

'I've heard of him, ma'am. I take it you're from the States too?'

The girl hesitated.

'Well – no. As a matter of fact, I was born in Birmingham. But the customers seem to like it, so I keep it up.'

'Customers?'

'I'm a dance-hostess at the Piccadilly Hotel. In London.'

'Then why are you down here?'

This young lady was very direct, and did not suffer from reticence. Her voice went up a little.

'Because I was so goddamned jealous,' she answered. 'I couldn't see straight. I knew he had a floosie down here, because I found one of the envelopes postmarked Lyncombe. But I don't even know who the floosie is. Look!'

Tears came into her eyes, and her shaky voice grew firm.

'I didn't come down here to make trouble. I wouldn't have started trouble anyway. I just wanted to see this floosie, that's all. I wanted to see what she had that I didn't have.' Belle Sullivan paused, and held out the flask-cup with her left hand. 'Pour me another drink, will you? I promise I won't pass out on you, or start getting gabby. Please, just pour me another drink.'

I poured it.

Craft, though he concealed it well, was a little shocked by this forthrightness. But I wasn't. Though it may show a certain lack of principle, I liked it and I liked her. She drained the second cup.

'Barry left on Friday night. By Saturday night I'd got myself into such a state I couldn't sit still. So on Sunday morning I just up and got on the train. Even before I started, I said to myself, "Belle, this is the craziest idea you ever had." I mean, you can't just walk up to somebody in a town and say, "Excuse me, do you know any woman who's sleeping with my husband?"'

'No, ma'am; I suppose you can't.'

'Besides, I didn't even want Barry to know I was there. But that's the kind of ideas you get when you feel the way I did.

'The trip down was awful. First I found I had to change at Exeter, and go on to Barnstaple. When the train got to Barnstaple, I found Lyncombe was still thirteen miles or so farther on. There's no train; and the buses don't run on Sunday. I had to take a taxi, though I hadn't a whole hell of a lot of money.

'The taxi-driver asked me where I wanted to go in Lyncombe. By that time I was wishing to the sweet Christ I hadn't come.

Excuse my language; I'll t-try to talk like a lady in a minute; but that's how I felt. I said to drop me at the biggest pub, and please, please go by the shortest way. He said he knew a short-cut. And so he brought me past here.'

Twilight was deepening in this curious room. The air was utterly still, and her shaky voice had a high carrying pitch. Every word must be audible to H.M. sitting in the car outside.

Belle Sullivan bit at her under-lip.

'That was *Sunday* evening, you say, ma'am?' Craft prompted.

'Yes. It was about half past eight, and still light. We came along this road. The driver was practically crawling along. We passed this studio place' – her eyes roved round – 'and . . . you know those huge double-doors downstairs, that open on the road?'

'Yes. Well?'

'The doors were wide,' Belle told us. 'And Barry's car was inside. I recognised the back number-plate.'

Craft's bushy eyebrows went up.

'Mr Sullivan's *car*?' he echoed in his sepulchral voice. 'Mr Sullivan's never had a car when he's been down here, to my knowledge.'

'Of course not. Anyway, where would he get the money to run a car? He's an automobile salesman. That was his demonstration-model. They don't let him take it out of London to go joy-riding, especially in times like these when he's going to lose his job anyway because there aren't any more cars to sell. Seeing the car there was what scared me.

'But I thought, "Wherever Barry's car is, that's where he'll be pretty soon, and very likely with his floosie too." So I told the taxi-driver to let me out right there.

'The driver, of course, thought I was nuts. He said nobody'd lived in this place for years and years, and that some artist guy cut his throat here once. But I paid him off, and sent him away, and then started to prowl around. Of course I didn't know about *this* part of the joint.' Her nod indicated the room. 'All I found was a locked door at the top of the steps. And a dirty studio room with a brick floor. And Barry's car in the studio.

'Swell place for assignations, isn't it? I mean, even aside from this over-decorated cat-house up here. You can come out here in a car. You can run the car straight into the studio like as if it was a garage. Then you close the doors; and who's to know anybody's here?'

I had been thinking the same thing.

'Then,' said Belle, 'it started to get dark.'

Involuntarily her large, grey, shining eyes moved towards the window. Outside, the tops of the trees were thin green. She shook her mop of disarranged brown curls, and uncrossed her knees. Her cigarette had gone out; she dropped it on the deep crimson carpet.

'I don't like the country,' she said. 'It gives me the jim-jams. I like some *noise*, and people near me who could come if I called out. Everything was dead quiet here. It got darker and darker. And I ran out of cigarettes.

'Then I started thinking how far away I was from anything or anybody. Not knowing any roads; not knowing anywhere to go even if I wanted. Stuck and stranded. Next I got to thinking about that damned artist who cut his throat here. That's when you begin to imagine things, and think there might be somebody just round the corner. I couldn't even turn on the lights of the car, much less use it, because there wasn't any key in the ignition. I sat on the running-board, and kept walking up and down. It must have been pretty late – anyway, it was nearly pitch dark – when I heard someone coming along the road.'

Craft and I had stiffened to such attention that she must have noticed it if she had not been so preoccupied.

'I thought it was Barry, naturally.' She hesitated, biting at her under-lip. 'And maybe it was. Or at least . . .'

Craft cleared his throat.

'Couldn't have been Mr Sullivan,' he said. 'Not on *Sunday* night.'

'Why not?'

'Never you mind that, miss.' Craft had a tendency to call her 'miss'; perhaps because she looked like one. 'Just take my word for it, that's all.'

'You mean he's gone away?' asked the girl, and her pretty face hardened.

'Well – yes. Just go on.'

Belle started to say something, but changed her mind.

'First,' she went on, 'I was sore as hell at him for getting me scared like that. But I've got *some* pride, and I didn't want him to find me there. And yet at the same time I didn't want to lose him and leave me stranded there. All that time I'd been walking up and down, you see, I never once thought what I'd actually *do* when Barry got back to his car.

'There was only one thing I could do. Barry's car is – I mean, was – a Packard roadster with a big rumble-seat. I climbed up, and opened the rumble-seat, and got down inside, and closed the top of the rumble-seat after me. I'm a little half-pint' – she held out her arms, inviting inspection – 'and it was easy. Besides, there's two little ventilators in those rumble-seats, and you get plenty of air. Then he came into the studio. That,' she added, and drew the back of her hand across her forehead, 'was when I heard him crying.'

Neither Craft nor I moved.

'Crying . . . I was going to say like a baby. But babies don't cry that way. It was that horrible kind of shaky sobbing, like as if he was sick and couldn't get his breath. It's pretty awful, hearing a man cry like that. It goes right through you. Once or twice he'd hit his fist against the side of the car.'

(Lost soul, damned soul, whoever you were.)

'And I was scared and wanted to cry too. But I thought, "Oh, you son of a so-and-so! You wouldn't be crying like that about *me*," and I hated him and kept quiet. Barry's like a kid; he's only twenty-five; I'm twenty-eight. There wasn't time to think about much. I heard him pottering around, and going upstairs once, and a key in a lock. Then he got into the car, and started it up, and we backed out. I thought, "My God, we're going to see the floosie; and here I am stuck in the rumble-seat."'

Belle paused, trying to laugh a little. The brandy had taken hold and was keeping her fairly steady, but she was far from being well.

Craft said quietly: 'Listen, miss. I want you to be careful about this. You're sure it *was* a man you heard?'

Belle's expression grew vaguely puzzled. 'Sure thing. I thought it was Barry. Naturally.' Again she paused. Her eyes widened. 'Wait a minute! Look! Are you trying to tell me it might have been the floosie?'

'I was only . . .'

Now she was even more thoroughly scared.

'If I'm shooting my mouth off and not doing justice to Barry –'

'Please, miss. It wasn't the floosie, if that word means what I think it does. I just want to know this. You only heard somebody crying, and walking about. You didn't hear anybody speak?'

'No. But if it wasn't Barry or the floosie, who else could it have been? Look. What's going on here? Why are you two looking so funny?'

'If you'll just go on with your story, miss, the doctor'll give you another drink of brandy.'

'No, the doctor won't,' I said. 'This young lady's not well. She's going back to Lyncombe, where we can get her some food and look after her.'

'I'm all right,' Belle insisted. She made an unsteady pout with her lips, smiled, and put down the flask-cup on the ottoman. 'I *want* to tell it. Because I'm coming to the part I don't understand and can't understand.

'The car backed out, as I said, and started off. The road was pretty bumpy, but I was all curled up on the rumble-seat and it didn't jar me much. I was only thinking what a god-awful sight I'd be when I had to get up again, specially my hat.'

She touched her hand to her head, vaguely.

'Then we got on a smooth road, and seemed to be going miles and miles. I think we were going uphill part of the time, but I'm not sure. There was a little ventilator on each side, down by the floor, but I couldn't see anything except a little moonlight going past.

'After that the road got bumpy again. It was much colder, too. I could feel the draught coming in and getting me round the ankles. We were going downhill a little; I was pretty sure of that from the way I had to brace myself. All of a sudden – just like that – we started to bump and jar so much that I banged my head against the side. My hat was awful; the veil had come all crooked; and my fur and handbag had slipped down on the floor.

'I knew we weren't on the road at all, because you could hear some sort of dry grass go *whush* against the wheels. There was a cold kind of mist, too; I could smell it. On we went, and I was trying to brace myself, and wanting to scream out at Barry, when . . .

'Well, the car slowed down. Barry – or somebody – changed gears. The door of the car opened, and I wondered what the dumb cluck was doing: opening a door with the car moving. It closed again in a second, so I supposed he'd got things under control, when we started forward again like sixty. Whiz! Just like that, and going on as smooth as grease. This was only for a couple of seconds, because we stopped as though something kept trying to push us back.

'It was like being on a feather-bed, only not quite so steady. I got the horriblest kind of idea that there wasn't anything under us. Then I heard the sounds: little gulpy sounds like air-bubbles, all around us. They sound *human*, like live things eating at you, and I heard one noise exactly like a belch. There was a smell, too.

'Then the car began to sink. It wasn't much movement, but you could feel it inside you. I reached down on the floor to find my handbag – I don't know why – and some sort of oozy stuff came through the little ventilator and touched my hand. Next the other little ventilator was stopped up, and I was in the dark. All of a sudden the whole car started to shake, and the front of it dropped about six inches, with the gulpy sounds getting louder all the time. So help me, that was the first time I caught on.'

Belle Sullivan stopped, held her shoulders stiff against trembling, and gripped the edges of the ottoman.

Superintendent Craft nodded.

'I see, miss,' he agreed grimly. 'Quicksand.'

11

Belle nodded in reply, winking her eyes very rapidly. 'I knew we were near Exmoor, naturally.' She swallowed hard. 'And I'd read *Lorna Doone* when I was a kid, or at least I'd heard about it. But I didn't think there really were such things. Not really honest-to-God, I mean, and away from the movies.'

Craft snorted.

'They're real enough, all right,' he assured her. 'Unless you know most parts of that moor, stay off it. Or, if you must go, follow the moor-ponies. They never make a mistake. Isn't that so, Doctor?'

I agreed with some vehemence. I have had to learn a good deal about Exmoor in the course of my professional life, but I don't like that windy, gloomy waste to this day.

'The next part was the worst,' said Belle, 'though it didn't last long. I can't tell you how I got the top of that rumble-seat open. At first I thought Barry had turned the handle and locked me in. I was as horribly cramped as though I'd been doing marathon-dancing. And there must have been less air than I'd thought, inside there. When I got the lid up, and tried to stand on the leather seat, I was so dizzy I almost fell over the side into the bog.

'I must have been a little bit cock-eyed. I screamed and screamed and screamed. But nobody answered me. And there was nobody in the front seat.

'Don't ask me where I was! There was a white mist with the moon behind it – you couldn't see a dozen feet – and it was so cold I could feel the sweat on my skin. It's funny what you think about at a time like that. I was furious because there *wasn't* anybody in the front seat: the dope had just jumped out and let her rip, of course.

'I remember the foggy stuff on the windshield. I remember what the upholstery looked like; and the clock and speedometer and petrol-gauge on the dashboard; and two little booklets like road-maps, one blue and the other green, stuck into the side pocket. But *he'd* gone. And there was the quicksand, sort of grey and brown and horrible, all spreading like oatmeal and pulling everything down in the dark. It moved, you see. *It moved.*'

'Steady, miss! There's nothing to be alarmed about now!'

Belle put her hands over her face for a moment.

'So I stood up on the edge of the car' – she spoke through her hands – 'and I jumped.'

Craft was looking rather white.

'God Almighty, miss,' he muttered, 'you've got your nerve right with you. That took a bit of doing. And you landed on solid ground?'

'Well' – she lowered her hands – 'I'm here. Aren't I? Ain't I? Whatever it is you say? I'm not out there dead under I don't know how many feet of sand, with that stuff still moving on top of me.'

Her lower lip quivered when she smiled.

'I'll tell you something else, too. You know that old phonus-bolonus about your whole past life going in front of you when you're just about to die? Well, it doesn't. But I'll tell you what does happen. I thought: "He can't be far away. He must have heard me yelling. But he's standing there letting me go down."

'And I thought: "He must have known I was in that rumble-seat." My cigarette-stubs were scattered all over the floor in the studio. I was wearing perfume, too: one he always liked. "Well," I thought, "this is as good a way of m-murdering a wife as any."'

There was a long silence.

'When I jumped out of that car, believe it or not, I saw Barry in every one of the ways I've seen him since we were married. He's well-meaning: he's childish; he's an awful dope; he's vain of his looks; he's fond of dough. The next thing I knew, I'd landed. I didn't feel sand grabbing me, like I expected. I felt ground. I crawled a little farther along, the way you do when you come out of water, and then I passed out. When I came to, I was locked in here.'

Belle lifted one shoulder. Her voice was almost casual when she added: 'What burns me up now is that I left my handbag with compact and lipstick and money and everything, back in that car. I left my fur and my hat too. But that's all. Gimme another cigarette.'

Craft and I exchanged glances. Before very long she would have to be told the reason why her husband couldn't have been the person who drove her on Sunday night. A very uneasy superintendent coughed, so to speak, in my direction as he produced cigarettes and matches. Belle Sullivan forced the decision herself.

'Now I'll tell you why I'm inflicting all this dreary stuff on you. Got that cigarette?'

Craft struck the match.

Its bright yellow flare contrasted with the deepening dusk. As Belle inhaled greedily – the smoke must have made her head swim, and I wanted to protest – you could see the gleam of tears against match light. You could see the soft line of the cheek tremble. Yet her voice remained conversational and even casual.

'I discovered something else when I was making that jump,' she told us. 'I'm not in love with Barry. And that's straight.'

'I'm rather glad to hear it, miss.'

'Oh? You think I've been a sap too?'

Craft was unhappy. 'If you'd just talk to the doctor about these matters, miss –'

'The way I figure it out is this,' said Belle. 'I've been kicked around just about long enough. Don't you agree?'

'Well . . .'

'You tell me it wasn't Barry who did that business. I don't know whether I believe you or not. You've got something up your sleeves, both of you.'

'Now, miss!'

'But I can't see *why* Barry should have done that, even if he did want to get rid of me. I mean, that car cost seven or eight hundred pounds. It's not his property. He'll have to make good to the company, and he can't. Anyway, if he wanted to get rid of me, why bring me back and throw me in here while I was unconscious?'

'Exactly!' agreed Craft.

'But look. If he didn't do that, what *is* the guy doing? Why hasn't he been out here? Why did he *let* somebody go and sink his car, with a key to the ignition and everything? And now, you tell me, he's gone back to London!'

'Not exactly to London, miss.'

'But you said he had!'

'No. I said he'd gone away.'

'Where?'

Craft turned to me and spread out his hands. It had to be faced. It was a risk; but if we refused to tell her she would become hysterical, and that would be worse. After debating it, I picked up the flask-cup from the ottoman, poured out still a third brandy, and handed it to her. She drank it as though she hardly saw it.

'Mrs Sullivan, your husband and this . . . floosie,' I said.

'Well?'

'I'm afraid you're never going to see her. And, if you do see him again, you must get ready for a shock.'

'They shot themselves and chucked themselves over a cliff on Saturday night,' Craft blurted out. 'They're lying down on a slab in the morgue now. Sorry, Mrs Sullivan; but that's how it is.'

I turned away and began to make an intensive study of the other side of the room. Each piece of furniture for this room must have been brought secretly, at one time or another. You could see Rita Wainright's hand in this. The carpet on the floor, the crimson velvet curtains which could be drawn across boarded windows, to shut out a real world for an imaginary. In one corner stood an ornate folding screen, and behind it – I went to look – a washstand with pitcher, bowl, and towels. Sordid? Well, yes. But Rita was Rita.

The thing which occupied me, with intense concentration, was what we should do with Belle Sullivan. Evidently she had brought no suitcase. Molly Grange would be only too glad to take her in. But a vision of Steve's face rose up against this. No: she had better come to us. Mrs Harping would take care of her.

So I stood there, with bitter black tragedy in my mind, and only wished I could take a drink out of the flask in my hand.

'It's all right, Doctor,' observed Belle. 'You can turn round now. I'm not going to throw a fit on you.'

Our pocket Venus was still sitting on the ottoman, one leg tucked under her, taking deep draws at the cigarette. The grey eyes looked at me steadily.

'I just want to ask you a couple of questions about this woman he was running around. *Was* she?'

'Was she what?'

'A floosie?'

'No. She was the Canadian wife of a professor of mathematics.'

'What was her name?'

'Rita Wainright.'

'Good-looking?'

'Yes.'

'High-hat?'

'Not particularly. Just an ordinary professional family, that's all.'

'Any mon . . . No, *that* won't do,' argued Belle, squeezing up her eyes, 'if they bumped themselves off. How old was she?'

'Thirty-eight.'

Belle took the cigarette out of her mouth.

'Thirty-eight?' she echoed incredulously. Then her voice grew suddenly shrill. 'Thirty-eight? Jesus Christ! Was he nuts?'

Superintendent Craft started as though someone had stuck him with a pin. This shocked him perhaps more than anything he had heard yet. He had been bending gloomy brows on the girl, ready to utter a word of praise for her fortitude, and now he didn't know what to say. But in Belle Sullivan this seemed neither callousness nor the brandy talking. It was sincere bewilderment, boiling up under every other emotion, because she knew her husband so well. I emphasised it.

'It's only fair to tell you, Mrs Sullivan, that I don't believe for a moment those two committed suicide.'

'Oh?'

'Somebody shot them both. You'll probably hear a different version from the police; but that's the truth. And now we're not going to talk about it any more, for the moment. You're coming along home with me.'

'But I haven't got any c-clothes!'

'Never mind. There's a girl near there who'll attend to that. You want food, and you want sleep. If you feel fit enough to walk now, let's go downstairs.'

This request was also underlined. A violent and prolonged squawking from a motor-car horn, in the road outside, droned out with such abruptness that Belle let out an involuntary cry. I went to the window. Sir Henry Merrivale, with a face of indescribable malignancy in the dusk, was leaning forward and poking with the end of his crutch at the button of the horn.

'I'm a patient man,' he said; 'but the dew is settlin' on my head and I got reason to suspect incipient pneumonia in my toe. What's more, my jailer has caught up to me. I just wanted to say goodbye.'

We had another visitor now. Paul Ferrars, in a very ancient Ford, had drawn up behind the police car and was getting out. To judge by his astonishment, when my face appeared at the window, he must have thought H.M. was being led into some very strange company.

'We're coming down straightaway,' I said.

Belle made no objection. I regret to say that her voice was marred by a slight hiccup, and her gait did not remain altogether steady. But mental anaesthesia was probably best under the circumstances. While Craft locked the door of the upper room, and put the key in his pocket, I assisted Belle down the steps.

When we arrived outside the studio, H.M. and wheelchair – the latter upside down – had already been transferred to the back of the Ford. It was a stroke of luck or thoughtfulness. If we had had to drive H.M. to Ridd Farm it would have meant crossing the edge of Exmoor. And that could have been no pleasant experience for Belle Sullivan.

Ferrars, in the old paint-stained flannels, lounged against the side of the Ford smoking a cherrywood pipe. His long-nosed intelligent face, topped by fair hair which he deliberately makes untidy, wore a complacent expression until he saw who was with us. Then his mouth fell open.

'Good lord!' he muttered, and caught the pipe clumsily as it fell. With the palm of his other hand he whacked the side of the car. 'Belle Renfrew!'

Belle turned round, blindly, and started back into the studio. I caught her arm to steer her back again.

'It's all right. Only some friends of ours. They won't hurt you.'

'Belle Renfrew!' Ferrars was repeating. 'What are you doing

in this part of the world? And what have they been doing to you? After all the good times we used to have together –'

'There's no Miss Renfrew, sir,' Superintendent Craft intoned. 'This is Mrs Sullivan. Mrs Barry Sullivan.'

'Oh,' said Ferrars. After a pause, while faint colour stained his cheeks, he added: 'Sorry.' After another pause, heavy with embarrassment, he climbed up behind the wheel of the Ford.

'We don't wear our wedding-rings,' Belle threw at him, 'when we're on duty at the Piccadilly. The customers don't like it.'

H.M., in the back seat, was contemplating us with an air of unwonted seriousness. He addressed Belle gently.

'Ma'am,' he rumbled, 'I'm the old man. I've notoriously all the tact of a load of bricks comin' through a skylight. I don't want to bother you much at a time like this. But I've also got a habit of helping lame dogs over stiles. About this story of yours . . .'

'You didn't *hear* it?'

'Well . . . now. You were talking pretty loud. There's more to being an invalid than just sittin' and thinkin'.' Here I handed him the flask, screwing on the cap firmly. 'If you wouldn't mind answering me a couple of questions, before the effect of that brandy wears off,' he went on, 'it might help a whole lot in the mess we're in.'

'Barry never killed himself!' Belle cried. 'He just wouldn't have had the nerve to! And you can ask me anything you want to.'

'All right. When and where were you married?'

'So you think I'm a liar about that, do you?'

'No! Burn me, no! I was only solicitin' information.'

'*I* don't do soliciting of any kind, thanks,' said Belle. 'Hampstead Registry Office, at the Town Hall. April 17th, 1938.'

'Was your husband's name really Barry Sullivan? Or was that a stage-name?'

'It was his real name.'

'How do you know?'

'Because . . . well, because it's his real name! He writes it. He gets letters with that name on 'em. He writes it on cheques, when he signs any. I can't see what more you'd want.'

H.M. looked very hard at her.

'Did you ever visit the United States, Mrs Sullivan?'

'No, I didn't.'

'Ever travel abroad anywhere?'

'No.'

'Ah,' said H.M. 'I thought not.' He touched Ferrars on the shoulder with his crutch. 'Start her up, son.'

The noise of the Ford's motor beat out against evening quiet. Ferrars backed up and swung the car round. The last thing we saw was the back of H.M.'s bald head, a malignant gleam in itself, as they moved away up the lane.

12

I am writing this in the middle of November, with a black wind flapping at the windows, and black death on the land. In September the bombers came to London. Only a few nights ago, first with Coventry and then Birmingham, they began their attack on our provincial cities. Bristol or Plymouth, they say, will be next.

And it occurs to me, too, how much life has changed and grown pinched since the time I am writing about. Up to the summer of 1940, there was a reasonable plenitude of everything. Petrol rationing provided no great hardship. Food, though partially rationed, remained abundant. You could invite a guest to dinner and never think twice about it.

I was thinking of this in connection with the Monday night in July when Belle Sullivan first came to stay with us.

We all fell for her, Tom and Mrs Harping and I. She was what the younger generation calls cute, and her large eyes did damage. Belle's recuperative powers were amazing. When we first got her home there were, as I expected, signs of delayed shock: cold, vomiting, pulse accelerated yet so faint as to be barely perceptible at the wrist. She could eat very little.

But Mrs Harping gave her a bath, and we got her to bed with a hot-water bottle in a pair of Tom's pyjamas. By eleven o'clock, even though Tom gave her some sulphonal to make her sleep, she was sitting up in bed with needle and thread, mending a rent in the frock which Mrs Harping – unbending amazingly – had sponged and cleaned for her.

Tom liked her; he was even more furiously didactic and insufferable than usual. A little past eleven o'clock, when I was sitting in my bedroom smoking the one pipe of tobacco I am allowed a day, I heard them talking through the closed door of the next room. And there ensued the following romantic dialogue:

'For God's sake, woman, if you must talk American, talk real American. Don't spout this film gabble. They're not the same thing.'

'Nuts to you.'

'And double nuts to you,' yelled my impolite son, whose bedside manner is noted more for its vigour than for its finesse.

'How does my hair look?'

'Terrible.'

'You go take a flying . . . look. There's a tear in the lining of your coat-pocket. You're the sloppiest damned man I ever did see. Let me fix it for you.'

'Take your hands off me, woman. I will not be mothered and pawed over by predatory females.'

'Who's a predatory female, you ugly son of a so-and-so?'

Belle did not say this heatedly, you understand. She could utter hair-raising words, and indulge in the most intimate franknesses, while speaking in a voice of soft sweetness, and even loving kindness.

'You,' said Tom, 'are a predatory female. All of 'em are. It's a question of glands. Let me go down and get my anatomical chart, and I'll show you.'

'One of those things that make you look as though you'd

been skinned?' Belle's voice shivered. 'No, thanks. I prefer my own outside.' A shadow seemed to come over her. 'Look, Dr Croxley. Do you know Superintendent Craft?'

'Yes. What about him?'

Belle hesitated. I could imagine her: the clear-glowing skin and brown curls, the needle and thread in her fingers, the homely bedroom that used to be my wife's.

'He says – there's got to be an inquest day after tomorrow.'

'Lie back in that bed,' said Tom, 'and go to sleep. That's an order.'

'No, but look! He says – maybe I'll have to go on the witness-stand and identify Barry.'

'Identification is usually done by the next-of-kin, yes.'

'Does that mean I'll have to *look* at Barry?'

'Go to sleep, I tell you!'

'Does he look – pretty awful?'

'You can't fall off a seventy-foot cliff into three or four feet of water without *some* injuries. But the doctor who did the post-mortem says there weren't many. That's because they were dead and limp when they struck. He says the worst of the damage was caused by bumping against rocks when the current carried them.'

Here I rapped sharply on the communicating wall. There should be limits to medical detail.

'Now go to sleep,' he roared at her.

'I won't be able to sleep. I'm just telling you.'

But she did sleep, when the sulphonal took over. It was I who couldn't close my eyes. I twisted and tossed, while the clock kept on striking, and I saw Rita's face in every corner. Finally, I went down to the surgery in my nightshirt, and got a mild sleeping draught for myself. This is a venial practice among doctors; not to be recommended. But, when I woke up again, it was past noon on a bright day which put new strength into my veins.

In fact, I felt almost cheerful when I took my bath. Super-intendent Craft and H.M., it appeared, had already been to the house to see Belle. The latter had gone so far as to hop upstairs on his crutch. They left word for me to join them at Alec Wainright's at three o'clock in the afternoon. And, going downstairs for a reprehensibly late breakfast, I met Molly Grange coming out of Belle's room.

I had been wondering how Molly, the quiet and reserved one, would get on with our guest. But one look at her reassured me. Though Molly's face was a little red, she smiled at me.

'Have you met Mrs Sullivan? Is she up?'

'Up,' answered Molly, 'and dressing.'

'How do you like her?'

'I like her tremendously.' Molly's face was perplexed. 'But I say, Dr Luke! Doesn't she use the most frightful *language*?'

'You'll get used to that.'

'And she would keep walking past the window,' Molly said, 'with practically nothing on. That crowd at the Coach and Horses were standing at the windows over there with their eyes popping out of their heads. If you're not careful, Dr Luke, you're going to get a very bad reputation in Lyncombe.'

'At my time of life?'

'I've just taken her in some stockings,' Molly went on. 'They were my last pair of silk ones. But, as Belle would say, what the hell? We mustn't introduce her to Father, by the way. He'd have a fit.'

'What did the police want to see her about?'

Molly's face clouded.

'They wanted to know if she had any pictures of Barry Sullivan. She said yes. But it seems the London police have been searching the Sullivans' flat in town, and they couldn't find any.'

'An actor without pictures of himself?'

'I know.'

'But, look here, Molly!' I was beginning to reflect. 'There must be dozens of snapshots of him out at the Wainrights'. Don't you remember? He and Rita were always photographing each other.'

'That's just it. The police were out there, too. And it seems' – Molly compressed her lips – 'it seems somebody has deliberately torn up every picture of them, out of pure spite. Can you understand that, Dr Luke? Can you understand anybody hating them so much that even the pictures had to be destroyed?'

The evil was back again. I shall always remember Molly at that moment, with her breast rising and falling, and the edges of her yellow hair kindled from the light of the window behind her.

'Somebody hated them enough to murder them, Molly.'

She was incredulous. 'You don't still believe that?'

'I believe it; and I'm going to testify so at the inquest.'

'But you mustn't!'

'I'm going to. Now run along while I get my breakfast.'

But Molly hesitated. 'Mrs Sullivan,' she said, 'isn't exactly without friends in this district. It seems she's acquainted with Paul Ferrars.'

'I believe so.'

'She informed me, out of a clear sky, that there's nobody quite so pleasant to get cock-eyed with – I suppose she means tight? – as he is. Very interesting. But you mark my words, Dr Luke: our little friend is going to cause considerable comment in this neighbourhood.'

The truth of this was made manifest when I went out to take the air at the front gate after breakfast. Harry Pierce, landlord of the Coach and Horses, came out of his own bar with the air of a reluctant emissary. Harry is an old-style barman, broad and with a glistening curl of hair across his forehead. His breath preceded him at some distance.

'Meaning no offence, Dr Luke,' he confided, 'but me and some of my customers wants to know what's going on in this 'ere place.'

'Going on in what respect?'

'First,' said Harry, 'those two un'appy people goes and chucks themselves off Lovers' Leap. Yesterday – Gawd-lummycharley!

– that big stout gentleman comes a-bustin' into my bar like a 'ole panzer division, and breaks eleven pint glasses, one table, two water-jugs, and an ash-tray.'

'I'm sorry about that, Mr Pierce.'

'Not that 'e didn't pay up 'andsome for it, mind!' Harry assured me, lifting one hand as though about to take an oath. ''E did, and that's a fact. I'm not saying nothing against the gentleman. But meaning no offence, Doctor: it's not the sort of thing a chap likes to 'ave 'appen to him, when 'e's just lifting his first pint of the day. Now is it?'

'Of course not.'

'It upsets the customers, that's what it does. Then, this morning, blow me if a young lady – and a very 'andsome young lady, I'm not saying she's not! – goes and exhibits herself practically stark naked at the window of your 'ouse.'

'*That* didn't upset the customers, I trust?'

'No, but it upset my missus,' confided Harry, lowering his voice. 'And there's other ladies 'oo don't feel too 'appy about it neither. Somebody told the parson down at St Mark's, and '*e* come a-charging up here; ah, and seemed a bit disappointed 'e got 'ere too late to give 'er a piece of 'is mind. Then, on top of that, there's Willie Johnson and this bloke Nero.'

'This bloke who?'

'The Emperor Nero, what fiddled while Rome was burning.'

'What about him?'

Harry shook his head despondently.

'Coo, you never 'eard anybody carry on like Willie done! Somebody gave 'im ten bob yesterday . . .'

'Yes, I know.'

'And down 'e goes to the pictures at Lynton. 'E comes back, first to the Crown and then to me and starts mopping it up. 'E can't talk about nothing but this bloke Nero. Willie says this Nero is the meanest, ugliest, wickedest brute 'e ever did see even in a film. Willie says 'e's awful. Throw fifty or a 'undred

Christians to the lions while 'e was polishing off a pint of bitter, Willie says.'

'Yes, but –'

''E went on about it so much I wouldn't serve 'im any longer, 'aving some respect for me licence. But down 'e goes to the Black Cat, and Joe Williams is fool enough to let 'im 'ave a bottle of whisky on tick.' Again Harry shook his head despondently. ''E'll be just warming up on whisky this morning, I reckon.'

'I shouldn't worry too much about him, if I were you. He'll be all right.'

'I 'ope so, Doctor. I 'ope so.'

'As for the young lady at my house –'

'Ah?'

I saw the quick, glutinous interest of the eye, and I didn't like it.

'You can go back and tell Mrs Pierce and the other ladies that the girl they saw was Mrs Barry Sullivan. She's lost her husband; she's very much upset; and she doesn't much like to be spied on. Will you tell them that?'

Harry hesitated.

'All right, Doctor. If you say so. But you can't blame 'em for 'ardly liking it. What with the war and all, it does seem like there's a curse on us, as you might say. Some of us are just wondering wot in the name of sense is a-going to 'appen *next*.'

Privately, this last was a view I shared. It was early, only a little past two, when I got into my car and drove out towards Alec's.

The sky was what they call a robin's egg blue; the countryside, with a sparkle on it, had never been more beautiful; but the bungalow at Lovers' Leap seemed to have aged, like its owner, and intensified the seediness I had noticed four nights ago. The bright beach chairs on the lawn were still there. Barry Sullivan, I remembered, had stayed behind when it started to rain on Saturday night, and said he was going to get those chairs in. But they remained.

I stopped my car in the drive. Martha, the old maid, admitted me to the house and directed me upstairs. You could hear your footsteps loudly on the hardwood in this place.

Alec and Rita had shared a big bedroom at the back of the house, overlooking the sea, when they first came to live here. As a matter of fact, Rita had been occupying a separate room for some time; she stayed in the rear room, while Alec moved to the front. But I had not remembered this when I carried him upstairs on Saturday night. It was to Rita's room I took him, and to Rita's room I went now.

Mrs Grover, the day nurse, was on duty now. She answered my tap at the door.

'How is he, nurse?'

'No better and no worse, as far as I can see.'

'Restless?'

'Not very. He calls for her, sometimes.'

'You haven't let him have any visitors?'

'No, Doctor. Miss Payne and I have been here day and night; and, anyway, there's been nobody to see him.'

I went in and closed the door. White linen blinds were drawn down on the two big windows facing the sea; the windows were open, and the blinds trembled in the draught from the door. The blackout material had been pushed back out of sight under heavy valances and curtains of flowered chintz.

Alec, asleep and breathing in thin gasps, lay in a big mahogany double-bed against the right-hand wall. The curious smell of sick flesh, so familiar and yet always so disturbing, pervaded this room. It was Alec's own fault; no system, at his age, could withstand shock on top of so many years' softening with whisky; but it is no good preaching after the fact. I took his pulse and glanced at the chart at the foot of the bed. In the dim whitish dusk of the blinds, I could see that Alec was holding something in the hand he held clasped on his chest outside the covers.

The skin of the hand was cracked and shiny, with congested veins. It rose and fell with the movements of Alec's chest. The object in his hand – at least, to judge by the top of it – was the chromium-headed key engraved with the word 'Margarita' and the true-love knot. Alec set great store by that key.

'Nurse!'

'Yes, Doctor?'

'You see that key in his hand. Do you happen to know why he's so attached to it, or what it's the key to?'

Mrs Grover seemed of two minds about answering. A nurse is not supposed to investigate her patient's private affairs; but, quite obviously, she *had* investigated this. Evidently deciding my question had no trap in it, she went to a dressing-table surrounded on three sides with mirrors, and pulled open the drawer.

'I should think, Doctor, it's the key to that.' She pointed. 'But of course I don't know.'

Inside, amid an untidy jumble of Rita's effects, was a biggish box of some material that resembled ivory. The word 'Margarita' was engraved in gold letters over the lock, and there was a true-love knot in blue just underneath.

'The pattern's the same, you see,' Mrs Grover pointed out.

I lifted the box, and it was very heavy. I shook it, without hearing anything. Its removal disturbed spilled powder, which made a scented dust from the drawer and was redolent of a dead woman who might have been standing at my elbow.

Rita's effects – those things which are so pathetic afterwards – were characteristic of her. There was one thin kid glove. There was an expensive wrist-watch without crystal or hands. There were gossamer-coloured handkerchiefs. There were hairpins, curling-pins, empty jars, and tubes of cold-cream, a bundle of ration-books, and a passport. All powder-dusted and drained of life.

I picked up the passport, whose photograph showed Rita and Alec at a much earlier date. Alec looked healthy and confident, with a smile on his lips even when he faced the passport photographer. Rita's was a wistful and naïve countenance in a bell-shaped hat. '*The bearer is accompanied by his wife, Margarita Dulane Wainright, born November 20th, 1897, at Montreal, Dominion of Canada . . .*'

So Rita had been forty-three instead of the thirty-eight she claimed. Not that it mattered. I put back the passport. I lowered the ivory box into its place again, and closed the drawer.

Mrs Grover cleared her throat. 'Doctor. I said there'd been nobody here. But there was a person who came to the house a while ago, and made a terrible row until Martha drove him away.'

'Who?'

'That horrible Willie Johnson, drunk as a lord.'

(By this time, the mention of Mr Johnson was beginning to exasperate me a good deal.)

'He claims Professor Wainright stole something from him,' said Mrs Grover. 'He carried on at a great rate, and wouldn't go away. Then he went out to the gardening shed at the other side of the garage; and I think he's still there, swearing and carrying on and I don't know what. We didn't like to ring the police, over a thing like that. Couldn't you do something about it?'

'Leave him to me, nurse. I'll settle him.'

I went downstairs in something of a temper. I walked through the sitting-room, where Rita's portrait greeted me with its half-smile. I went through the dining-room into the kitchen, and down the steps to the back yard.

It had not rained since Saturday night. Past the sparse grass which formed what might be called a back lawn, the great expanse of damp, soft, reddish soil stretched out to Lovers' Leap. There were the geometrical designs in tiny white pebbles. There were the pebbles which outlined the form of the path to Lovers' Leap. There were the two sets of footprints, still sharply marked, of the lovers who had not come back.

You could see along and out over the mighty curve of the

cliffs. Distantly, a grey trawler idled against dark-blue water stung with light-points under sunshine. A mild breeze blew inshore.

And a voice shouted: "Ere!'

Round the left-hand side of the house, from the direction of the gardening-shed near the tennis-court, came Mr Willie Johnson.

He walked not rapidly, but with exaggerated care. You might even have said he was stalking something. His broad-brimmed hat was pulled down almost to his eyebrows; beneath it, bloodshot eyes made an effort to focus by concentrating along the line of the nose. From the pocket of his coat projected the neck of a bottle considerably depleted. While still some distance away, he stopped, swayed, pointed his finger at me with great concentration, and spoke huskily.

'I've 'ad,' said Mr Johnson, ''orrible dreams.'

'Have you?'

''*Orrible* dreams,' emphasised Mr Johnson, sighting along the line of his extended finger. 'I've 'ad 'em all night. Somebody is a-going to pay for them dreams.'

'You'll pay for them yourself, if you don't keep off the booze.'

Mr Johnson was not interested in this.

'I dreamed,' he said, 'that the Emperor Nero was a-sitting in judgement on me. 'E was smoking a 'alf-crown cigar and 'aving people coated with pitch so's 'e could burn 'em up. Such a ugly 'orrible face you never saw on any 'uman being; and be'ind 'im was all his gladiators with swords and pitchforks. 'E leans over like this, and 'e says to me –'

Here Mr Johnson paused to clear a husky throat. There was, it seemed, another remedy for this. Drawing the bottle from his pocket, he carefully wiped its mouth on his sleeve, measured its contents with one eye by holding it up to the light, and elevated it to his lips.

And then something happened.

13

For several seconds, it is true, I had been conscious of a faint steady noise of *pop-pop-pop*, suggesting a light motor vehicle in motion. I did not need to look, because I knew what it was. It inspired in me, I must confess, much the same sense of impending disaster as was inspired in Captain Hook by the approach of the crocodile with the clock inside it.

But I never guessed how much disaster.

This vehicle, unseen, popped steadily nearer round the opposite side of the house. The *pop-pop-pop* grew in volume as it approached, round the angle of the house behind my back. Something, describing a broad and skittish curve, appeared and bore down steadily in our direction. And Mr Willie Johnson, with the bottle still tilted at his lips, lowered one eye to look.

I have never, I think, seen on any human face such an expression of living horror as froze then on the countenance of Mr Johnson. I did not see his hair actually rise, since he was wearing a hat; but in his case I am prepared to admit the phenomenon. It utterly paralysed him. It would have moved a man of stone to pity. It was, in fact, so terrible that I whirled round to look.

The approaching wheelchair contained a figure which was at once familiar and unfamiliar. On its bald head the figure wore what was later described to me as a laurel-wreath. The laurel-wreath was set there firmly, with some suggestion of a bowler hat on a bookmaker, and its two little ends stuck up like horns.

Round and round the barrel-figure was wound in many folds, like a badly tied bandage, a voluminous garment of pure white wool with a deep purple border. It left only the right arm bare, and this arm was decorated – so to speak – by brass ornaments which glittered in the sun. On its feet, propped up against the footboard of the chair, it wore sandals. The big toe of the right foot was bandaged. On its broad face, with the spectacles pulled down on the nose, it wore an expression of terrifying malignancy; and it was smoking a cigar.

Ensuing events were a little chaotic.

The unearthly yell which burst from Willie Johnson could have been heard, I think, as far as the trawler in the bay. Only for a second did he remain completely paralysed. The bottle left his lips. He lowered his arm, screamed again, and flung the bottle straight at the apparition which was bearing steadily towards him at a speed of about twenty miles an hour.

Afterwards, merely to say that Johnson ran would be a powerful understatement. He moved with such speed as almost to baffle the eyesight – he collected a bicycle. So far as I recall, he did not stop to mount the bicycle. Man and bicycle, so to speak, seemed to melt together and become man-on-bicycle without a second's interruption of progress.

But my attention was on other matters.

To have a half-filled whisky bottle fired at your head is enough to destroy the composure of even the noblest Roman.

The bottle whizzed past the head of Sir Henry Merrivale, and fell between Superintendent Craft and Paul Ferrars as they came pelting round the side of the house. Ferrars, who was carrying a suit of clothes across his arm, stumbled over it.

As it flew, H.M. put his hands up instinctively to shield his face. The steering-handle, left to its own devices, brought the chair round in a broad curve; and the motor, as though inspired by a diabolical life of its own, put on the burst of speed which made him travel as steadily as an express-train straight towards the brink of the cliff.

'Turn it!' Ferrars was screaming. 'Turn it! Mind the cliff! For God's sake mind the –'

What saved H.M.'s life, undoubtedly, was the softness of the soil and his own weight. Two deep grooves followed his jolting and bouncing passage across the earth. The crutch flew out of his hand. The motor coughed and died. The chair lurched, sank deeper, put on a last burst of speed; and then came to rest, deliberately, on the very edge of the cliff. His sandalled feet, in fact, stuck out over nothingness.

Then there was silence, under the warm sunlight.

The pause was broken by Ferrars. Carefully taking a pair of trousers from over his arm, he held them by the braces like a whip, and brought them down violently on the ground.

'This,' he said, 'is the end!'

'What are you doin' to my pants?' howled an irate voice from the figure sitting very rigidly on the cliff and facing out to sea. 'You mind my pants! I can't turn round, but I can hear you doin' something to my pants. What are you doin' to my pants?'

'Nothing,' Ferrars answered with some restraint, 'compared with what I'd like to do to you. Listen, Appius Claudius. If you're ruddy well determined to kill yourself, why don't you take a gun and do it cleanly? I can't stand this sort of thing much longer.'

'Don't move, sir!' shouted Superintendent Craft in some agony. 'Whatever you do, don't move!'

'Now that,' said H.M., 'is what I'd characterise as the irrelevant advice of a blazing fathead. What in the name of Esau do you think I'm goin' to do – take two paces forward and float?'

'I only meant –'

'Chuckin' whisky bottles at people!' said the irate voice, coming back with ghostly effect after being directed at the sea. 'You come round the side of the house and they up and sling whisky bottles straight at your dial. Y'know, son, it's not only the dogs in this place that are demented. It's the people too. And what about a little action from you two, now that the fun's all over? Are you going to leave me sittin' here like King Canute, or are you going to pull me back?'

Superintendent Craft considered him dubiously.

'I don't know that we dare pull you back, sir.'

The figure in the toga put both hands up to its laurel-wreath, and pulled down the wreath more firmly on its head, as though H.M. were corking himself.

'Speaking personally,' he said, 'there's nothing I admire more than a sea-view. This is a very fine one, I admit. But I can't help feelin' that after the first forty-eight hours it's goin' to pall a little, and what if I have to go to the lavatory? Burn it all, *why* can't you pull me back?'

We all went out to the stranded wheelchair. H.M. had even lost the steering-handle, which projected straight out ahead of him over the gulf.

'Well, sir,' said Craft, 'you're bogged pretty nearly to the axles in that soil. We can't just pull you out. We'll have to lay hold and give you a yank. But, if we give a yank, I'm afraid it might jerk you right out over the edge.' Craft considered deeply. 'Couldn't you sort of ooze round and get out yourself?'

'"Ooze round",' repeated H.M. 'That's fine. That's very helpful. What do you think I am: a goddamn snake? Can't you two stop drivellin' and think up something practical for a change?'

'After all,' Craft consoled him, 'it might be a whole lot worse, even if you did slip. It's nearly high-tide now and you'd only fall in the water.'

The back of H.M.'s neck turned purple.

'I'll tell you something we could do, though,' Ferrars suggested.

Very slowly, and with infinite caution, H.M. craned his neck and a part of his body round so that he could get a glimpse of us. The laurel-wreath was now inclined rakishly over one ear, and the cigar was gripped in one comer of his mouth. The look he directed at Ferrars was one of the deepest suspicion.

Despite himself, Ferrars' lips were twitching; he had difficulty keeping a straight face. The wind blew flat his light hair, and his greenish eyes were not exactly innocent. Still holding H.M.'s trousers by the braces, he slapped idly at the ground with them.

'I'll tell you what we could do,' he amplified. 'We could get some clothes-line and tie him to the chair.'

Craft nodded. 'That's not a bad idea, sir!'

'Then, of course, we could yank as much as we liked. And he wouldn't necessarily fall over.'

'What I like,' said H.M., 'is that word "necessarily". It's so comfortin'. Believe it or not, and strange as it may seem to you, I prefer to do my swimming when not attached to a two-hundred-pound motor wheelchair. Y'know, you fellers can think up games that would embarrass Houdini.'

'We won't let you slip,' Craft assured him. 'If we don't do that, what else can you suggest?'

'I don't know,' yelled the noble Roman, and began to whack his fist on the arm of the chair. 'I'm only askin' you to use a little of the sense that the Lord gave Assyrian monkeys, and –'

'*Look out, sir!*' shouted Craft, as the chair tilted about two inches.

H.M. spat out the cigar, a good effort which carried it high into the air and over the brink. Then, craning cautiously round again, he caught sight of me.

'If that's Dr Croxley, will you just tell the old man why that feller was chuckin' bottles at me? Hey? If I remember rightly, it's the same chap I gave ten bob to yesterday. Oh, my eye. You give a man ten bob, and he goes and buys whisky with it, and then comes back and slings the bottle straight in your face. If that's not gratitude, son, I never heard of it.'

'Johnson must have thought you were the Emperor Nero.'

'He thought I was who?'

'He saw a film last night, *Quo Vadis?* or something of the sort, and he's got Nero on the brain. You must admit you were fairly paralysing when you came tearing round that corner.'

To my astonishment, H.M. looked considerably mollified.

'Well . . . now. Maybe there is some resemblance, at that,' he conceded. 'I told you, didn't I, that Ferrars here was painting my picture as a Roman Senator?'

'Yes,' said Ferrars, 'and that's another thing. If we get you out of this –'

'*If* you get me out of this?'

'That's what I said. If we get you out of this, you're going to promise to put on your clothes like a civilised human being. You're also going to get out of that infernal wheelchair for good. Otherwise, so help me, we'll leave you stuck just where you are until you turn into a statue.'

'How in Satan's name can I get out of my chair? I'm an invalid.'

'Nonsense,' retorted Ferrars. 'The doctor took off that splint this morning. He said it was quite all right to walk on it if you went gently.'

Again H.M. laid violent hands on his laurel-wreath.

'Some people,' he observed offhandedly, 'might think that the proper place to hold elegant and witty converse was the edge of a nice cosy cliff while stickin' half-way over. Maybe you might. Maybe G. B. Shaw might. But burn me if *I* do. I tell you straight, son: I feel more like the third episode of the *Perils of Pauline*, and it's underminin' the old man's composure. Are you goin' to drag me away from here, or aren't you?'

'Will you promise to put on your clothes?'

'All right! All right! Only –'

'*Look out, sir!*' shouted Craft.

'What we need now,' said H.M., 'is a good spectacular landslide. I feel this thing movin' under me, I tell you! People who could do what you're doin' to me would poison babies' milk and steal the pennies from a blind man.'

Ferrars nodded as though satisfied. He took one last slap at the ground with H.M.'s trousers, dislodging some money and a key-ring. Then he piled all the clothes on the ground, and turned to me.

'Come along, Doctor,' he said. 'There ought to be some clothes-line in the kitchen.'

Though Martha was not there, we found the clothes-line in one of the lower cupboards. We bound H.M.'s body securely to the back of the chair. Then, with infinite care, we yanked and dragged while a flood of vituperation and obscenity directed us. There was one bad moment when the chair lurched. But we got him back safely. We were all feeling a little queasy when we untied him.

The only one unaffected now was the noble Roman himself. Majestically, he arose from his chair. Exaggerating the limp in his right foot, he took a few turns up and down. He made a striking figure against the skyline, his toga stirred by the breeze, and had an electrifying effect on two fishermen passing in a boat below. He was just gathering up his clothes, after an evil glance at Ferrars, when Martha came down from the back door.

Nothing, I think, could ever startle Martha. Even H.M.'s appearance failed to shake her. But there was awe in her voice when she delivered her message.

'If you please,' she said. 'Scotland Yard is calling Superintendent Craft on the telephone.'

There was dead silence on the sunlit cliff. Your skin seemed to crawl with it. I spoke merely from lack of something to say.

'The telephone's been repaired, then?'

'Oh, yes,' growled H.M. 'And now maybe we're goin' to get

some news about the little joker who cut it. Come along, all of you.'

Ferrars handed him his crutch, and we went to the house. We went through kitchen and dining-room, and into the sitting-room. There, not far from the radio round which four persons had listened to *Romeo and Juliet* on Saturday night, was the telephone. The sun was on the opposite side of the bungalow, and this room remained gloomy. While we all sat down – I had almost said crouched – Craft picked up the receiver.

'Yes,' he said. 'Speaking.' The telephone seemed to be chortling in deep amusement. Craft's good eye moved over towards H.M. 'Yes. Yes, he's here now. Sitting beside me.'

H.M. sat up with some violence. '"Who's that speaking?' he demanded.

'Chief Inspector Masters.' Craft put his hand over the mouthpiece of the phone. 'Have you got any message for him?'

'Yes. Tell the dirty dog I hope he chokes.'

'Sir Henry says to give you his kindest regards, Chief Inspector . . . What's that? Yes, certainly I'm sober! . . . Yes, his toe is much better . . . Well, no. No, I can't say he's enjoying himself.'

'Enjoying myself,' said H.M. 'Twice on successive days I nearly get killed, and then they ask if I'm enjoying myself. Here, let *me* talk to the blighter!'

Again Craft put his hand over the mouthpiece of the phone. 'You're too mad, sir,' he insisted. 'And besides – they've got it.'

The telephone talked at great length, though we could distinguish no word. Nobody else spoke. Ferrars was leaning back in a padded chair, his legs crossed in their paint-stained flannels, and his hands thrust deep into the pockets of a grey sweater. His shirt was open at the neck, so that you could see his Adam's apple move. His eyes rested on his own portrait of Rita, above the fireplace; there was pity in his look, I thought, and also regret. Then he closed his eyes.

Superintendent Craft's whole expression grew as fixed as the one glass eye. Fumblingly, he reached into his inside pocket, manipulating notebook and pencil with one hand while he listened. He dropped the notebook on the telephone table and started to write rapidly. At length he drew a deep breath, said a word of thanks, and replaced the receiver. His face was even more sepulchrally gloomy when he swung round.

'Well, sir,' he admitted, with another deep breath, 'it seems you were right after all.'

'Sure I was right, son.'

'And maybe' – Craft looked at me – 'the doctor was right too.'

'Right about what?' inquired Ferrars, opening his eyes.

'Go on, son!' H.M. urged impatiently. 'I'm staying at that feller's house. I know him. He won't blab.'

Craft consulted his notebook.

'Have you ever heard,' he asked, 'of a theatrical publication called *Spotlight*?'

'Sure. It's a kind of advertising medium for actors. What about it?'

'They couldn't find a photograph of Barry Sullivan anywhere else. But they eventually ran one down at the *Spotlight* office: an old one. This morning they took it round to the American Consulate in Grosvenor Square.'

Craft examined the point of his pencil. His mouth was worried and grim. It was only after a long pause that he continued.

'There's no "Barry Sullivan" on the records at the Consulate. But, when they saw the photograph, one of the girls in the American passport department recognised it like a shot. They've got both his photograph and his right thumbprint there – it's a new war-time measure – so we can check it easily enough.

'Barry Sullivan's real name was Jacob McNutt. He was born in 1915 at Little Rock, Arkansas. I've got all the details.' Craft tapped the notebook. Then he raised his eyes. 'Maybe you saw in the papers recently that the American liner *Washington* would be calling at Galway this week?'

'Yes,' I said. 'Alec Wainright mentioned it.'

'To take Americans and their families who wanted to get back to the United States?'

'Yes.'

'Jacob McNutt, alias Barry Sullivan,' Craft spoke slowly, 'together with his wife, booked passage to sail aboard the *Washington* some time ago.'

A dim glimmering of the truth, a foreshadowing that came gradually into focus, stirred at the back of my head.

'His wife?' Ferrars echoed.

Craft made a slow and portentous nod.

'We couldn't get a photograph of Mrs Wainright,' the superintendent explained. 'But one of the gentlemen at the American Consulate recognised her from the description. The "wife" was Rita Wainright. And he ought to know, because he gave her a visa for the United States.'

I got up from my chair, but sat down again.

'She carried a British passport, made out in the name of Rita Dulane McNutt. Across the bottom was the official notation, "wife of an American citizen". That's the law, you see. An English-woman who marries an American doesn't – by American law – assume her husband's nationality. She carries her own passport.'

'But Rita,' I protested, 'didn't *marry* Sullivan?'

Craft snorted.

'She went through a form of marriage with him, though. Because she had to have that passport.'

'Rita's got a passport! I saw it upstairs in the dressing-table drawer!'

'Which,' said Craft, 'would have been no earthly good to her. You see, Doctor, this ship was sent to take *only* Americans and their dependants. Also, if she meant to disappear and start a new life, she had to have a new identity. So she had to get a new passport under false pretences.'

It was H.M., twiddling his thumbs, who explained.

'Looky here, Doctor,' he said patiently. 'You saw the whole thing unroll in front of you. But you never noticed what was happening. These two, Rita Wainright and Barry Sullivan, never had the least idea of killin' themselves. The whole "suicide pact" was a fake, carefully planned, carefully designed; and acted out, burn me, in a way that rouses my admiration! It was intended to deceive not only Alec Wainright, but the rest of England too.

'That woman (don't you see?) thought it was her only way out. She really was fond of her husband. She couldn't bear to hurt him. But she couldn't give up her boyfriend either. So that hysterical, romantic nature of hers thought of a plan that she imagined suited the case. She wouldn't just up and run away with Sullivan. But if the husband, and the rest of the world, thought she and Sullivan were dead, they wouldn't bother any longer.

'Charmin' idea. Also characteristic. Dodgin' the responsibility. Don't you follow it even yet?'

14

'And if you don't,' added H.M., 'think back!'

Automatically he reached for the pocket that should have held his cigar-case, but found only a toga. He regarded this dismally, and then forgot it.

'Rita Wainright came to your surgery, in a terrible stew, on the twenty-second of May. She wanted you to do something for her. What were the first words she said to you? I'll tell you. She said: "I've quarrelled with my solicitor. No clergyman would do it, naturally. And I don't know any J.P.s. You've got to . . ." And then she stopped. Is that true?'

I could not help nodding.

'Yes. It's true.'

'Sure. And what is it you apply for,' said H.M., 'where you've got to be recommended and vouched for on personal knowledge by a physician, a lawyer, a clergyman, or a justice of the peace?'

It was Ferrars who answered, sitting up straight.

'A passport,' he said.

The image of Rita in my office, with her red finger-nails and her harassed eyes, looking at corners of the ceiling, always stumbling and drawing back on the edge of telling me something, returned in cruel vividness. 'It's all such a mess,' I could hear her saying. 'If only Alec would die, or something like that.' And then a quick, furtive look at me, to see how I took it.

But still I protested.

'It's fantastic, I tell you! What would they have used for money? Sullivan had practically none, and Rita certainly hadn't any.'

'If you remember,' grunted H.M., 'you asked her the same question. And it didn't bother her at all. Not the least little bit in the world, son! Because, d'ye see, she had an answer for it – What about diamonds?'

His eyes travelled up to the portrait of Rita over the fireplace. Only then did I stop concentrating on the face of the portrait, the tantalising half-smiling face, to remember what I have indicated in this record: that Ferrars had painted her in diamonds. Diamond necklace at the throat, diamond bracelets on her wrists. As the centre of interest shifted, those painted diamonds seemed to wink with sly reminder.

'You yourself,' pursued H.M., 'kept telling me how Professor Wainright loved hangin' her with diamonds. There'll be a rule soon that jewellery can't be taken out of the country; but in the meantime they're awful negotiable.'

'But Alec Wainright,' I said, 'is practically broke. Those diamonds must be all he has left. Rita would never have taken the diamonds and left him without . . .'

'Practically broke,' murmured H.M. 'Uh-huh. Did she know he was broke?'

(Truth is a dizzying thing.)

'Well – no. Come to think of it, she didn't. Alec told me so himself.'

'He kept his business affairs strictly under his hat?'

'That's right.'

'And she still thought he was a wealthy man?'

'Yes, I suppose so.'

'Let's clear up the question while we're at it,' said H.M. 'Does anybody know where those diamonds were kept?'

'I can tell you that,' interposed Ferrars. 'In fact, I told you last night. She keeps 'em – or used to keep 'em, anyway – in a biggish ivory box lined with steel, up in her bedroom. You open the box with a little key, like a Yale key only smaller, that's got "Margarita" and a true-love knot engraved on it.'

H.M. contemplated me, continuing to twiddle his thumbs. His expression remained sour.

'The husband guessed, of course,' he said. 'Every word you quote him as sayin' on Saturday night proves that. "Kill me? I can see you don't know my wife. They aren't planning to kill me. But I can tell you what they are planning to do." Only, d'ye see, he had it slightly wrong. He didn't bargain on any fancy fake suicide pact. He thought they were just goin' to run away.

'For what happened? You came in and told him those two had thrown themselves over Lovers' Leap. And it hit him like a mule's kick. It dazed him. He screamed out that he didn't believe it. Then what did he do? He ran upstairs to see if her clothes were there. "Her clothes are still there," he said when he came down; "but –" and that's where he held up the little key. Meanin', my fatheads, that the diamonds were gone.'

There was a silence.

Ferrars, slowly shaking his head from side to side, kept his gaze mainly on the carpet. Once he glanced up at the portrait, and muscles tightened down his lean jaws.

'Are you saying,' Ferrars interposed, 'that Mr Wainright was going to *let* them take the diamonds?'

'Sure.'

'Even though he'd have not very much money left?'

'There are people like that, son.' H.M.'s voice was apologetic. 'The evidence shows Alec Wainright was one of 'em. But can you wonder he's feelin' a bit tired and sick and disgusted with the world?'

As I saw the picture take form, as I recognised the essential rightness of each detail, it seemed impossible to argue any longer or to doubt H.M.'s version. And can you doubt, even if you wish, the evidence of a consulate which shows you passports and visas?

But, even granting this were so, why was it necessary to curse and thrash at the memory of Rita? As H.M. had suggested, the thing was absolutely characteristic of Rita. She brought down destruction; but she meant well. She had nearly killed Alec; but that had not been her intention. If it was essential to praise Alec, was it also essential to blame Rita?

'As for Mrs Wainright and Sullivan – we'll call him Sullivan – you can see what they had to do,' continued H.M. 'She had to get a new passport. He had to bring his car down here from London, and hide it away in the studio, so they could slip quietly away when the trick had been worked.'

'Away, sir?' prompted Superintendent Craft.

'Sure. First up to Liverpool. Then, gettin' rid of the car, across to Ireland and Galway. Next, they had to destroy *every* photograph of themselves. Why? Lord love a duck! They were shortly goin' to figure as the victims of a terrible tragedy. The newspapers would come snoopin' after photographs to print.'

Craft nodded.

'I see,' he said thoughtfully. 'They couldn't have someone – from the American Consulate or the British Passport Office, for instance – see the newspaper pictures and say, "Here! That's not Mrs Alexander Wainright and Mr Barry Sullivan. That's Mr and Mrs Jacob McNutt, who are now on the high seas headed for America."'

H.M. spread out his hands.

'If you want any more evidence,' he growled in my direction, 'just think of what happened on Saturday night.

'Who chose a Saturday night, which was the maid's night off? Rita Wainright. Who had the gardener Johnson sacked, because he was a snooper? Rita Wainright. Who vetoed her husband's suggestion to make the party bigger, and insisted on just you four? Rita Wainright.

'Finally, what *time* did these love-birds choose for their dramatic hocus-pocus? Nine o'clock, naturally. And why? Because Alec Wainright is a news-fiend. As soon as the soothin' voice of Joseph Macleod or Alvar Liddell is heard in the land, he becomes deaf and blind to everything else. He wouldn't interfere when they left this room. Nobody would interfere. The husband was too engrossed, and the guest was too embarrassed.

'Mind you, Rita's conduct then wasn't all actin'. Not by a jugful! All that emotionalism, all that carryin' on, was almost as real to her as though she meant to kill herself. When she stroked the hair on her husband's head, she meant it. When the tears started streamin' out of her eyes, she meant that too.

'In a sense, gents, she *was* leaving this life. She was sayin' goodbye. She was cutting off, with what she thought was a sharp knife, her old life and her old associations. You can call it affected nonsense, if you like; but the point is that she didn't see it as that. Oh, no. Out she goes. And the handsome Sullivan – who's a little bit nervous about walkin' off with five or six thousand pounds' worth of diamonds – goes after her.'

H.M. scowled, and cleared his throat.

Ferrars, who was lighting the familiar cherrywood pipe, glanced up briefly. The glow of the match showed his sinewy wrists, and the hollows under his cheek-bones as he drew in smoke.

'Tell me one thing, governor.' He blew out the match. 'About this Barry Sullivan, or Jacob McNutt.' Again the catlike smile flickered under the long nose. "Was he really in love with the woman, or was he only interested in diamonds?'

'Well . . . now. I never met the feller. Judgin' from the descriptions of him, notably his wife's –'

'You mean Belle?'

'Yes. I should sort of hazard a guess that it was a good deal of both. His conscience didn't prevent him from doin' what he oughtn't to do; it just prevented him from enjoying it. But you can follow their conduct on Saturday night. They rushed out of this room. And then . . .'

Superintendent Craft spoke softly.

'Yes, sir. And then what?'

'I don't know!' roared H.M. 'I haven't got the ghostiest trace of a notion. The old man's completely stumped and flummoxed.'

This, evidently, was what bothered him. Immense in his purple-bordered toga, apparently forgetting his toe altogether, he lumbered up and down in front of the fireplace. He removed the laurel-wreath, eyed it distastefully, and put it on the radio. Then he said: 'Now follow this, my fatheads. This is what we know. *Between nine o'clock and nine-thirty, those two walked out to Lovers' Leap. There they disappeared. But they didn't jump and they didn't mean to jump.*'

Craft nodded, though he had a dubious frown.

'Son, there are two possible explanations,' H.M. pursued fiercely. 'Either (a) they somehow got down the face of the cliff. Or (b) they somehow walked back to the house again, ready for their getaway in Sullivan's car.'

Craft sat up abruptly. Ferrars glanced at me in a puzzled way, taking the pipe out of his mouth, but I could only shrug my shoulders.

'Stop a bit!' the superintendent urged. 'In that case, what becomes of the murders being committed on the edge of the cliff?'

H.M. made a face.

'Oh, my son! You don't still think the murders were committed on the edge of the cliff?'

'It's the assumption I've been proceeding on, yes.'

'Then it's a wrong assumption.'

Craft came as near a sputter as the intense gloominess of his expression would permit. He tapped the point of his pencil on the notebook.

'I'd like to hear some proof of that, sir.'

'All right. We'll try a little.' H.M., hitching up the toga as though he were carrying a load of bed-linen, turned to me. 'Doctor, you were sittin' in here with Professor Wainright. The back door of this house was open. Between you and the outside there was only that thin swing-door to the kitchen' – he pointed – 'with a space under it where you could feel a draught. Right?'

'Right.'

'If those two were shot on the edge of the cliff, a Browning .32 automatic was fired twice out there. Did you hear any shots?'

I thought back. 'No. But that's not necessarily unusual or anything like proof. It's fairly windy up here. When the wind is blowing in the wrong direction, to carry sound away . . .'

'But the wind wasn't blowin' in the wrong direction, dammit! You yourself kept saying, several times, how the wind blew straight in your face when you went out there. You even felt it in here.' H.M.'s sharp, disconcerting little eyes fixed on me. 'How was it the sound of the shots didn't carry? Oh, and if anybody starts gibberin' about silencers, I retire to bed.'

There was a long silence.

Craft tapped the point of his pencil on the notebook.

'What's your idea, sir?'

'It's this,' H.M. returned with hideous earnestness. 'Those two love-birds thought they had an *aes triplex*, fool-proof method of provin' they'd committed suicide. And so they had.

'They went out and worked it. It probably didn't take 'em long. Then they'd go *away* from here, away from this district, to get their car and hop it. They were probably gone at shortly past nine o'clock. But the murderer caught 'em. The murderer shot both of 'em at close range, and pitched the bodies into the sea.'

'H'm,' said Craft.

'Y'see, it's not the conduct of the murderer that's puzzling to the point of the magical. This murderer is a fairly straightforward chap. You notice what he had to do on the followin' night, Sunday? He had to get rid of Sullivan's car, so that nobody would suspect any hanky-panky on the love-birds' part, and the business could still pass as a suicide pact. So he drove the car out to Exmoor and ran it into quicksand. Don't you remember that Belle Sullivan saw "two little booklets like road-maps, one blue and the other green, stuck into the side pocket"?'

'Well, sir?'

'They weren't road-maps. They were passports. A blue British and a green American. But Belle Sullivan had never travelled abroad, so she couldn't tell.'

H.M. sniffed.

Hurling one corner of his robe over one shoulder, he took a broad and challenging look at all of us, and sat down again. His manner remained as earnest as ever.

'Let me repeat,' he insisted. 'It's not the scheme of the murderer that's baffling to the point of the magical. Here we got a reverse twist. What we want to know is the scheme of the ruddy *victims*.'

Ferrars tapped the stem of his pipe against his teeth. 'You mean to go out there and not come back?'

'Sure. Son, it's really got the old man dizzy this time. I said a minute ago that they either (a) somehow got down the face of the cliff. Or (b) they somehow walked back again without leavin' any trace. I know, I know!' He shushed Craft with a fierce gesture as the superintendent started to protest. 'Both of those explanations are absolute eyewash.'

'You're quite sure of that?'

'I'm dead sure of it. A fly couldn't get up or down the sheer face of that cliff. As for the footprints . . .'

Superintendent Craft spoke with decision.

'And *I* say again,' he declared, 'that there was no funny business about those footprints. Mrs Wainright and Mr Sullivan walked out there, and they didn't come back. That's what *I* say.'

'Agreed,' said H.M.

'But look here,' protested Ferrars. He spoke from behind a cloud of smoke, with a gleam in his eyes which might have been malicious amusement or a real desire to help. 'Do you realise that this bit of enlightenment leaves you in a worse position than you were before?'

'*I* do, anyway,' snapped Craft.

'First you only had a murderer who could walk over soft soil without leaving a track. Now you've got two levitating bodies. Or worse. You've got a man and a woman who can walk out to Lovers' Leap and there vanish like soap-bubbles, only to reappear somewhere else . . .'

'Stop it!' said Craft.

Ferrars put his head against the back of the chair and blew up a smoke-ring. I could see the cords in his neck, and the gleam from under his half-closed eyelids. Resting his elbow on the arm of the chair, he drew a slow circle in the air with his pipe-stem.

'This intrigues me,' he remarked.

'Thanks,' said H.M. 'I hope we're amusin' you.'

'I meant that seriously.' The pipe-stem described another circle. 'Do you mean to say that we – the collection of intelligence assembled here – can't solve a problem set by Rita Wainright and Barry Sullivan? With all due respect to them, they weren't exactly intellectual giants.'

Superintendent Craft was brooding in a corner, with folded arms; I might have guessed what was going on in his mind; but he roused himself to ask a question here.

'Were you well acquainted with those two, Mr Ferrars?'

'I knew Rita pretty well, yes.' Ferrars' eyelids raised towards the picture. He put the pipe into his mouth, and puffed reflectively. 'Sullivan I hardly knew at all. I'd met him once or twice. He struck me as being a good-looking, well-meaning moron. Why a girl like Molly Grange should see anything in him . . . !'

Ferrars' face seemed to assume sharper lines and angles,

ending in an expression of cynicism as he bit at the stem of the pipe.

'But he did have one talent,' the painter went on, 'which people like that often have. He was damned good at puzzles.'

'That's it!' I exclaimed.

They all turned to look at me.

'That's what?' H.M. inquired suspiciously.

'I've been trying to think when and where I'd heard mention of puzzles in connection with those two. It was from Alec himself. When he invited me out here for the famous Saturday night, he said that both Rita and Sullivan were fond of puzzles; and that we might have some puzzles.'

'Professor Wainright,' grinned Ferrars, 'seems to have been prophetic. And he kept his word like a gentleman.'

'*He's* a wallopin' hand at puzzles, I expect?' demanded H.M.

'He was very good, yes, before he started to go to pieces. But it was that mathematical stuff which bores me green. You know the kind of thing. A crafty nuisance named George comes in and says, "I have a certain number of hens in my fowl-house. If I have twice the number of hens that I had yesterday, and three and one half times as many hens as my Aunt Matilda had on Tuesday, how many hens have I got today?" You want to reply, "For God's sake, George, don't make life so complicated. You know how many hens you've got, don't you?"'

Again Ferrars blew up smoke, drowsily.

'But this isn't mathematical. This calls for some real imagination. What the not-very-clever Sullivan devised, we ought to be able to solve by the simple process of examining the tracks.'

'Simple,' groaned H.M. 'Oh, my eye! The brashness of youth! Simple!'

'I stick by my guns. Our Mr Sullivan' – Ferrars' nose wrinkled – 'is not going to beat me. I propose to settle his hash. If the maestro admits he's in trouble' – he nodded towards H.M. – 'I'll have a shot at it myself. What do you think, Superintendent?'

Craft was still brooding. His face smoothed itself out as he looked up. But his arms remained folded, and it was as though he were bracing himself.

'Well, gentlemen,' he said, 'I can tell you short and sweet what I think. I'm still not convinced that any murders were committed at all.'

15

There was a minor explosion then. Though both H.M. and I protested, Craft remained unimpressed. He lifted his hand for silence.

'Just what are the facts now?' he asked. 'Sir Henry's proved, I admit, that those two *intended* to do a bunk for America.'

'Thank'ee, son. I'm real obliged.'

'But he's trying to turn the whole case wrong-side out. Now he says those two weren't shot on the edge of the cliff at all. Where were they shot, then?'

'How should I know?' howled H.M. 'Maybe in that private brothel out in the studio. Maybe in one of the caves along this coast. This feller here,' he nodded towards Ferrars, 'has been goin' on about caves.'

'Do you call that evidence, sir?'

'Maybe not. But . . .'

'It's evidence I've got to have,' the superintendent pointed out, not unreasonably. 'And, so far as I'm concerned, the actual evidence in this case hasn't changed since yesterday.'

'You mean that they still killed themselves? Oh, my son.'

'Well, has it changed? Suppose they did intend to run away!'

'You don't doubt that, do you?'

'Wait. I was thinking of a question I asked you yesterday. I said, "Who would murder them when they meant to kill themselves?" And you said it didn't matter: that they might have intended suicide, but didn't have the nerve.'

'Well?'

'Take it,' suggested Craft, 'the other way round. They decide to bolt with the old gentleman's diamonds. They make all their plans. But at the last moment Mrs Wainright – who's clearly the moving spirit in this – can't face it. Dr Croxley tells us, and you admit, how fond she was of Mr Wainright. I may not know much about women, but that "I'd rather be dead!" rings pretty true to me.'

'Uh-huh. So?'

Craft tightened his folded arms.

'She changes her mind. She gets Sullivan out to the edge of the cliff. She shoots him, and then herself. Later Dr Croxley, who can't bear to think of her in connection with a double suicide, removes the gun from the edge of the chff and takes it away. Just as we decided yesterday.'

We were back to it again.

It seemed useless for me to break out once more into protests. But this time, I thought, H.M. was on my side.

'There's one little detail,' he rumbled apologetically, 'that I hate to trouble you with. It's only my innate cussedness makes me bring it up. Somebody took Sullivan's car out to Exmoor on Sunday night, and ditched it in some very gooey quicksand. Hadn't you forgotten that?'

Craft's slight smile did not extend to his dead eye.

'No, sir. I hadn't forgotten it. But there's one person here who admitted to us yesterday he's familiar with every corner of Exmoor, and would know exactly where to dispose of that car: which most of us wouldn't. Excuse me, Doctor, but what *were* you doing on Sunday night?'

If this can be credited, it took me several seconds to realise what the man meant. Perhaps I am dull, but the thing was so preposterous that it simply didn't penetrate. It was only when all their eyes turned towards me, and Ferrars burst out laughing, that I did realise. Ferrars had no doubt been posted by H.M. about every detail.

'You know, Dr Luke,' remarked Ferrars, going over to knock out his pipe against the top of the fireplace, '*I* could believe that. It's exactly the sort of damn-fool chivalrous thing you *would* do.'

I must have made a queer spectacle of myself, for H.M. spoke hastily.

'Easy, Doctor! Remember your heart!'

'It's a fact, though,' declared Ferrars. 'I can see him going out in the middle of the night to do just that. Protect a lady's good name. Destroy the evidence that she was intending to run away with Sullivan.'

I am afraid I raved for some time. Then I said: 'Whatever I say, you don't seem to believe it. But do you think anybody with a sense of decency – with a sense of anything – would have left Mrs Sullivan screaming in that car while it went down in quicksand?'

'Was the young lady hurt?' asked Craft. 'I don't seem to remember it.'

'Nor I,' agreed Ferrars. I guessed he was only doing this for devilment, but he was doing it. The smile curved again under his long nose. 'I should say Belle was treated rather tenderly. I couldn't have done a better job myself.'

'She was brought back somehow,' Craft went on, 'though a murderer, you'd think, would have left her lying in the mist on the moor. Not caring particularly whether she caught her death of cold or not. When she woke up, she found she was in that room above the studio. What do you say, Sir Henry?'

H.M. did not appear to be listening. He was bending forward in the chair, elbow on knee and chin on fist. If it had not been for his spectacles, he would have suggested less the Emperor Nero than the late Marcus Tullius Cicero meditating a blast in the Senate.

'Found she was back in the studio,' he muttered vacantly. The corners of his mouth turned down. 'Found she was back in the . . . oh, my eye!' Then he woke up. He made fussed gestures and pulled up the spectacles on his nose. 'Excuse me, son. The old man was wool-gatherin' a bit. What new dirty work has the doctor been up to now?'

'I'm not saying anything. I'm not even intimating anything,' lied Craft. 'I'm just asking him where he was on Sunday night.'

'Confound you, sir, I was at home!'

'I see. What time did you go to bed, Doctor?'

"Very early. Before nine o'clock. They said I'd been exerting myself too much the night before.'

'Did you see anybody after that time?'

'Well . . . no. I wasn't supposed to be disturbed.'

'So you couldn't prove you were at home, if you had to?'

I clutched at my collar.

'Now I'll tell you what it is,' Craft spoke very seriously, unfolding his arms and pointing a pencil at me. 'I've tried to be reasonable about this; but you won't give me any choice. Somebody removed that gun from the place where they'd shot themselves, and somebody got rid of that car. All to protect Mrs Wainright. I warn you, Doctor, you're going to be in a lot of trouble at the inquest tomorrow morning. And I'm going to cause it.'

He turned to H.M.

'Don't you see, sir, that all I want is evidence? Just show me some evidence that those two didn't kill themselves! You say they devised some new way of floating in the air or walking without footprints . . .'

'I still say it.'

'Then how did they do it?'

H.M. drew a deep breath. 'Y'know,' he volunteered off-handedly, 'I've always had a name for this.'

'For what, sir?'

'For this kind of situation. I call it the blinkin' awful cussedness of things in general. And for getting us into this mess' – H.M. blinked sourly at me – 'you can thank your persuasive solicitor friend, Mr Stephen Grange. Of all the rare ones I ever heard for poisonin' coppers' minds, he's it.'

'If you ask me, Sir Henry, I'd say he was the only one who has talked sense,' Craft objected. 'And he's got a lot of influence with the coroner.'

'I'll bet he has. At the ringing of the curfew, Dr Croxley is goin' to find himself in the cooler or I'm a Dutchman. That's why I've got to do some sittin' and thinkin'.' Inflating his chest deeply, H.M. glared round at us like a noble Roman wrestler about to enter the arena. 'There's nothing else for it. I've *got* to find some way of working that levitation trick!'

'With my able assistance,' said Ferrars. 'And I'm going to make a suggestion. In fact, I think I can solve it for you now.'

'You?' said H.M., with a sneer so vast that his young friend might have been a worm made articulate.

'Don't be so snooty, governor. You're not the only person in this world who enjoys funny business.'

'No. But I wasn't thinkin' of your particular type of funny business. With Belle Renfrew Sullivan, or . . .'

To my surprise, colour came into Ferrars' face. Though he tried to lounge back in the chair, tapping the stem of his empty pipe against his teeth, there was a curious rigidity about his muscles.

'My dear Commodus,' he said, 'there never was anything between Belle and me. I must have had too many drinks late last night, and exchanged confidences over the fire. And look here, I'd rather you didn't say anything about that to Molly Grange.'

'So?'

'Just a whim of mine.'

'I can't quite make you out,' said H.M. 'Sometimes you talk like the world-weariest rip that was ever bored with life. Other times you talk like a brat just down from Eton for the holidays.'

'So far as I remember, governor, I was trying to solve your puzzle.' Ferrars remained urbane. 'You say our eloping friends couldn't have climbed down the face of that cliff?'

'That's right.'

'No, but suppose they came down by parachute?'

H.M. regarded him austerely.

'Don't gibber, son. I hate gibberin'. Besides' – he rubbed his nose – 'I already thought of that.'

'Is it gibbering?' Ferrars asked softly. 'Is it? We've seen some amazing things done with parachutes recently. I'm not sure whether you can make one of 'em open enough to hold you in a relatively short drop like seventy feet; but why is it impossible?'

'Because I say so!' bellowed H.M., tapping himself on the chest. 'It might remotely be possible for a trained paratroop, with a special 'chute and a whole lot of experience at landing on a reasonably smooth surface. What chance would there be for those two, without experience and without 'chutes as far as we know, jumpin' down on to rocks in the dark of a windy night? No, son. It won't do.'

'Then how in blazes *was* it done?'

'That's what we're goin' to find out. Come on.'

'Not in those clothes you don't!'

'What's wrong with these clothes? Hey? You wanted to paint me in 'em, though I got a deep suspicion it was your idea of bein' funny. And if it was . . .'

'They're all right in my studio. But I don't want you to go parading round the country in 'em. Hang it all, what would old man Grange say if he heard I had a guest who ran around dressed up as an ancient Roman?'

'So that's it. Hey?'

Ferrars merely pointed to the clothes.

It was twenty minutes later when we stood, in the pallor of the late afternoon light, staring at the last footprints made on earth by Rita Wainright and Barry Sullivan.

They were framed in the path outlined by the tiny white-painted pebbles. Their very simplicity made them so maddening. Superintendent Craft stood at one side, stroking his chin with the indulgent air of a man who has a winning hand. Ferrars, frankly beaten, sat on the back steps. H.M. – now much less offensive to the eye in ordinary attire except for one carpet slipper – bent as far over as his corporation would permit to peer at the tracks.

'Yes, sir?' promoted Craft, with a high and lofty air of amusement.

H.M. lifted his head.

'There are times,' he said, 'when you remind me so much of Masters that my gorge rises. Oh, lord love a duck! These are perfectly honest footprints. There's no flummery about 'em.'

'That's what I kept telling you, you know.'

H.M. put his fists on his hips.

'You noticed,' he suggested, 'that the toes are indented? As though they'd been running?'

Craft's tone was dry. 'Yes. We noticed it. They *were* running, as you can tell by the length of the stride. But not running very fast. Just hurrying, as you might say.'

H.M. shook his head dismally from side to side.

'I say, son, do you mind if I walk on top of 'em? I notice they're the only part of this stretch that hasn't been messed up.'

'Go ahead and walk all you like. As I told you, we've got plaster casts at the police station.'

H.M. started down the path. Even with no rain since Saturday night, his own footsteps sank heavily. Using great caution with his injured toe, he limped down towards Lovers' Leap. Here, stepping on the little semi-circle of humped, coarse grass, he deliberately peered over the edge. It was a sight which made my stomach turn over, even at that distance; a head for heights must be a fine thing, and it did not seem to bother him in the least.

'Find anything?' called Craft.

H.M. turned round, his fists on his hips, against the skyline. The breeze from behind belled out his linen coat. His eye moved first right, and then left, over the rest of the expanse – now scored with many footprints, including all our own and the track of his wheelchair. He looked long at the geometrical designs in white-painted pebbles. Then his voice came loudly down-wind.

'Oi!'

'Yes, sir?'

He pointed with a big flipper.

'This place was kept pretty neat and smooth before people started gallopin' all over it. Those pebbly bits, like Euclid having some fun at the seaside. And the pebble-edged path. Could they be used for any hocus-pocus?'

'You mean could anybody walk on them? Just try a few and see.'

With the heel of his right foot, gingerly, H.M. tested them; and they sank into the ground. That was no good either.

'But see here, son. Haven't they got any purpose?'

'Nothing will grow here,' Craft pointed out. 'They're ornamental. Also,' he grinned sepulchrally, 'you can see them in the dark.'

An expression of vast bewilderment overspread H.M.'s face. Still shaking his head, he lumbered back up the four-foot path towards us. Once again he stopped to peer at the footprints.

'It's a bit rummy,' he said, 'how those two kept step in their runnin'. Almost as though –' He paused, massaging his chin, and he did not continue.

'Now come on.' The abrupt sharpness of Craft's voice startled me. 'Let's not waste any more time. In the name of sense, Dr Croxley, why don't you *admit* you stole that gun out there, and let's all go home to tea?'

'You're making an awful mistake, son,' H.M. said quietly.

'Very well, sir.' Craft spoke from deep in his throat. 'I'm making a mistake. Let's leave it at that, until tomorrow morning at the inquest. Shall we?'

'But listen, man! This suicide pact business is all eyewash! You say they made all these elaborate plans to run away. Then, on the spur of the moment, while listenin' to *Romeo and Juliet*, they suddenly changed their minds and rushed out to glory. If they did that, where did they suddenly pick up the gun – which nobody's been able to identify since?'

Craft shook his head.

'I don't say that's what they did, Sir Henry.'

'Then what do you say?'

'As I see it, they first intended to go, just as you showed. But before then, maybe several days before, Mrs Wainright had a change of heart. She persuaded Sullivan to join her in the suicide pact. They had a last fling at listening to the *Romeo and Juliet* play, and then they did it. Remember: there's no sign that they took any clothes with them. Not a suitcase or bag or anything. And they must have had clothes ready, if they meant to bolt.'

(This, I had to admit, was true enough.)

For a moment H.M. stared straight ahead of him. Then he snapped his fingers.

'Diamonds!' he muttered. 'I was almost forgetting the diamonds!'

"What about them?'

'The diamonds they took with 'em!'

'But we don't know they did take any diamonds. That's a deduction of yours. We haven't looked in this famous ivory box, because the nurse wouldn't let us in. Consequently –'

H.M. stopped him.

'But if the diamonds are gone, or there're imitations substituted for real ones, ain't that good enough evidence those two meant to do a bunk? Rita Wainright wouldn't rush away with thousands of pounds' worth of jewellery if she meant to commit suicide.'

Craft pondered this.

'Yes, sir, that sounds reasonable enough. Unless, of course, she'd converted them into cash beforehand.'

'We'd better get up to that bedroom, Doctor,' H.M. said to me. 'That is, if it can be managed?'

'It can be managed.'

Here, at last, was hope. Nobody comprehended better than your obedient servant that I was in both an awkward and a dangerous position. Craft was in no pleasant frame of mind. He meant business. If they were going to press this charge of taking a very expensive motor car, in order to sink it in Exmoor quicksand, I failed to see what I could do about it. The mere grotesqueness of the charge made me boggle and splutter, as though I had been accused of holding up a bank or dynamiting a railway line. But it was no less serious for all that.

When we went into the house, I am ashamed to confess, there was one time when I had tears of wrath in my eyes.

I explained the situation to Mrs Grover, the day nurse, who stood aside disapprovingly as we went in. Alec was still asleep. The room was dim now, its furniture making shadowy outlines against the whitish blinds.

H.M. went over and gently took the key out of Alec's limp hand.

'Please!' said Mrs Grover.

Her voice seemed to rap out harshly, too loud a noise. Ferrars, who lurked outside the door and would not come in, merely pointed to the dressing-table. Craft went over and raised a blind, again to the disapproval of the nurse. Opening the drawer of the dressing-table, H.M. lifted out the heavy ivory box. Into its lock he fitted the key with the engraved word and the true-love knot.

When he opened the lid, we saw that the box was lined first

with steel and then with dark-blue velvet. Cases were piled inside: cases long, cases round, cases square, cases oval: all of the same dark-blue velvet, with white satin inside. I counted sixteen of them as H.M. put them out on the dressing-table. Only one of them, a bracelet-case, was empty. The only stone represented was a diamond.

'Imitations,' growled H.M., as little heaps and curves of glittering stones built up into a kind of fiery scrap-heap. He was rapidly opening one case after another, and flinging it aside. 'Imi . . .'

But he did not go on. Instead he rested his hands for a moment on the dressing-table, as though supporting his own heavy weight. He picked up one of the cases – it contained a diamond pendant, I remember – and limped over to the light of the window.

There he studied it, hitching up his spectacles firmly, and turning down the corners of his mouth. I remember the slate-blue sea behind him, the red horizon, and the shifting glitter against his hands. Each one of those articles he scrutinised with a fiendish care, taking each to the window. When he had finished, and closed his eyes as though to rest them, his face had taken on a poker-playing impassiveness; it might have been made of wood.

'Well?' I said.

'Slight miscalculation.' His tone was without inflection. 'They're not imitations. They're real diamonds.'

On the bed, Alec Wainright opened his eyes. Though it was difficult to tell, I think he smiled.

And softly, just behind us, Superintendent Craft was laughing.

16

Molly Grange and Belle Sullivan were standing at the gate when I got back to Lyncombe.

They made an attractive picture. Molly was taller than Belle, perhaps less well developed in what Tom would portentously call the mammary and gluteal regions. Belle's grey eyes were intensified by thin black pencilling, her mouth was dark red and even her brown curls seemed to shine, whereas Molly had none of these things. Yet, despite the charm of our visitor, my money is and always will be on Molly.

Instead of driving into the garage, I left my car at the front door and got out into the half-dusk. It was Molly who spoke.

'Dr Luke, where on earth have you been? You look tired to death.'

'Out at the Wainrights'. I'm all right.'

'Do you realise this is the second time you've missed your tea in two days? Tom's furious.'

'Then Tom will just have to be furious, my dear.'

'You're a prodigal parent, that's what you are,' said Belle, who was smoking a cigarette and getting lipstick all over the end of it. 'Who were with you? That big fat guy with the wheelchair?

The one who called me a liar when I said I was married?'

'Yes. And Superintendent Craft and Paul Ferrars.'

Molly's blue eyes narrowed. 'What's Sir Henry up to now, Dr Luke?'

'To tell you the truth, he was dressed up like a Roman Senator.'

Both girls stared back at me, with slowly dawning enlightenment. Then they turned to each other and spoke together.

'The Emperor Nero,' they said.

'Have you heard about him too?'

'Have we heard about him?' echoed Belle. 'Jesus H. Christ!' She took a quick puff at her cigarette before removing it to make an excited gesture with it. 'Have we heard about anything else?'

'It was Harry Pierce,' Molly explained, 'and that man Willie Johnson.'

'And I was right in the middle of it,' amplified Belle.

'Johnson! Where is he now?'

'He's in the can.'

'What can?'

'The hoosegow,' Belle said impatiently. 'They arrested him.'

'I can't say I'm exactly surprised. But –'

'Boy,' said Belle, 'you should have seen what happened! I was standing here at the gate, like this, talking to that fellow Pierce. He'd been over here about six times. It wasn't more than twenty minutes after two, not closing-time yet.

'This Pierce was just saying to me, "And I 'ope, ma'am, we'll 'ave no more of what I might term the reign of terror in these parts," when I looked up and saw a guy on a bicycle, just coming like a bat out of hell. Boy, was he travelling!

'Pierce's eyes start to pop out, and he runs out in the road and waves his arms and yells, "You keep away from my house, Willie Johnson, you keep away from my house." And I guess that must have scared the guy on the bicycle. Because he skids, and turns clean over, and goes bicycle and all straight like a bat out of hell through the doors of Pierce's saloon-bar.'

'Not *again?*'

'Yes, again,' returned Molly. 'It was the most dreadful crash you ever heard. Much worse than yesterday.'

'But that wasn't the worst of it,' Belle assured me. 'Up comes the cop, and up comes everybody. He started – I mean Johnson started – telling a story we could hear clear across the street.'

'About the Emperor Nero?'

'That's right. He said the Emperor Nero met him on the Baker's Bridge road yesterday, and gave him a ten-shilling note. Then, because he – I still mean Johnson – was a condemned sinner, he spent the money on liquor and today the Emperor Nero started chasing him in a flying throne with wings. Of course, they just figured he had the screaming mimis and they threw him in the hoosegow. But now I'm not so sure.'

Molly did not seem certain about anything.

'Father was here too,' she volunteered. 'He had to see a client at Lynmouth. I asked him whether he could do anything for the Johnson man, and he surprised me.'

'How?'

'He said he would,' Molly replied naïvely. 'Or at least that he'd try.'

'Come into the back garden, both of you,' I said. 'I want to talk to you. There's news.'

They must have seen it was serious. I could even have guessed Molly had been expecting it.

'We have news for you too,' she said.

In the garden, where the wicker chairs stood under the apple-tree, I motioned them to sit down and wondered how to start.

'*You've* been all right?'

'Oh, I'm swell.' Belle's face was expressionless. She dropped her cigarette on the ground and trod it out. From her sleek appearance, the trim green frock, the tan stockings and shoes, you would never have identified her as the hysterical girl of twenty-four hours ago.

'They tell me,' she went on, 'that I'll have to stay and identify Barry's body at the inquest tomorrow. I've probably lost my job at the Piccadilly, but what the hell? I persuaded a nice bank-manager down in Lynton to cash a cheque for me, so everything's fine.'

'They've treated you well?'

'People have been swell.' She smiled at Molly. 'The men have been sympathetic, too. They say my mind needs distraction, and they've all tried to date me up. One wants me to go to the Valley of Rocks. Another to Dartmeet, whatever that is. Another says to see the caves in the cliffs. I'd kind of like to take a boat-ride and see those caves.'

'My dear Belle,' cried Molly, 'those caves are way up the cliffs. You can't reach them by boat except at high-tide, four o'clock in the afternoon, or one o'clock in the morning. And you mustn't do it anyway! People would talk.'

'Would they? What the hell?'

'I mean it!'

'Anyway,' said Belle, 'the person who invited me was your old man, so I'd be well taken care of.'

Molly was so amazed that she must have wondered whether she had heard aright.

'*My* father?'

'Yeah, sure.' Belle smiled again; but sympathetically, and without any trace of the sardonic. 'Baby, my business is to size up men. Haven't you guessed from the way he dresses that he likes to be a natty squire of dames? Don't get me wrong, either! He's a nice guy underneath that manner. If he wants to play Sir Galahad at his age, where's the harm?'

Molly folded her arms. By the rise and fall of the arms, you could see her breathe. The blue eyes moved sideways, studying Belle briefly; then moved back to contemplate the tips of her shoes.

'What's your opinion, as a connoisseur,' she asked, 'of Mr Ferrars?'

'Paul? He's a good egg,' Belle answered promptly, 'who's so thin-skinned that everything worries him, and then he thinks he has to be nasty about it. You ought to hear him when he gets eight or ten drinks under his belt. Quotes romantic poetry and everything.'

'I'm sure he does.'

'And not so much of the "connoisseur", either.' Belle wrinkled her nose. 'I may be able to size up men, in a way, but I sure am one terrible frost when it comes to picking 'em for myself.'

I couldn't dodge it any longer.

'Mrs Sullivan. About your late husband . . .'

Belle lifted her shoulders. 'For Pete's sake, Doctor, don't talk that way. Don't call him my "late husband". It gives me goose-flesh; it sounds like something out of a family Bible. Just call him Barry.'

'But that's just the trouble, my dear. His name wasn't Barry, and it wasn't Sullivan. You'll hear it all tomorrow, when they hit you over the head with it at the inquest, so you'd better hear it from me.'

Though an afterglow of sunset remained in the sky, the garden had turned shadowy. Belle had her head turned slightly away from me, and she kept it poised, there. Her body had grown tense, as though she were about to get up and run.

'Then the old guy was right, after all,' she said.

'The old guy, as you call him, has a habit of being right. Tell me one other thing. Do you still feel as you did yesterday – about not loving your husband after all?'

'I'd better go,' observed Molly, and got to her feet.

'No you don't!' Belle cried fiercely. Turning round, she stretched out her left hand to Molly, and Molly took it. There they were, one in green, one in grey, one sitting, one standing, against the colours of the twilight garden.

'Anything I say,' Belle went on, 'and practically anything I think, can be shouted from the roof. Don't you go!'

'All right, Belle.'

'As for being in love with that cluck,' Belle said to me, 'what I told you yesterday still goes and more so. Naturally, I'm sorry he's dead. But as for being in love with him . . . I mean, so much so you want to bite the pillow and scream . . .' Belle looked at Molly. 'You're what they call a nice gal, baby. You wouldn't understand that.'

'Perhaps not,' agreed Molly. Her eyes seemed to hover over Belle in a curious way.

'You can wash that out, Doctor,' Belle said firmly. 'This little chicken isn't wearing any widow's weeds. I'm heart-whole, fancy-free, and only twenty-eight.'

I could not help drawing a breath of relief.

'Your husband's real name was Jacob McNutt. He was going to elope with Mrs Wainright. They had planned to take the liner *Washington*, which calls at Galway some time this week.'

'I knew it!' cried Belle, after a long pause while her eyes widened. She slapped her right hand down on her knee. 'Didn't I tell you he'd never have the nerve to knock himself off?' And then, presently, she said: 'Mrs Jacob McNutt. Oh, my God,' and started to laugh.

'You never saw his passport or his alien's registration certificate, evidently. If you didn't travel, there was no reason why you ever should.'

'But wait a minute!'

'Yes, Mrs Sullivan?'

Belle put up a hand to shade her eyes.

'I remember about that ship. We were talking about it. Barry said, "Darling sweetheart, I'd like to take you to America and out of this, but we simply haven't got the money." His floosie had the money, I suppose? But how did she think she was going to get aboard that ship? Being British and not married to him?'

'She got a new passport under false pretences. Some professional man recommended her from personal knowledge . . .'

'Suitcase!' Molly exclaimed softly, but with such emphasis that we both looked at her.

'What you're saying, Dr Luke,' Molly announced, 'doesn't surprise me at all. I said I had some news for you. It's all over the village. This morning one of the fishermen hauled up something heavy in his net and found it was a suitcase – a grey leather suitcase – with a woman's clothes in it. I haven't seen the things, but I think I guessed whom they belonged to.'

(Part of the missing luggage. I hoped fervently the news would reach Craft in short order; but he had the bit in his teeth and it was going to be difficult to convince him.)

'Where did they find it, Molly?'

'I haven't heard, exactly. Fully half a mile away from the Wainrights' place, though.'

'Half a mile?'

'But wait a minute!' Belle was repeating. She made elaborate gestures, like a temple dancer, and withdrew her hand from Molly's. 'I still don't see how this floosie worked. Didn't she have to have a birth certificate?'

'Yes. She just used a copy of her original Canadian birth certificate, claiming she'd never been married. But the written recommendation from the professional man had to be genuine, in case they checked up.'

'Who recommended her?'

This was the difficult part.

'Well, my dear, they're now claiming *I* did.'

Both girls stared at me.

'You see, it's a little involved. Willie Johnson isn't the only one who's likely to be confined in what you call the hoosegow. I'm the next candidate.'

'Dr Luke, you're smiling!' cried Molly. 'I don't believe a word of it!'

'This, my dear, is what the novelists call a wry smile. There's going to be a terrific rumpus at the inquest tomorrow morning, unless a miracle happens tonight; and I wanted to warn you in advance.'

'Rumpus? How?'

'Sir Henry Merrivale and I claim those two were murdered when they were on the point of running away. But we haven't a single card in our hands to play.

'Craft, on the other side, has a whole handful of trumps. He claims they changed their minds about running away, and backs it up with the undeniable fact that they *didn't* take the diamonds which were the only thing they could have used for money. He claims – on so far unbreakable evidence – that they committed suicide. Afterwards he claims I stole the gun and got rid of their car to remove what he romantically calls the stigma of suicide.'

Molly stood up straight.

'But you didn't, Dr Luke? Or did you?'

'Not you too, Molly? Of course I didn't.' And I gave them a sketch of the facts.

'Look,' said Belle, feverishly lighting another cigarette and sweeping it away from her lips in a broad gesture. 'They don't claim *you* were the man who nearly soaked me in quicksand on Sunday night?'

'Yes.'

'I never heard of such goddamned hooey in all my born days,' cried our pocket Venus. 'Why, the guy was crying his eyes out! Crying his heart out! I heard him!'

'Unfortunately, Mrs Sullivan, at my age the blood gets thin and the emotions aren't always under control. When they were accusing me today, I got so mad that the tears did come into my eyes, and . . .'

Belle's jaw grew square.

'You let *me* get into that so-and-so witness-chair,' she declared, attributing to witness-chairs a lascivious habit not common to them. 'I'll tell 'em a thing or two that'll curl their hair.'

'Yes, my dear, that's just what I'm afraid of. I want to warn you: try to control your language in front of the coroner. He's a Scotch Presbyterian, a friend of Molly's father, and you're supposed to be a stricken widow. Don't get into any more trouble than is necessary.'

Molly's face was flushed.

'But what are you going to do, Dr Luke?'

'I'm going to tell the truth. If they don't like it, Mrs Sullivan can probably suggest a course for them to adopt.'

'Dr Luke, you mustn't! They'll have you for perjury and not a doubt about it! After all, what does it matter? Hasn't this thing been horrible enough already? Why don't you say what Superintendent Craft wants you to say?' Molly whirled round. 'Don't you agree, Belle?'

'Oh, so-and-so, I've got no objection to telling lies,' Belle announced broadly. 'I'll tell lies by the bucket and like it. What burns me up is to have a good guy like Dr Croxley get up and swear he left a gal sinking in quicksand and never lifted a finger to save her.'

Molly has, as I have indicated before, inherited a good deal of her father's practical instinct.

'But don't you see?' she insisted, clenching her hands. 'He doesn't *have* to say he sank the car. I admit that would be bad, because it was an expensive car – or at least I've heard it was – and he'd have to replace it at the very least. But they can't *prove* he sank the car. Whereas they can prove this point about his being the only one who could have moved the gun. Just let him admit that; bring in a double-suicide verdict; and Craft will be satisfied.'

Belle was evidently deeply impressed by this point about the car.

'That's right,' she admitted, and puffed furiously at the cigarette while she pondered. 'Look!' she said at length. 'I've got an idea.'

'Well?'

'Suppose I said I *saw* the guy who sank the car, and it wasn't Dr Croxley?'

Molly considered this.

'Who would you say it was?'

'Well, suppose I said it was a little guy in a derby hat. Or with whiskers, or something like that. Nothing definite, but enough to prove it wasn't him. I'm the stricken widow. They'd sure as hell believe me.'

'It might do.' Molly nodded thoughtfully. 'It might do.'

Though it is dangerous to make generalities, this was far from being the first time in my life when I have observed the absolute incapacity of any woman for telling the truth when truth becomes unsuitable. There is no intent to do wrong in this. To the female sex, it simply does not matter. Truth is relative; truth is fluid; truth is something to be measured according to the emotional needs, like Adolf Hitler's.

'I appreciate your intentions, both of you. But it won't work. Don't you understand?'

'No,' said Belle.

'Rita Wainright was murdered. Deliberately and swinishly murdered. I'm going to find and punish the person who did it if I have to spend the rest of my life in the . . . in the . . .'

'Hoosegow?'

'Hoosegow or can. Yes. Don't you feel like that about your husband?'

This took her a little aback.

'Sure, I want to have the guy caught. Don't misunderstand! But my husband happens to have been a cheap, chiselling – !' Belle caught herself up; tears of rage were coming in her eyes. 'They weren't either of them any prize packages, if it comes to that. It makes me sore to see you stand up for this floosie, that's all.'

'And I still think, Dr Luke, you're not being very sensible,' insisted Molly, with that soft, enveloping smile of hers. 'It's not as though we were asking you to do anything dishonest. Why don't you talk it over with my father? He's coming down the path now.'

I felt so sick and beaten that I didn't even turn to look.

Steve Grange, as immaculate as ever in a blue double-breasted suit which was fashionable without being too noticeable, joined us under the apple-tree. He touched his hat with grave gallantry to .Belle, who instantly – and rather revoltingly – became almost coy. He addressed Molly in a friendly voice.

'My dear, I'm afraid you'll catch your death of cold sitting out here when it's nearly dark. Besides, your mother will want you. Hadn't you better run along?'

'But you've got to speak to Dr Luke!'

'Speak to Dr Luke? Why?'

'He wants to go to the inquest to tell them Rita Wainright was murdered. And they won't believe him. What difference does it make if it *is* true?'

Steve looked at me.

'We must always tell the truth, Molly,' he informed her, seriously, but rather absently. 'Truth is the only sound, sane, conservative policy. Haven't I always told you that?'

'Well . . .'

'Haven't I?'

'Yes, you've always said you said so.'

Steve regarded her sharply, but did not pursue the matter. Smoothing at his thin line of moustache, he addressed me with a sort of dry and ordered jocularity.

'But we've always got to be sure we know what truth is, and not what we think it is. What's on your mind, Dr Luke?'

'Steve,' I said, and I remember clasping my hands, and turning them over, and looking at the knuckles that are of a clumsier size than they ought to be, 'if I get into trouble with the authorities tomorrow – as seems likely – it's just as well to accumulate all the information I can now.'

His eyes were quizzical.

'What's all this nonsense about getting into trouble with the authorities?'

'It's a long story. Molly will explain. In the meantime as I say, I want to tap any possible source of information I can about Rita Wainright. Will you tell me something I very much want to know?'

'Certainly, if I'm not violating any confidence.'

Molly had sat down again; and Steve, in disobedience of his own rule about damp air, perched on the arm of her chair. He sat very gingerly, very stiff-backed, and was all attention. I continued to look at my hands, at those infernal big knuckles and heavy fingers, while I searched round desperately for some key that would unlock this door before morning.

'Well,' I said, and humped my shoulders and tried to stir my brain, 'will you tell me what was the cause of your original quarrel with Rita? I mean, the time she asked you to do something unethical?'

17

Steve laughed. It was a homely and pleasant sound against the quiet.

'Luke, old man! You don't think that's got anything to do with this business?'

'No. But – for instance, did she ask you to write her a recommendation for a passport?'

Steve looked astounded, as well he might.

'No, certainly not. Besides, what's unethical about that?'

'In her maiden name, I mean. As Miss Margarita Dulane.'

It was Molly who interposed here.

'But that won't work either, Dr Luke,' she protested. 'Don't you remember? She and Father had that row before ever she *met* Barry Sullivan. I remember particularly, because it was the day war was declared. Barry and I met you and the Wainrights outside here . . ."

Then memory returned.

'And I hesitated about introducing Barry to them, because I knew there'd been a quarrel of some kind. Rita couldn't have been wanting a false passport as long ago as that.'

I am a mutton-head. Of course it was true, and I have noted

it in this record; but I caught at blowing straws wherever they were. Steve was much amused when I explained to him, though less amused at the conclusion of the whole story. He kept smoothing at his moustache, and smoothing at his withered cheek while the garden grew darker and darker.

'I absolutely refuse,' he said, enunciating the words carefully through stiff jaws, 'to have an old friend of mine give any such testimony as you intend. Remember: I warned you about that yesterday.'

'Confound it, Steve, isn't there anybody who wants poor Rita to get her due?'

Steve tapped one finger into the palm of his left hand.

'If this whole account is true, and I say *if*, I consider the woman has had her due. (Mark that, Molly.) She was deliberately deserting her husband. She was overturning the foundations of home and family life. She deserved whatever punishment Providence accorded her.'

'Steve, we're both old enough to stop talking nonsense, even for the benefit of the children. You can't change human nature with sermons, or the clergy would have cleaned everything up ten centuries ago.'

'The fact remains,' he retorted, 'that she shirked responsibilities and broke up a useful family. Even Johnson admits –'

'What *about* Johnson, by the way?' interposed Molly.

Though Steve appeared ruffled and annoyed at being interrupted, he did not crush her.

'Johnson's getting sober, and he's heavily repentant. He says he forgives everybody for everything.' Steve snorted, forgiving Johnson nothing. 'He says he even forgives Professor Wainright in the case of a garden-roller he claims Professor Wainright stole from him. He'll go before the beak in the morning, and get fined ten shillings. There's nothing I can do for him.'

'Never mind Johnson. Can you honestly say now you believe this was still a suicide pact?'

Steve spoke blandly.

'The important thing, my boy, is what can be proved. And they can *prove* it was a suicide. Legally –'

'Damn the legal aspect!'

'Oh, no. Never say that. That's foolish. The point is this: those two didn't take the diamonds. Therefore they didn't mean to run away.'

'What about the suitcase found by the fishermen? The suitcase containing women's clothes?'

'Were they Rita's? That's the point,' returned Steve, 'and the only point. If they can't be proved to be Rita's, they might be anybody's. And I'll tell you something else.' He tried to examine his fingernails in the gloom. '*If* Rita had meant to run away to a new life, she would have taken good care not to have any of her effects marked "R.W.", or marked in any way. They'd all be new clothes, too, unidentifiable by anybody. So I can almost assume they will never be proved to be hers in any case.'

I put my head in my hands.

'I keep saying "Rita",' Steve added. 'Of course I mean "Mrs Wainright".'

'But you don't feel like telling why it was you two quarrelled?'

Steve hesitated.

'We-ell. In confidence, no. Perhaps I don't mind. As a matter of fact, she asked me to sell some diamonds for her. I refused, and we had words.'

'Why did you refuse?'

Steve's voice came querulously out of the gloom.

'Reason one, I am not a broker. Reason two, diamonds so bestowed are considered in legal ethics as the joint property of husband and wife, like a joint bank-account. I said I might undertake the negotiation if I had Professor Wainright's instructions as well as hers. She flew into a temper, I regret to say. She forbade me ever even to mention the matter to him. One thing led to another, and . . .'

Steve lifted his well-tailored shoulders.

'But that was before she met Sullivan?'

'Long before. I imagine Mr Wainright must have been keeping her a little short on her personal-allowance money.' As though finishing and underlining the whole thing, Steve slapped his knees, got up, and turned to Molly. 'We'd better be getting along, young lady. I only want to warn you, Luke: no indiscreet words in the coroner's court tomorrow.'

So we went up the path between the tall blue delphiniums, with the rocks on either side painted white so that you might see them in the blackout. Belle and I went towards the back door, and Belle suddenly ran ahead of me. Though Molly and Steve started for the front, Molly returned alone to have a last word.

It was not yet blackout time, and a bright light shone out from the uncurtained scullery windows. Inside Mrs Harping was dishing up dinner. In the light from the windows, I could see Molly clearly; it brought out the colour of her blue eyes, as shining as Belle's own, and the fine teeth behind her half-open lips.

'Dr Luke, you were talking about human nature.'

'Yes?'

'If human nature told you to do something, and yet all your training and traditions were against it, would you do it?'

'Is it anything that would be on your conscience afterwards?'

'No!'

'Then I should say do it.'

'Thanks. I believe I will,' said Molly. Then she ran.

Dinner that night was pretty gruelling. I didn't say anything to Tom about my plans for the next day, because he would have had a fit; and, as it was, I got a lecture for missing tea. I also cautioned Belle against saying anything.

I don't know whether I have conveyed that I am very proud of that boy, since you can't say such things and it seems poor taste even to write them. But he had now been doing ten men's work instead of five, and looked it, and I lectured him in return.

Tom, however, was full of an interesting if non-lethal case of carbolic-acid poisoning at Elm Hill. I was left to my own thoughts while he gave a minute description of it to Belle, firmly under the impression that the subject enthralled her.

'The first thing to do,' I remember him saying, as he helped himself to steak-and-kidney pie, 'is to wash out the stomach with lukewarm water.'

'Oh, Tom!'

'Yes. In that you want to dissolve a little magnesium sulphate – or you can use saccharated lime if you prefer –'

'Speaking personally, big boy,' said Belle, 'I always use saccharated lime myself. But don't let it influence you, please.'

'So that the phenols combine and form a harmless ether-sulphate, to . . . look here, you little swine, I don't believe you know a damn thing about it.'

'What a sense of humour we've got! You take that salt-cellar and cram it down your throat.'

(But Belle was watching me nevertheless.)

How to prove that Rita and Sullivan had been murdered? How in Satan's name to prove it before ten o'clock the next morning?

'See here, governor, you're not eating anything!'

'I'm not hungry, Tom.'

'But you've got to eat! You couldn't stow away less these days if you were on a diet or in jail.'

'Let him alone, Tom!'

How to prove that? How? How? How?

'And I think, if you don't mind, I'll not stay for the sweet either. Excuse me.'

I got up and left the table. I had a glimpse of them as the dining-room door closed: Tom large and freckled and hollow-eyed, and Belle with her shining curls and fresh-red finger-nails, under the mosaic-glass dome of lights which has hung over that table for thirty years.

Mrs Harping came out of the kitchen to expostulate, and

I think I spoke to her irritably. I went into the sitting-room. Presently I turned on the news, heard a depressing bulletin, and switched off. This brought my thoughts to Alec, lying out at 'Mon Repos'.

After that I switched out the light in the hall, opened the front door, and took a look outside. There was a bright moon over the pitch-black village, making the windows gleam. From across the road, faint noises of jollification issued from the Coach and Horses. Someone was walking along the road, with the hollow clop-clop which footfalls make at night, and whistling 'Over The Rainbow'. We were all whistling 'Over The Rainbow' in that summer, perhaps the most tragic summer in our history.

I noticed I had left my car in the street, but I could not be bothered to put it away now. I didn't want company and couldn't stand company. I went up to my bedroom, shut the door, and turned on the light.

There were the familiar things, the old Morris chair and the picture of Laura, Tom's mother, over the bed. Tom and Belle now had the radio on downstairs; and, curse the B.B.C., they were playing 'If You Were The Only Girl In The World'.

There were the shelves of familiar books, but I did not touch them tonight. I undressed, and put on nightshirt, slippers, and dressing-gown.

'Luke Croxley,' said a voice inside my head, 'this situation is nonsense. It's so intolerable that it's got to be dealt with.'

'Oh? And how am I going to deal with it?'

'You are going to work out,' said that voice, 'from the evidence in front of you, how those two managed to disappear like soap-bubbles on the edge of the cliff, and how they were murdered.'

'Is it likely I can do that, when Sir Henry Merrivale himself so far admits he can't?'

'It doesn't matter whether you can do it,' said the voice. 'But it's got to be done. Now begin with the admitted facts . . .'

I sat down in the Morris chair, filled my solitary permitted pipe of the day, and smoked it. When that was finished, I deliberately filled and lit another one. This gave me a sense of guilt, but also an exhilarating sense of freedom or 'going the whole hog'.

Tom went clumping up to bed at a little past eleven. I was uneasy in case he should notice the amount of smoke in the room, but he only said good night through the door, and went on. A few minutes later Belle tapped at the door, and came in carrying a smoking cup in a saucer.

'Look, Doc.' She held up the cup and saucer. 'I've made you some hot Ovaltine. Will you promise to drink it before you turn in?'

'Yes, if you insist.'

'Yes,' persisted Belle, 'but will you promise to drink it before it gets cold? You say you will, but will you?'

'I promise.'

She came over to put down the cup on the little table beside my chair.

'Look, Doc.' The small dark-red mouth twisted. 'I was all full of fight and ginger this afternoon, but it's no good. The cards are stacked against you. Why not give it up? Say what they want you to say tomorrow.'

'Go to bed, please.'

'Honest, if you had any chance against that set-up –'

'Go to *bed*, please!'

'All right, old-timer. By the way, about our friend Molly Grange.'

'What about her?'

'I guess you must have noticed she's wild, blind crazy about Paul Ferrars?'

'I more than half noticed it, yes. Go to bed.'

Belle eyed me curiously. 'Well, I hope she has better luck with her boyfriends than I've had with mine. G'night.'

I waved her out; she went as though she still had something to say. She was the one who needed consolation, no doubt, and yet I was too infernally selfish to do more than grunt. I regretted this when she had gone, but nothing could be done about it by that time.

And, as you will imagine, I let the Ovaltine get cold. I lit still another pipe, and let the evidence unreel as though on a moving screen, while the clock went on chiming against deepening quiet.

Beginning with the bungalow, and a glimmering path leading to Lovers' Leap, I let my mind wander out across roads and valleys and cliffs and waters and caves of this countryside, to Exmoor and the Baker's Bridge road: bringing back a residue of facts and persons to the bungalow again. I thought of the tantalising footprints, closing my eyes to see them first on a rainy night and then on a brilliant afternoon. I thought of Alec and Rita and Sullivan and Ferrars and Molly and Steve and Johnson and Belle . . .

Even if you explained so many of the events that happened at 'Mon Repos' on Saturday night, others had not even been touched in H.M.'s reconstruction that afternoon. There were facts which remained not only puzzling, but meaningless.

The cut telephone-wires and the petrol let out of the cars, for instance. Why had the murderer done that?

It must be a part of the design, unless it had in fact been done by Johnson. H.M. himself had remarked on it forcibly yesterday. Nothing was proved. Nothing was gained. It could not possibly have prevented discovery of the crime. A dangerous risk would be run by any outsider, for instance, who crept in to cut the wires and stick them back into the box again. Severing communication with the outside world would only have prevented the arrival of the police until –

Out in the hall, the clock struck half past twelve.

I had to put down my pipe carefully in the glass ash-tray, since now my hand was shaking.

I saw the explanation of the whole thing.

18

And, once you grasped the essential clue, it was frightening in its simplicity.

I stood up in the smoke-filled room. I could feel my heart beating, but that's not a cardiac sign: when you feel your heart heavily, it's nearly always your stomach.

I knew where to look now. Unless the murderer had been phenomenally careful, it might be possible to prove my case tonight. But was it sensible, or even possible, to go tonight?

If any of the household caught me sneaking out, I should be due for a lecture from Tom that would last a fortnight. But why not? The biggest difficulty in getting away from any house unheard is in starting up a car. But my car wasn't in the garage; it was standing at the front gate. I could coast down the High Street, which has a slope, then turn round and come back again.

As I got dressed again very hurriedly, there moved in front of me an image of Paul Ferrars' face, and a recollection of Ferrars saying he could see Dr Luke going out in the middle of the night to do some fool thing. Evidently, they knew my character better than I knew it myself. But this had to be done.

I had finished dressing, all except my shoes, and put an

electric torch in my pocket, when I noticed the cup of Ovaltine standing neglected on the table. It was stone cold, but a promise is a promise. I swallowed most of it at a gulp, switched out the light, and opened the door.

The great thing was to get downstairs without being heard. Yet I knew every creaky board in the house; I learned them years ago, when I tried to get in from night calls without waking Laura. A clock ticked asthmatically in the dark hall. Carrying my shoes, I tiptoed downstairs and only once made a board squeak. I was at the front door when something else occurred to me.

A witness.

I must have a witness for what I hoped to find, else they might not believe me even when I found it. So I tiptoed back to the surgery and softly opened the door. It wasn't necessary to turn on any light. Surgery, nine paces long. Against the opposite wall, the bookcase with calf-leather volumes and the skull on top of it. In line with that, take four paces forward – find the desk – then the chair – sit down – reach the telephone.

And ring Ferrars' number at Ridd Farm.

A sleepy exchange rang that number for a long time. I could hear the two little ghostly buzzes, pealing insistently in the dark, far away out there on Exmoor. Then it was answered.

'Uh-huh? What in blazes do you want, wakin' people up at this time of the night?'

'Is that you, Sir Henry?'

There was a long pause.

'I'm sorry to bother you, but this is so important there wasn't any choice. I've got it.'

The voice sharpened. 'Got what?'

'The solution. I know how it was done.'

Again a pause.

'Well . . . now,' said the voice. 'I wondered if you would.'

'You mean you've got it too?' (He seemed oddly evasive.) 'Then listen. Could you possibly meet me at the corner of the main road and the Baker's Bridge road?'

'Now?'

'Yes, now. Tomorrow may be too late. I know it's an imposition to ask you, but we may be able to prove a case. Sir Henry, I know exactly *where* those murders were committed.'

There was another curious thing. It was so dark that I could not even see the telephone. This darkness, unaccountably, appeared to have a cotton-wool quality which padded round my head and even partly obscured the tiny voice at the other end of the line.

'Son, I can't!' muttered the voice, coming from far away. 'I've been walkin' on this toe of mine all day.'

'Get Farrars to drive you.'

'Ferrars isn't here.'

'Not there? At half past twelve? Where is he?'

'I dunno. But he's out, and he's got the car with him.'

'Then come in your wheelchair! Come somehow! Come any-how!' I was whispering to the phone with fierce urgency, yet my voice sounded distant to my own ears. The cotton-wool padding thickened round; there was a faint prickling at my scalp, extending to the ear-drums. 'I shouldn't have asked it except that it means preventing a miscarriage of justice! Will you come?'

'I'm a loony, I am. All right. Main road and Baker's Bridge road. When?'

'As soon as you can make it!'

When I put back the telephone receiver and started to get up, two things happened.

A vertical line of dim light appeared on the wall facing me. The door behind my back was slowly opening, and someone had switched on one bulb in the passage. The dim yellow light broadened and fanned out as the door opened. Someone's shadow appeared on the opposite wall, where stood the bookcase with the skull on top of it. To me there came a fancy – I could always say a dazed fancy – that the head of the shadow rested exactly on the face of the skull opposite, and blotted it out.

Belle Sullivan's voice whispered: 'What's the idea, Doc? What are you doing?'

Then, as I got to my feet, a wave of dizziness flowed up into my head and made it spin. It was only momentary; but for a second I felt I was rocking back on my heels and about to fall.

'Be quiet!' I remember whispering.

I got hold of the back of the desk-chair, which creaked slightly, and the dizziness passed. It left only a cotton-wool feeling in the head and a dry taste in the mouth.

'What's the idea, Doc? Why are you dressed?'

She was wearing a pair of Tom's blue-and-white striped pyjamas, which overflowed her small body even though they were turned up many inches at the wrists and trouser-edges. She was also wearing a pair of my slippers. I remember her silhouetted figure, and the dim light touching the worn brown linoleum on the floor.

'I'm going out,' I whispered back. 'I've got to.'

'Why?'

'Never mind why. And please don't talk out loud.'

'Doc, you can't go out!' The whispering voice was almost crying. 'I mean – did you drink that Ovaltine?'

'Yes.'

'It had dope in it,' said Belle.

Such is the power of suggestion, the effect of mere words, that the bright brown silhouetted curls seemed to swim round.

'Tom gave it to me, but I thought you needed it more than I did. So I put it in that Ovaltine to give you a good night's rest. You ought to be sleeping like a baby this minute.'

I took my own pulse, and there could be no doubt it was slowing down.

'What was it,' I said, 'and how much?'

'I don't know! It was a little red capsule.'

'One capsule?'

'Yes.'

Seconal, probably. I held tightly to the back of the desk-chair, and then straightened up.

It is possible, within limits, for the power of the human will to fight a sleeping-drug. We find this in cases of hysterical patients who have a phobia that they can't sleep. And, since I had taken the drug only a few minutes ago, its full effect would not lay hold and drag down the wits, as into a whirlpool, for many minutes longer. But it sickened me just the same, a physical nausea to have victory perhaps snatched away now.

'I'm going out just the same.'

'Doc, I won't let you!'

My face must have scared her, for she drew back. I patted her shoulder reassuringly as I passed her, feeling a little light and shaky at the knees, but reasonably clear in the head. At the front door I put on my shoes, having a bad wave of dizziness when I lowered my head, and slipped out.

The night air was cold and pleasant. I got into the car, let it coast downhill in the opposite direction until I was some distance from the house, and then started the motor. I backed around, started up again, and – once clear of the dark houses lining the High Street – I travelled that night at a pace I never want to travel again.

What was more, I knew the murderer. It sickened me to think how easily we had been fooled by someone we all knew and liked; but there it was.

The moon was round, bright, and clear white: what they later came to call the bombers' moon. It was while I was bucketing round a curve past Shire Oak that the 'unreal' feeling started to creep over me: a sense of flying through time and space, of being alone with the moon and the hedgerows. I flashed past a car which seemed vaguely familiar, doing about seventy miles an hour. Alone here with . . .

Look out!

A tree sprang up at me. I felt the thudding lurch of the car, the screech and squeal of brakes, coming from far away. Then I was back on the road again, and flying once more.

Darkness on its way.

Unconsciousness coming.

Steady.

Ahead was the entrance to the Baker's Bridge road, turning off to the right. I pulled up the car and stopped.

H.M. wasn't here. He could hardly have got here in this time, but I didn't think of that. I climbed out, buoyed and upheld by some mysterious force which made me seem to float along, very pleasant except for a tingling in scalp and finger-tips.

Also, I was talking to myself like a drunken man. Every idea that came into my head had to bubble out at the lips. H.M. wasn't here. I couldn't wait. I couldn't wait.

'Doesn't matter,' I remember saying aloud. It seemed fiercely important to impress some invisible auditor with this. 'Doesn't matter at all! He'll follow me.'

It never occurred to me that he couldn't possibly follow. When I said, 'Meet me at the corner of the main road and the Baker's Bridge road,' he must have thought I meant to go to the old studio where so much of terror and anguish had already taken place.

But I wasn't going there at all.

Instead of turning right, I turned left and crossed the road in the direction of the sea. Between the main road, and the cliffs running parallel with it, lies a vast waste of open ground. It is hilly and hummocky, with sparse scrub trees bent to a permanent slant by the force of the wind. As I staggered over the hummocks, I remember praying aloud – like a wandering seventeenth-century parson – that my wits shouldn't be pulled away, down a dark and whirling drain, before I could reach the tunnel leading down into the Pirates' Den.

The caves along our coast were never, contrary to popular belief, smugglers' caves. For that you must go to South Devon or Cornwall. In the eighteenth and nineteenth centuries, it would have been awkward for a smuggler from France to reach North Devon. The caves are natural phenomena honeycombing the cliffs. They have been given picturesque names: Dark-Lantern Hole, Inferno, Caves of the Winds, Pirates' Den.

And the cave called the Pirates' Den was the one I wanted.

Its entrance, on the land side, was a tunnel sloping down gently some forty feet underground. Its other entrance, in the outer face of the cliff, was some thirty feet or more above the rocks below. And it was fully half a mile away from the Wainrights' house along the line of the cliffs.

I took one bleared look back over my shoulder, across the moonlit waste where nothing moved. There was my car in the distance. There was the main road and the Baker's Bridge road. Then I started to descend.

At first it was a nightmare. You have to crawl into what seems the side of a hill, twist round, and go down three wooden steps that the authorities have put there for sightseers. I had my electric torch, but its light seemed dim.

The entrance here is about a hundred yards from the edge of the cliff. At the foot of the wooden steps you can walk along the tunnel, provided you keep your head down.

This was the worst part, keeping my head down and having black waves come sweeping up across the brain. Once I fell flat. But I didn't break the torch, and the pain of bruised hands helped to keep me steady. The air in the tunnel was quite fresh, except for its earthy smell; the slope of ground made you stagger and slide on sand, but you could brace yourself with one hand against the damp wall.

Then a strong salt breeze fanned over my face, gushing out of the dark. I could even hear the faint *slap-slap* of water. It must be close on one o'clock – high tide against the face of the cliff.

Ten steps more, and I was in the Pirates' Den.

The opening giving on the sea showed as a jagged bluish-white arch of moonlight. Beyond moved sullen black water, reflecting back the light of my torch. It was cold and perishing damp here. Roughly circular, with ribbed and hollowed walls moisture-plastered, this Pirates' Den might have been fifteen feet across by ten feet high. A rock formation on the wall, vaguely suggesting a skull and cross-bones, had given the place its name.

The light of my torch was growing dim. I played it round, and saw nothing.

Nothing.

The chuckle of the water echoed back hollowly from uneven walls; the skull and cross-bones formation, scratched with people's initials; the candle-grease on the uneven stone floor, where my footsteps rasped on sand: nothing else.

'But there's got to be something!' a voice cried out, and I heard it din in my ears from echoes. 'There's got to be something!'

I couldn't hold out much longer. Even I recognised that, from far away. The skull and cross-bones blurred; the light of the torch grew more dim. All I could find was the stump of a candle stuck in one ribbed niche of the walls, sheltered from the breeze which blew straight in.

I tried to light the candle, and got it burning on the fifth match. A blurring of eyesight caused its flames to appear several, and to move round each other in slow procession. The skull and cross-bones got more vivid, on the other hand, and became a real death's head.

'An automatic pistol,' the voice started repeating beside my head, 'ejects its cartridge-cases high and to the right. An automatic pistol ejects its cartridge-cases high and to the right.'

I put the torch in my pocket, shrieked aloud for the strength to hold on to consciousness five minutes more, and began to feel – like a blind beetle – along the walls. The ridges and pits and crevices seemed interminable.

This hundred-to-one chance didn't seem much. My fingers crept and poked and fumbled and blundered. When I did touch that tiny metal object, lodged away in a furrow of the rock where it had been flung from an exploding .32, it rolled away from me. I had to chase it, frantically fumbling, clear along the crevice before I got it.

Holding it enclosed in two hands, as you might hold a captured insect, I backed and stumbled away from the wall. I closed one eye, steadied the other in a swimming head, and looked at it.

It was the brass cartridge-case of a .32 bullet.

But that wasn't all. Some dim recollection of another surface brushed, another kind of feeling momentarily under my fingers, sent me back to the wall again. Presently I dragged out – they were as hard to pull as weeds – two objects which I had dreamed of finding but never expected to find. They had been pushed down deep into one crevice. They showed guilt. The cartridge-case was sagely in my waistcoat pocket. I stumbled away still further from the wall, holding one of these new finds in each hand.

Two bathing-suits.

To be exact, one was a pair of men's bathing-trunks, coloured dark blue, with a white belt and metal buckle. The other was a woman's bathing costume, light green, which half of Lyncombe could identify. Both were now grimy, dark-coloured, and still damp.

'We've got it, H.M.,' I said aloud. 'We've got the murdering devil now as sure as I'm alive.'

Behind me, from the shelter of the tunnel, somebody fired a shot.

I didn't, in that second, identify the explosion as a shot. But the *whing* of a bullet ricocheting from rock – a hideous wiry noise like the singing of a metallic whip or snapping piano-wire – can be recognised by anybody who has ever been under fire.

As the cavern blasted with echoes, a little white nick appeared in the face of the skull carved on the wall. Somebody fired again, and the flame of the candle went out.

I suppose I should have been grateful for that. But I don't recall thinking about anything much, or even feeling anything much. I held those two bathing-suits against my chest, hugging them as though they were my most cherished possessions. I took a couple of steps forward on the uneven floor, and fell.

It was dark here, except for the moonlight streaming through the sea-opening of the cave. The water, gurgling and slapping, black tinged with gleams of grey, reached up to two feet or less below the mouth of that opening.

When the whirlpool got me at last, I grabbed at consciousness with both hands. I tried to roll over, but the ribbed floor was damp and slippery. I concentrated fiercely as the dark world swung round. I just managed to turn over on my side, and get the electric torch out of my pocket. Though I was completely helpless – as helpless as a man drained of blood – I did have strength enough left to press the button of the torch.

Its beam, as dazzling to my eyes now as though it were a headlamp, swung round crazily before I got it focused on the entrance to the tunnel.

There was somebody standing there.

19

An old Morris chair, and the edge of a lace curtain with sunlight against it, were the first two things to emerge.

I failed to recognise the chair, or even my own bedroom overlooking the back garden, for a little while after I opened my eyes. I felt refreshed, completely rested, and at peace. The bed under me might have been made of swansdown. Then I saw the face of Sir Henry Merrivale looking down.

"Morning, Doctor,' was all he said. Casually.

While I propped myself up on one elbow, H.M. dragged out a chair and sat down, wincing, by the side of the bed. He carried a cane on which he rested his folded hands, and he sniffed.

'You've had a good long sleep,' he went on, 'and it's done you a lot of good. Belle Sullivan did you a good turn, more of a good turn than she knew, when she shoved that Seconal into your Ovaltine.'

This was when recollection smote me fully.

'Oi! Now don't try to get up!' H.M. said warningly. 'Just sit back comfortably until they bring you some food.'

'How did I get here?'

'*I* brought you here, son.'

'It's tomorrow morning, isn't it? The inquest! What time is the inquest?'

'Oh, son!' said H.M. dismally. 'The inquest has been over hours ago.'

The windows were open, open and peaceful. I could hear hens clucking in the fowl-run next door. I leaned on one elbow, wondering if ever the Good Lord would send me a bit of luck and not put the last drop of bitterness into everything I did.

'Our friend Craft,' pursued H.M., 'says it's a good thing you weren't in shape to testify after all. You'd have been in an awful mess if you had. You know that as well as I do.'

'*What was the verdict of the inquest?*'

'Double suicide while the balance of their minds was disturbed.'

I sat up in bed, propping pillows behind me.

'Sir Henry, where are the clothes I was wearing last night?'

He moved his big head without taking his eyes from me.

'Hangin' up across that chair there. Where?'

'If you'd like to look in the lower right-hand waistcoat pocket, you'll find out why.'

'There's nothing in any of the pockets, Doctor,' answered H.M. 'We looked.'

After a light tap at the door, Molly Grange put her head in. She wore a house apron, and looked radiant. Behind her appeared the anxious face of Belle Sullivan.

'Is the doctor,' Molly asked, 'ready for breakfast?'

'Uh-huh,' said H.M. 'Better bring it up to him.'

Molly surveyed me for a moment in silence, her hands on her hips.

'You've given us scares before,' she said at last, 'but I don't think you've ever given us such a scare as last night. All the same, I think I'll leave preaching about it until later.'

And she went out, firmly closing the door. I was now in a state so helpless, so beaten and outfaced at every turn, that I could look at the thing calmly.

'Well, Craft's had his way,' I said. 'He's got his verdict and he doesn't have to exert himself any longer, whatever the rest of us do. And that's a pity. Because *I* know the true explanation of the whole thing, and it's not Craft's explanation.'

H.M. took out a cigar and turned it over in his fingers.

'You're quite sure you know how it was done, son?'

'At one o'clock last night I could have proved it. Now . . .'

'At the end of most cases,' growled H.M., lighting a match by whisking it across the seat of his trousers, and applying it to the objectionable cigar, 'it's the old man who sits down and explains to the fatheads where they get off. Let's reverse the process this time.'

'Reverse the process?'

'*You*,' said H.M., 'tell *me*. Do you also know who the murderer is?'

'Yes.'

'Well . . . now. I might have a stab at it myself, Doctor, if a bloke like Masters got mad and challenged me. But we might compare notes. Is it anybody who's been suspected so far?'

The image of a certain face rose up in front of me.

'It's certainly nobody I should have suspected at first glance,' I told him. 'But it's a murdering devil just the same; and I can't understand how we were all gulled by somebody we knew and liked.'

Again there was a tap at the door. This time it was Paul Ferrars who came in.

'Glad to see you looking healthy again, Dr Luke,' he said. It was the first time I had ever seen him wearing a necktie. 'Molly said you were awake. If you feel up to it, we all want to know what in blazes happened to you.'

H.M. blinked round.

'Sit down, son,' he invited Ferrars in a wooden tone. 'Dr Croxley is just goin' to tell us who did the murders, and how they were done.'

For an instant Ferrars stood motionless, his hand at his necktie. His forehead wrinkled, and he directed a doubtful look at H.M. The latter only made a gesture with the cigar. Ferrars sat down in my Morris chair, dragging it round. The empty cup of Ovaltine was beside him, and my pipe. Ferrars, smiling and clean-shaven, kept his eyes fixed on my face while I talked.

'I was sitting here last night, mulling over the evidence. It was all out in front of me, as though I had a lot of exhibits in a court-room. But nothing seemed to fit together, until I remembered the cut telephone-wires and the petrol let out of the cars. Who did that, and why was it done?'

H.M. took the cigar out of his mouth.

'Well?' he prompted.

I shut my eyes to bring the picture vividly back again, and then I went on speaking.

'On Saturday evening, as the rain started to fall, Barry Sullivan made quite a point of it that he had to get some beach-chairs in out of the rain. He sent Rita and me ahead to the house, while he stayed behind to attend to it. But he didn't take in the beach chairs. I saw them still on the lawn when I went out to "Mon Repos" yesterday. On the other hand, Sullivan did do something; because he came back into the house wiping his hands on a handkerchief. That, I'm almost sure, was when he let the petrol out of the cars.'

Ferrars sat up.

'*Sullivan*,' he queried, 'did that?'

'Yes. Just as he and Rita cut the telephone-wires. And why did they do it? They did it so that either Alec Wainright or I would have to walk in to Lyncombe or further to get in touch with the police.

'Both Alec and I have to walk very slowly. I for obvious reasons, and Alec because he's got stiff joints. Neither of us could do those four miles in much under two hours. Then, on reaching Lyncombe, we should have to telephone the police further on. The police would have to get themselves together and come on out to "Mon Repos". For various reasons – including Alec's collapse and my delay – they didn't actually get there until one o'clock in the morning.'

H.M. continued to smoke woodenly.

Ferrars' forehead was wrinkled in perplexity.

'But I still make the old objection,' he protested. 'Stranding you two at that place wouldn't have prevented the police from getting there.'

'No,' I said, and raised my voice. *'But it would have prevented them from getting there until the tide came in.'*

This time I hadn't heard Molly Grange enter.

That is what feverish concentration does for you. I saw Molly, with something of a shock, standing at my elbow and holding a breakfast tray. Belle was behind her. I took the tray mechanically, though I never felt less like eating in my life, and set it in my lap.

Both girls, evidently, had overheard what was being said. They did not leave the bedroom. They stood there, very quietly, without speaking.

'At half past nine on Saturday night, when I went out to Lovers' Leap and found those two had apparently jumped over, the tide had turned. It was now coming in, and rising. I pointed that out to Alec, when he asked if the police wouldn't look at the foot of the cliff.

'Now, how far does the tide actually rise up the cliff at its full?' Here I looked at H.M. *'You* know, Sir Henry, because Craft mentioned it himself when we were driving out to the studio on Monday.' I looked at Belle. 'And *you* know, young lady, because Molly mentioned it in connection with a visit to the caves by water. The tide rises thirty feet up the cliff at high water.

'True, that cliff is seventy feet high. But at high water, or even anywhere near that time, such a drop isn't much to two expert swimmers and divers – as we know both Rita Wainright and Barry Sullivan were.'

The bedroom was absolutely silent.

Ferrars opened his mouth, and shut it again. H.M. continued to smoke. Belle was staring out of the window. Molly, who had sat down on the foot of the bed, dropped one small monosyllable into that immense quiet.

'But . . .'

'Let's return,' I said, 'to my own adventures at half past nine. I found that they'd apparently jumped over the cliff. I was very badly shocked and upset. Either Alec or I would have been badly shocked and upset: that's why we were chosen as witnesses.

'As I told Sir Henry, at the time I was too upset to notice anything much. All I saw were some tracks, on an overcast night with a hooded torch. And I'm no criminologist. But I did fleetingly observe something' – in fact, I have been careful to include it in this record – 'about the footprints. One set of them went ahead firmly. The other lagged behind, with slower or shorter steps.

'But yesterday, when we saw the steps by daylight, Sir Henry pointed out several things about them. The prints were indented at the toes, as though the people had been hurrying or half-running. But both sides of prints went in even steps, stride for stride, and *side by side*.

'That's what made my subconscious memory wake up.

'The whole scheme was planned round one effect. It was to make everybody think that the footprints I saw at half past nine were the same footprints to which the police gave expert examination at one o'clock.'

Again there was a silence.

Molly Grange did not even point out that my toast and coffee and bacon were growing cold. She sat at the foot of the bed, one hand on her breast and her eyes widening. There was almost a stealthy look about her.

'The puzzle-book!' she cried out.

And then, as startled heads were turned in her direction, she went on to explain.

'I mentioned to Dr Luke that we might get some help from a book of puzzles I've got at home. In that book, two people apparently jump over a cliff. One of them simply walks out to the edge in his own shoes; then puts on the other person's shoes and walks backwards. Rita and Barry Sullivan could have done that, because there's a patch of grass to change shoes at the edge of the cliff. But Sir Henry said it was no good . . .'

Her eyes strayed towards H.M., who continued to puff out clouds of smoke with no change of expression.

'Yes,' I said. 'That was how they made the first set of footprints. The set only intended to deceive *me*. They knew it wasn't good enough for the official police, of course.'

Ferrars, sitting bolt upright in his chair, moved the back of his hand slowly before his eyes as though he were testing his own sight. I could see his Adam's apple move convulsively in his neck.

'That may have been all very well for the first set,' he said, 'but how in all blue hell did they make the second set?'

This was the hardest part to forgive Rita. Yet let me repeat, over and over, how well she meant.

'The two of them waited, probably close at hand, until I came out to see the false prints. They'd made sure somebody would come by leaving the back door open. I was the logical candidate. Alec would be half stupefied with whisky by that time, and there had to be a sober witness whom the police would believe.

'I saw the prints, and believed in them. I went back to the house, feeling – pretty badly. Never mind that.'

'You still think you have something good to say about that woman?' Belle Sullivan almost screamed.

Molly looked a little shocked, and I silenced them.

'Then they walked in a leisurely way across the open ground to a cave called the Pirates' Den. You all know it. They had their suitcases in the Pirates' Den: everything ready. There they took off their ordinary clothes, put on bathing-suits, and returned.

That bungalow is four miles from any living human habitation; they wouldn't be seen if they kept away from the road. Finally, both were wearing shoes.

'They waited until the tide got high enough. The soil in that backyard is almost as soft as sand at any time; and on that particular night it was made still more moist with rain. So they simply walked out the path to Lovers' Leap again, this time pushing ahead of them ... do I have to elaborate? What did they push ahead of them?'

Molly Grange put her hands to her forehead.

'*A garden-roller,*' she breathed.

Then again the immensity of silence took us all. The sun was broadening and strengthening against the windows; it felt uncomfortably hot now, under the crazy-quilt spread.

'The same garden-roller,' Molly persisted, 'that Willie Johnson says Mr Wainright stole from him.'

I admitted it.

'Sir Henry there,' I said, 'noticed yesterday that the whole expanse of ground had been kept in smooth, very smooth, condition. That meant rolling, of course: though I was ass enough never to think of it.

'So those two went down the path. An iron garden-roller, weighing four hundred pounds or more, would easily flatten out and obliterate the first false sets of footprints. They simply walked behind it and left honest footprints about which there need be no hocus-pocus. We can see now why the toes of the prints were indented – they were not running, but pushing. We can see why the length of step was exactly the same in both people – it had to be.

'No *track* of the roller would be left, because the path was outlined by lines of pebbles. The roller was four feet wide. Now I remember it: Johnson told us so when we met him full of beer, on the Baker's Bridge road Monday; only he said "long" instead of "wide". The path was four feet wide, as we know. All they had to do was keep the roller inside the pebbles, so it wouldn't run over any of them and make them sink into the earth.'

'But could they *see* to do that?' demanded Ferrars, whose throat was working. 'After dark?'

'Easily. The sky had cleared then, as I told Molly on Monday. And the pebbles, if you recall, were painted dead white – which is the colour we use to guide us during the deepest blackout. Craft himself joyfully pointed out how they could be seen in the dark.'

Belle, who was still staring out of the window, had lighted a cigarette. The sun must have blinded her. She spoke viciously.

'I wonder who thought of that stunt?' Belle said. 'Barry or the floosie?'

Molly made a sharp gesture, disregarding this.

'And then?' she prompted.

Now I came to the ugly part.

'The mechanics, my dear, were simple. When they got to the edge at Lovers' Leap, they just pushed the roller over. Craft himself admitted he hasn't looked at the foot of that cliff.

'They dived or jumped over, whichever suited them best, into very deep water. All they had to do was swim along the line of the cliffs until they reached the cliff-face hole leading to the Pirates' Den. The water comes almost to its edge at high tide. If they did it earlier, they could have left a rope hanging over.

'And if they weren't certain of finding the place, that would be easy too. They could have left a lighted candle – I found one there myself, last night – in a niche where it would be shielded from draughts, would make the water gleam, and yet wouldn't throw much light out at sea.

'They climbed into the Pirates' Den, took off their bathing-suits, and got dressed again. It was simple; it worked like a charm; nobody was ever likely to suspect. In a few more minutes they'd be on their way, with suitcases, to the old studio and Sullivan's motor car. There was only one thing they hadn't taken into their calculations. I mean the murderer.'

It was a situation at once normal – a bright Wednesday with the chickens clucking in the fowl-run – and yet at the same time grotesquely abnormal. Three faces – Molly's, Belle's, and Ferrars' – were turned towards me. I started to take a sip of lukewarm coffee, but my hand shook and I had to put the cup down.

I was thinking of that cave, the Pirates' Den, on Saturday night. The dim candle burning in the niche. Sullivan and Rita getting dressed, guiltily scurrying, and Rita crying because she was leaving her home. And then someone who crept down the tunnel from the land-side, with white and distorted face, to fire point-blank against their bodies before they could lift a hand.

'Look,' Belle said rather hoarsely.

Stubbing out her cigarette in a soap-dish on the wash-stand, she coughed out a gust of smoke and slipped round the edge of the bed.

Afterwards – I was thinking blankly – it would have been easy. Simply roll the dead bodies out into the sea, and drop the suitcases after them. They received so few injuries from the fall, as the post-mortem doctor had pointed out, not because they were dead when they fell from a height, but because they never had fallen from a height at all. It was the current, banging those limp corpses against rocks, which had battered them half unrecognisable.

I put my hands up over my eyes.

'Are you saying,' continued Belle, 'that you know who knocked off Barry and that floosie?'

'I rather think so.'

You could hear Molly Grange's breath whistle; she could hardly seem to breathe. She was now half standing, with one knee on the bed.

'Not – somebody we know?' Molly asked.

'Who else could it be, my dear?'

'Not somebody from – *here*?'

A throbbing in my throat wouldn't stay quiet.

'It depends on what you mean by "here", Molly.'

'Well?' demanded Ferrars. 'This strikes fairly close to home. We're listening. Who did kill them, then?'

I took my hands away from my eyes.

'Forgive me, Mr Ferrars,' I said, 'but I think *you* did.'

Pause.

I hated the man and I couldn't help hating him. Acting may be an admirable thing in its way, but we have had too much of it in this business.

To judge by his look, you would have imagined him to be a man almost startled out of his wits. Ferrars very slowly got up out of my Morris chair. One lock of fair hair fell across his forehead, after the fashion of the Führer.

'Me?' he yelped, and made an elaborate pantomime of pointing at his own chest. '*Me?*' Then his breath came out in a great gust. 'In Satan's name, why?'

As for myself, I wasn't in any too good shape either. I upset the coffee-cup, and Belle had to come and take the tray away.

'Why?' Ferrars kept shouting.

'You were friendly enough with Rita,' I said, 'to paint her picture with an expression on her face which nobody has ever noticed there except perhaps Sullivan. Do you understand what I mean?'

Ferrars swallowed. His glare flashed towards Molly, who stood as though transfixed.

'I understand what you mean, yes. I – I painted her as I saw her. Come-hither and – and that kind of thing. But that doesn't necessarily mean anything.'

'In addition to being no anchorite, Mr Ferrars, you live on Exmoor and you would know very well where to sink a car. Then there's your very gentle treatment of Mrs Sullivan, when she fainted just after she jumped out of that same car in the quicksand on Sunday. You were acquainted with Mrs Sullivan and you're fond of her. But there's another thing too.'

'Lord of high hell,' cried Ferrars, and passed his hand across his forehead, 'but this is a fine way to go on before the one girl I actually do . . .'

'When we were bringing Mrs Sullivan out of the old studio late Monday afternoon, you saw her and you said, "Belle Renfrew!" But that's not all you did. You whacked your hand against the side of the car.'

'Well? What if I did?'

'Mrs Sullivan had just been telling us how the murderer, the man in anguish, the man who drove her to the quicksand the night before, had walked up and down that studio striking his hand against the Packard car. I'm suggesting, Mr Ferrars, this was what made her – when she saw you – turn round and run blindly back towards the studio. Even if she did not, and does not, consciously recognise you as the same man.'

Belle's eyes moved slowly round.

Ferrars lifted his hand as though to stroke something again; but he only stared at it, and dropped it at his side.

'Whatever else you do,' he begged, 'don't go psychoanalytic on me. I can't stand it. This is too serious. Have you got any *proof* of all this tommy-rot?'

'Unfortunately, no. You saw to that.'

'I saw to it? How?'

'If I had been allowed to keep a spent cartridge-case and two bathing-suits, which I found in the Pirates' Den last night, I might have shown Superintendent Craft a good deal. What can I show him now? I suppose I ought to be grateful to you for not shooting me; but gratitude isn't exactly the emotion I feel towards the man who killed Rita Wainright. It *was* you with the gun, wasn't it?'

Ferrars took a step forward.

'Half a second,' he said sharply. 'You say last night. At what time last night?'

'At just one o'clock in the morning, to be exact. You were absent from home in your car, if you remember, at half past twelve.'

Molly, still half standing with one knee on the bed, now got to her feet. Well repressed anger, incredulity, perplexity, and also perhaps jealousy had all been present in her expression to some degree; she showed, in a few seconds, more emotion than I had ever observed in her before. I told them the whole story, then.

'But Paul couldn't have been anywhere near the Pirates' Den at one o'clock this morning!' Molly cried. 'He was . . .'

'Just a minute, son,' interposed a quiet voice.

If this can be credited, we had entirely forgotten Sir Henry Merrivale. Throughout the whole turmoil he had said not a word. He was sitting only a few feet from my bed, his big hands folded over the head of his cane. The cigar had burnt down to within a quarter of an inch of his mouth. He squinted down at it to see whether it was still lighted; finding it was not, he took it out of his mouth and dropped it into the ash-tray.

Then he sniffed, and got up.

'Y'know, Doctor,' he remarked, 'I got to congratulate you.'

'Thanks.'

'That's a real good reconstruction,' argued H.M., 'and burn me if it's not! It's neat, it's simple, it's well thought out. The two sets of footprints, the roller, the miracle that wasn't a miracle. I like it myself. It's a pity, in a way –' he ruffled his hands across his big bald head, and peered down over his spectacles – 'it's a pity there ain't a word of truth in it.'

Ferrars did not sit down into his chair; he dropped down into it.

Since I was sitting down myself, nothing of this sort could have happened to me in bed. But I now know what it feels like when your ordered universe flies apart even more than under the shock of war.

'Y'see,' he went on with an air of apology, 'I thought of that myself. Last night I had a lot of fellers in gum-boots explorin' the foot of the cliff at low tide. And there wasn't any garden-roller there.'

'But it's got to be there! Maybe it was . . .'

'Pinched? By one man? Oh, my son! Four hundred pounds of iron, among jagged rocks with the water pourin' in?'

I tried to hold hard to reason.

H.M. rubbed the side of his nose, glowering at Ferrars.

'And one other thing, Doctor. Be awful careful how you tell this story, especially since you've got that lad there mixed up in it. For last night, anyway, he's got an alibi as cast-iron as the garden-roller.'

Belle looked around wildly.

'Are we all going nuts?' she inquired. 'I could have sworn the doctor had it bang on the nose. It sounded right, every word of it. It was tied up so you couldn't have doubted it if you wanted to. If that didn't happen, what in the name of the sweet Christ did happen?'

H.M. regarded her very steadily for a long time. Then his face smoothed itself out again to blankness. He sounded troubled and tired and old.

'I dunno, my wench,' he said. 'It appears we've got to start again, and do a whole lot of sittin' and thinkin'.'

Here he rubbed his nose again.

'But I expect,' he added, 'they've got the old man licked at last. In London, as maybe you've heard, they say I'm no good any longer. I'm outmoded and an old fossil and I don't know how things ought to be run. And I expect they're right. Anyway, goo'bye. I'm goin' across to the Coach and Horses and sink myself in a pint of beer.'

'But see here!' I shouted after him. 'How did you know I was out at that cave, if you say you found me?'

He hesitated in the doorway, but he did not return and he did not reply. Leaning on his cane, he lumbered out into the hall. Mrs Harping later said he passed her with a scowl so ferocious and evil that she dropped her duster and nearly screamed. All I can say is that I heard him going slowly, bumpingly – and, I thought, rather blindly – down the stairs to the front door.

Postscript and Epilogue
by
Paul Ferrars, RA

Here ends the manuscript prepared by Dr Luke Croxley. It is not finished as its author intended it to be finished, but it can stand as a separate entity.

Dr Croxley met his death during the night of the first great air-raid on Bristol: November 25th, 1940. He died in circumstances characteristic of him. He died performing an emergency operation in a blazing building, at utter disregard of his own life, after toiling for seven hours in the midst of that inferno from the foot of Castle Street to the top of Wine Street.

The irony of this story I do not mean to discuss. But I must mention it. This manuscript was written to prove – as he contended to the end – that Rita Wainright and Barry Sullivan did not commit suicide, but were murdered.

Therefore it is fortunate he never learned that the murderer of those two, the murderer he had been pursuing with such patient determination, was his own son Tom.

20

In my studio at Ridd Farm, on Exmoor, this affair may be said to have ended on a very cold and foggy night towards the beginning of February, 1941.

Molly and I – Molly has been Mrs Ferrars since July – had built an immense fire in the cobblestone fireplace, which in itself is big enough to drive a small car through. The burning logs threw red-and-yellow light up across brown rafters and a glass roof obscured by blackout curtains.

Molly was sitting cross-legged on the bright Navajo rug in front of the fire. I sat on the opposite side, smoking the Tried Mixture in the best domestic tradition. And on a cushioned settee facing the blaze was H.M., the old maestro himself, who had come down from London for the weekend to tell us the truth.

And the shock of it was still lingering.

'Tom!' cried Molly. 'Tom! Tom! Tom!'

'Then,' I said, 'Dr Luke was right in his reconstruction after all? That's exactly *how* the murders were committed Only . . .'

H.M. had Dr Luke's manuscript in his lap. He held it out and riffled the pages, in that fine painstaking handwriting, just as you have finished reading them in print.

'Y'see,' H.M. went on, putting down the manuscript on the settee, 'it's all here. The doctor himself says, in all innocence, that you can be too close to a man to see him. If that was true when he talked about Alec Wainright, it was a whole lot truer when he talked about his own son.

'The interestin' thing about this is how he writes about his son. Study it carefully. In his manuscript, Tom is all over the place. We hear what he said. We hear what he did. We can form a pretty good idea for ourselves of what his nature must have been. But it wasn't the old doctor's idea at all.

'Dr Luke, y'see, never even thought of Tom as a character in the story. Tom was just there, a well-loved piece of household furniture, only mentioned at all because every detail has to go in. He never *watches* Tom. He never understands Tom, or even thinks it's necessary to understand him.

'In the first glimpse we get of Tom, he's snappin' shut his medicine-case and giving a violent lecture about fools who are indiscreet enough to get themselves talked about over a love affair. In the last glimpse we get of him, he's sitting "hollowed-eyed" under the dome of lights in the dining-room, emotionally exhausted and at the end of his string. And the old doctor attributes it to overwork, and chivvies him a bit about it.

'He never once dreamed he was livin' in the same house with a robust, strongly repressed man who'd fallen so violently for Rita Wainright that he went stark mad and killed both Rita and her boyfriend when he learned they were goin' to run away. And, if you watch, you can see the whole thing move towards inevitable tragedy.'

H.M. tapped the manuscript.

'But d'ye know,' he added apologetically, 'it's awful easy to understand. I've got an idea, if you or I were going to write an account that included some member of our own family, we'd write in just exactly the same way that the old doctor did.'

Though the burning logs were exploding and snapping out sparks, nevertheless Molly shivered.

'What on earth,' she asked, 'ever made you think of Tom?'

'Oh, my wench! Couldn't you see for yourself, as early as the Tuesday afternoon, that Tom Croxley was quite literally the only one in the whole blinking case who could possibly be guilty? That was the end and the final crownin' point.' H.M. blinked at me. '*You* saw it, son?'

'No, I'm hanged if I did!'

'But I mean,' persisted Molly, 'whatever made you think of him in the first place?'

'Well, my wench,' said H.M., and looked at her over his spectacles, 'I think you did.'

'I did?'

'Uh-huh. On Monday, after Craft and Dr Luke and I had come from seein' you and your old man, we were driving out on the main road. Craft asked me what I thought of you. I said I thought you were fine . . .'

'Thank you, sir.'

'But that I generally distrusted these wenches who say they've got no interest in the opposite sex. It generally means they've got a whole lot of interest tucked away somewhere.'

'Drat you! *Damn* you!'

Molly turned as red as certain sections of the Navajo rug. Despite the reputation for sneering which Dr Luke's manuscript has given me – it worries me even yet – I did permit myself a modest grin. But Molly came over to sit in my lap nevertheless, and I kissed her in public: which, in Mrs Ferrars, is practically a sign of wantonness.

'You cut out the canoodlin'!' howled H.M., blasting back a gush of smoke from the fireplace. 'It was canoodlin' that got that poor devil into all his trouble.'

'I'm sorry,' said Molly. 'Go on.'

'Well! I thought of the young feller who'd attended to my toe.

Tom Croxley. There was somebody, on the other side of the fence, who before me and you too was always goin' on about how he had no use for women. He professed to be a real Trappist monk, he did. Women were predatory. Women were this. Women were that. He was one of nature's bachelors, and don't you ruddy well forget it. I wondered if he mightn't be protesting too much.

'After all he was Rita Wainright's doctor. *Somebody* had to write that passport recommendation for her, if Dr Luke didn't. Why, for instance, was Rita so infernally upset when she came chargin' in on that twenty-second of May to see Dr Luke – claimin' she wanted sleeping-tablets, but really to wangle a passport recommendation? Why? He asked her himself why she didn't go to Tom. And she hadn't any adequate answer to it. Was it because, if she couldn't face Luke with the request, she'd have to go to Tom? And if so . . .

'Oh, my eye!

'A little bit of the picture started to emerge. Y'see, I didn't at all like one part of Dr Luke's conversation with Alec Wainright on the very night of the two murders.

'In Dr Luke's office, Rita swore to him she'd never been unfaithful to her husband. She seemed almost too dewy and sweet about it. Dr Luke, in turn, told this to Alec Wainright. And Alec *laughed*. "But then," Alec said, "I can see why she wouldn't tell." It meant nothing at all to the bewildered doctor. But to my nasty suspicious mind it meant a good deal. What about Tom and Rita as lovers?

'Next, on Tuesday morning, we fell slap over the explanation to a point that had bothered me like blazes since the beginning.'

Here H.M. paused abruptly.

A vague and vacant expression came over his face, as though he were turning over something in his mind. He seemed to be mumbling to himself. With a muttered word which sounded like apology, he reached into his inside pocket and took out an envelope. On this he began to write with the stub of a pencil.

His voice now sounded hollow and ghostly, as though he were tasting the words.

'Rothbury. Rowfant,' he said. He cocked his head on one side, the better to study what he had written. 'H'mf. Roxburgh? Royston? Rugeley? Palmer the poisoner lived at Rugeley. Uh-huh.'

We stared at him.

Molly was too polite to comment, and I was too startled. H.M. thoughtfully returned the envelope to his pocket, and sniffed.

'The point that bothered me from the beginning,' he argued, with a ferocious scowl, 'was this. This murderer – whoever he was, and however he did it – has got a practically perfect crime. First, it's five to one the bodies will be washed out to sea and never found. Second, even if they are found, the status quo won't be much different if nobody ever comes across the gun that did it.

'Then why, why, WHY did the silly dummy go and chuck down the .32 automatic in a public road? It gave me burnin' pains in the brain. It just wasn't sensible, however you looked at it. The only reasonable explanation seemed to be that he didn't mean to chuck it down and couldn't help chuckin' it down: in other words, he lost it.

'On Tuesday morning, Craft and I went to see Belle Sullivan at Dr Luke's house, when the little gal had just spent her first night there. We wanted to ask her about photographs of Barry Sullivan. But, just incidentally and in passin', we learned something that made my hair curl. Tom Croxley had a hole in the lining of his coat-pocket. The little gal wanted to mend it for him.'

Molly sat up so abruptly that, perched across my lap, she nearly burned her cheek against the bowl of my pipe.

'It's in the manuscript,' said H.M. 'The old boy chronicles it in innocence and faithfulness, when those two were talkin' the night before.

'But it made me gibber a little. Here was another bit of evidence fittin' in about the poor, blind, crazy bloke who committed those murders and cried like a baby beside his victim's motor car. Next, only a little later, came the point that put the tin hat on it.

'My whole case – my whole ruddy case – was based on the assumption that Rita and Barry were goin' to do a bunk to America, taking Alec Wainright's diamonds with them. It was made of diamonds. It was built for diamonds. Then we went up to the bedroom and opened that ivory jewel-box. And there were the blinking diamonds, as large as life and twice as shiny. For a second, I admit, it had the old man floored completely.'

'I still don't understand about those diamonds,' said your correspondent. 'They were what turned the scale at the inquest. People hereabouts still firmly believe it was a suicide pact. If the diamonds were there . . .'

'Oh, my son!' said H.M. 'Don't you see that the diamonds were in the jewel-box because somebody returned 'em?'

Here he bent forward.

'Looky here. What about Alec Wainright himself? Hasn't *he* had anything to say about it?'

Molly looked at the floor. 'Professor Wainright's moved away from here. He never has said anything at all. Dr Luke was his only friend anyway. He – I think he got over the tragedy; but he can't get over the war.'

'On that thrice-celebrated Saturday night, just after Dr Luke discovered the footprints, Alec hurried upstairs to see whether Rita's clothes and the diamonds were there. You got that?' H.M.'s forehead wrinkled hideously. 'He found the clothes, but he didn't find the diamonds when he opened the box. So he came downstairs with the little key. Now follows the curious and very significant adventure of that key.

'When Wainright collapsed, Dr Luke absent-mindedly stuck the key in his own pocket and walked away with it. When he remembered it next morning, you remember what he did. He gave it to . . .'

'To Tom,' supplied Molly. 'Dr Luke told me so himself.'

'To Tom, that's right. And asked Tom to take it back to Alec. Which Tom did, because we found the key in Alec's hand. And that's not the most fetchin' and rummy part of the business either.

'What was the situation at "Mon Repos"? Two nurses, a day nurse and a night nurse, were with Alec Wainright every second of the time beginnin' late Saturday night. Tom Croxley didn't take the key back until Sunday morning, when the nurses were on duty.

'If somebody – the murderer – returned those diamonds to the box, it was done between Sunday morning and late Tuesday afternoon. Who could 'a' done it? Here we come up against the very revealing if at first upsetting fact of the nurses' testimony. The nurses say that *nobody, nobody at all*, has set foot in that sick-room day or night. Burn me, haven't Craft and I had good reason to know it? They wouldn't even let the police in.

'But when the nurses say "nobody", of course they wouldn't include the doctor in attendance. For, as we know from Dr Luke, Tom Croxley had been goin' out to see Alec twice a day. If nobody but the doctor had been there, it must have been the doctor who returned the diamonds.

'Ain't that fairly simple?

'And nothing easier. What would be the only occasion when a nurse would dare leave her patient for any time at all, when he's in a condition like that? It would be when the doctor ordered her to go out of the room for something, leavin' *him* on guard.

'Tom Croxley knew Alec Wainright was broke, with very little between him and starvation. Why? Because Dr Luke told him all about it – see manuscript – after that conversation Dr Luke had with Alec on Saturday morning, when the party for the night was arranged.

'Tom liked Alec. He also felt guilty as blazes. He wasn't any leerin' monster: he was a violent-tempered feller of thirty-five who'd gone completely scatty on the subject of Rita Wainright. He didn't give a curse about money – Superintendent Craft can tell you that – any more than his father did. He certainly had no use for the five or six thousand pounds' worth of diamonds he snaffled in the luggage of those two when he murdered 'em in the Pirates' Den.

'And it was no good chuckin' 'em into the sea with the rest of the luggage, when the husband needed 'em. So he returns 'em. They weren't taken away in those blue-velvet cases, unless I miss my guess: they were taken loose when Rita removed 'em. All Tom had to do was carry 'em back in his pocket, send the nurse out of the room, open the ivory box with the key that was there, and replace 'em in their separate cases. Finish.

'But you can see now why I said Tom Croxley was the only one in the case who could 'a' been guilty. Because he was the only one, by the evidence, who could have returned the diamonds. Any objection?'

We hadn't.

Molly got up again and moved to the other side of the fireplace, where she sat down cross-legged. The fire was flaring higher, now, a streaming and crackling pillar which turned Molly's face pink, so that she had to shield her eyes, and illuminated every corner of the old stone studio.

H.M. spoke vacantly.

'St Ives, Saltash,' he murmured. 'Scarborough. Scunthorpe. Sedgemoor. Southend. Sutton Coldfield . . . the Ashford gal was drowned there . . .'

But here I had to protest at this gibberish, whatever it meant.

'Listen, maestro,' I began. He gave me no chance to continue.

'You'll now be able,' he said, with an evil look which silenced both of us, 'to fill in the details for yourselves. Rita's mysterious boyfriend, who used to sneak out to the studio with her on Baker's Bridge road, was Tom Croxley.

'He was the feller that you' – H.M. looked at Molly – 'almost saw that afternoon in April, when Rita came tearin' away from the studio in her car. How do you describe her after that incident?' He picked up the manuscript and leafed through it. 'Uh-huh. "She looked all tousled and mad, with a martyred expression as though she hadn't been enjoying herself at all."

'And of course she hadn't. Tom wasn't any beauty – Belle Sullivan called him an ugly son of a so-and-so – but I expect he suited her well enough until the grand passion came along. Barry Sullivan.

'Then she did feel sick and martyred; and he stood by in agony, watching her grow more and more infatuated with Sullivan, while there wasn't anything he could do about it. As a climax to the whole thing at the end of May, while he was tearin' his heart out, Rita came to Tom and threw herself on his mercy and said she wanted a passport recommendation to go away with Sullivan.

'That tore it.

'It wouldn't have been hard for him to get the whole story out of her. Don't you see that a flighty, romantic, star-gazin' female like Rita Wainright would be very easy to gull in one particular way? If Tom said to her something like this: "Yes, little gal, I renounce you to a better man and God bless you," that would be exactly the sort of thing Rita would *expect* him to say.'

Molly compressed her lips.

'Yes,' Molly said shortly.

'It was the way her husband always treated her,' H.M. continued. 'The way he treated her to the end. She'd have tears of gratitude in her eyes, and she'd kiss Tom in a chaste way and say how noble he was. But he wasn't noble. Oh, my eye, no. He was only human, and just a little crazy.

'He learned all about their scheme with the garden-roller,

just when and where and at what time they were goin' to do it. Why not? He was their self-sacrificing friend. And it would arouse no suspicion in the district if Dr Tom happened to be out late at night: a country G.P. is the one person who usually is.

'At some time on Saturday night – we can't say just when, but it must have been before one in the morning – he drove out to the Baker's Bridge road and parked his car there. He walked across to the tunnel entrance to the Pirates' Den, and down the tunnel holdin' a stolen gun behind his back. He was comin' to say goodbye.

'He found those two just finished dressin' after their swim. They'd had no reason to be suspicious. They were all eager and breathless for a new life. He had a glove on against the back-fire of the gun. Maybe he was a bit white round the gills, but in candlelight they wouldn't notice that. He walked straight up to Rita and shot her through the heart at body-range. Sullivan, who must have been too paralysed to move, felt the gun jab into his own chest too.'

H.M. paused.

In imagination, I heard the shots echo.

'Tom rolled the bodies out into the sea. The suitcases went after them, all contents except diamonds and passports. Unmarked clothes didn't matter, but passports were too dangerous. He took those with him. But he forgot the bathing-suits, which they had stuffed out of sight in a crevice of the walls; and he couldn't find one of the spent cartridge-cases. Then he put the gun in his pocket and went back to his car.'

I intervened here.

'But why take the gun with him? Why not drop it after them?'

H.M. eyed me over his spectacles.

'Oh, my son! They were supposed to have shot themselves – *if* the bodies were ever found – on the edge of Lovers' Leap. Hey?'

'That's right.'

'But a steel automatic pistol has a nasty habit of not floatin'. If he chucked it in at all, he had to chuck it in somewhere near Lovers' Leap and not half a mile away. That's where he had a very bad bit of luck, a crusher, the thing that did for him. That same night, probably while he was gettin' into his car, the gun slipped through his pocket. And he was so shaky and upset he never noticed it.'

H.M. took out a cigar, turning it over in his fingers.

'Well . . . now. The next thing he had to do was get rid of Sullivan's own car. But he didn't dare to do it that night, because shortly the roads would be hummin' with coppers and he couldn't stay away from home *too* long.

'He never knew Rita and Sullivan had left those studio doors standin' wide open, with the car exposed to the public eyes. Then, the next afternoon, Belle Sullivan came stormin' past and stopped. When Tom came out that night to get the car, by this time so full of remorse he ruddy near did lose his reason, we had the quicksand business.

'Undoubtedly, he'd already left his own car near the patch of quicksand he intended to use, and walked back for the other one. He must 'a' been petrified when he saw a little gal pop up screamin' out of the dickey-seat.

'You'd all been spoutin', by the way, about who knew Exmoor and where to dispose of a car. Craft was down on Dr Luke; and Dr Luke, young feller, was down on you. It didn't seem to occur to anybody that, if the father had to be acquainted with Exmoor in the course of his work, so had the son.

'Well, Belle Sullivan jumped and fainted. Tom didn't know what to do. His conscience was all over him like delirium tremens. He wasn't goin' to risk more trouble. He'd done everything in darkness, and she couldn't have recognised him if she'd seen him again.

'But what could he do with her? He couldn't claim to "find" her there without sayin' how he came to be there himself, away off the road, and perhaps causin' considerable curiosity as to why he was there at all. So he bundled her into his own car. He took her back to the studio. He put her into the upper room – he had a key to that, from previous experience – where she'd at least have a bed to lie on. He locked her in, fully expectin' she'd have the sense to push the key through and fish it under the sill when she woke up.

'She didn't. She lost *her* head, too.

'It must have given him still another jolt when he found the same little gal appearin' next day as a guest in his own home.

'Dr Luke's got an interestingly blind account of it. "Tom," he says, "liked her. He was even more furiously didactic and insufferable than usual." Didactic? Insufferable? He was scared. Listen to the tone of his voice! See how he shies back, this chap who'll tell you all the details of a post-mortem while eatin' bread and butter, yet feels his throat go dry when Belle starts talking about the injuries to Rita Wainright.

'All that remained for Tom, now, was another visit to the Pirates' Den to make sure of what had happened to that missing cartridge-case. By this time (let me repeat) he'd gone through the phase of mere remorse and was now good and scared for his own skin.

'One: they'd found the bodies. Two: they'd found the gun. Three: the coppers suspected hocus-pocus. If there happened to be any other little thing he'd left behind in that cave, he might be for it.

'But he couldn't go on Monday night. Because why? Because they had a guest – Belle Sullivan – who kept 'em up late. Even when she'd been put to sleep with dope, the old man himself was restless and stayed awake most of the night. Tom couldn't go. So it had to be Tuesday night, the night before the inquest.

'Where Tom got a second gun I can't tell you. I'd hazard a flyin' guess he got several to choose from for his great effort; and, as Molly's father said, they're floatin' about as common as gooseberries nowadays. When he went to the Pirates' Den that night, he had blood in his eye and he meant business.'

Molly pulled her skirt over her knees and cried out in protest.

'Surely,' she said, 'Tom Croxley wouldn't have shot his own father?'

'Ho ho,' said H.M., with a chuckle of such ghoulish mirth that little children would have fled from him. 'But he had no idea on this good green earth it *was* his own father.

'If the parent misunderstood the son, just see how the son misunderstood the father. It happens in the best families, they say. To Dr Tom, Dr Luke was an old dodderer fit only to he gaspin' in the sun and get lectured to when he wouldn't eat his porridge.' H.M.'s face grew murderous. 'Of all the people Tom *didn't* expect to run into anywhere, especially in a cave at one o'clock in the morning, his old man led the list.

'What he saw at a distance, in dim candlelight, was the bent back of a man holdin' a bathing-suit in each hand. He'd guessed somebody was there, right enough. Because he'd seen a car parked in the road, even if he didn't get close enough to identify the number-plate.'

'And then?'

'Tom completely lost his head. He fired a couple of blind shots, not hitting anything. But the man keeled over just the same, against the moonlight streamin' in from the sea entrance.

'We will now,' H.M. added, with emphasis and dignity, 'return to *me*.'

For some time he had been twisting the cigar in his fingers. At this point he condescended to put it into his mouth, indicating that he wished it lighted. I then took a – perhaps fairly large – burning brand out of the fire, and extended it politely in the general direction of his face.

This may have been unwise, since it provoked an outburst in which he inquired whether I thought I was a goddamn lion-tamer, and intimated that I must be in the habit of lighting the kitchen fire with incendiary bombs. It was Molly who got him soothed down presently.

'When we found the diamonds back in their box on Tuesday afternoon,' he was persuaded to continue, 'that tore it. Tom Croxley was the feller we wanted. No doubt about it now.

'Up to then I hadn't been absolutely certain. And I still didn't see how Rita's and Sullivan's levitation trick had been worked. But when we went in early in the evening to pay Willie Johnson's fine in advance – after all, could we blame the poor fellow if the majesty of my appearance made him think I was Nero? – I heard about the garden-roller. That finished up everything.

'I'm not joking, son. I *was* scared.

'Here was the blinkin' awful cussedness of things in general, back on my neck again. Here was the father, as fine and honest an old boy in his way as I've ever come across. He was dead set on solving this problem. And the murderer, if he did solve it, would turn out to be the son he was so proud of that you can hear Dr Luke's chest-buttons burstin' every time he mentions Tom.

'I don't want you to think, curse you, that I was actin' from any motives of human sympathy. I've got no human sympathy. Grr!' said H.M., leaning forward and looking us both in the eye. 'But it did seem a good idea to bribe the crew of a fishing-boat to (a) get that roller to blazes away from the foot of the cliff; and (b) to keep their mouths shut afterwards. I expect I'll be payin' blackmail for the rest of my life.

'I hoped the doctor wouldn't tumble to it: to the mechanics of it, I mean. But he did. I knew that when he rang me up in the middle of the night.

'The worst of it was that you two were out canoodlin' in the car until three o'clock in the morning . . .'

Molly smiled placidly.

'Maestro,' I said, 'for many mortal months I had been trying to persuade that girl to give up her so-and-so father and her so-and-so principles. I wanted her to throw in her lot with a reckless

Bohemian like me, who stays up almost until midnight every night. And do you know what finally did the trick?'

'Bah,' said Molly.

'Belle Sullivan, and Belle Sullivan's philosophy. For the first time, that girl looked at her home and said what the hell? I hear Belle has a boyfriend nowadays, and I wish her very much luck. She did the trick.'

Again Molly smiled placidly.

'Nonsense,' she declared. 'I asked Dr Luke if it would be all right, and he said yes, so I went ahead. Father was dreadfully annoyed. But,' added Molly, 'what the hell? If it weren't for poor old Dr Luke . . .'

H.M. spoke quietly.

'I told you it was tragedy, my wench. It couldn't have been anything else. But it might have been a much worse tragedy if Tom Croxley had hit his father when he fired those blind shots into the cave.

'You'd left *me* stranded out here, curse you. I couldn't get in to head the doctor off when he started investigatin'. Naturally, I had a most excellent idea of where he was going. As I told you and Craft and the doctor, you'd been goin' on about caves ever since I'd been here. The Pirates' Den seemed to fit the bill.

'My wheelchair wasn't any good since you fellers tried to push me over the cliff in it and busted the motor. So I walked. Toe and all, I walked. When I got there . . .

'You see what had happened, don't you? Tom slipped out of the house before his father. Croxley Senior, speedin' like a maniac to get to the Pirates' Den before that drug overcame him, passed his son without recognisin' him any more than Tom saw the old man.

'When Tom fired those shots, that shape ahead of him, that "somebody", fell. Dr Luke managed to get out an electric torch. Its beam wobbled round, and up over his own face, before he flopped down again with the drug in him.

'And when I got there, a pretty long time afterwards, I found Tom sittin' at the outer mouth of the tunnel in just about a demented state. The moon was shining down on him and he had his head in his hands. Y'see, he thought he'd killed his father.'

H.M. took several puffs at his cigar, yet he did not appear to enjoy them. He cleared his throat.

'I went back into the cave with him. Dr Luke wasn't even scratched; he was only full of Seconal. Tom and I didn't talk much. I didn't *say* I knew, but he knew I knew. I told him to help me get his father back up to Dr Luke's car. Then to hare off for home himself, and sneak in, and never let on to anybody he'd been out of the house that night.'

'But Tom,' Molly suggested, 'took care to dispose of the spent cartridge-case and the two bathing-suits?'

H.M. sniffed.

'Well, no,' he admitted. '*I disposed* of 'em. I slung the bathing-suits into the sea – Devon morality must 'a' got an awful shock if they were washed up anywhere – and I found the cartridge-case in his waistcoat-pocket, so I kept it.

'I took him home, and you know the rest. He never got a real glimpse of the figure with the gun; he was too far gone. And he never could prove afterwards, thank God, that those two had been murdered.'

There was a long and uncomfortable silence, while we all thought round one subject without daring to approach it.

'Of course you heard . . .' Molly began.

'All about Dr Luke's death . . .' I said.

'In Bristol . . .'

'Uh-huh,' said H.M. He glowered at the floor, and seemed to be wriggling his toes inside his shoes. 'Y'know, I think I'm a little bit sorry.'

'He was only there for the day,' Molly said clearly. 'Visiting a friend of his. He didn't have to stay. He was under no obligation to stay.'

As for me, I couldn't look at either of them.

'Tom,' I said, 'went into the Army a week after his father died. Of course we never guessed . . .' I stopped. 'Tom's in Libya now.'

H.M. shook his head.

'No, he ain't, son. I saw the *Gazette*. That's why I came down here. Thomas L. Croxley has been awarded a posthumous V.C., and that's the very highest award for bravery they give.' After a pause he added: 'There was good stuff in that family, even if one of 'em was a murderer.'

Again a long silence.

'Paul,' Molly observed at length, 'goes next month.'

'Oh, ah? What branch?'

'Field-artillery, maestro. To the devil with this Camouflage stuff. And Molly, of course, with her typewriting training . . .'

'We're all going somewhere,' said Molly. 'Maybe we don't know where, or very much about it, but we're going. Where are *you* going, H.M.?'

H.M. threw his cigar into the fire. He sat back, twiddling his thumbs across his corporation, and turned down the corners of his mouth.

'Me?' he said drearily. 'Oh, I'm only goin' into the House of Lords.'

His voice was ruminative when he spoke again.

'Taunton, Ticklebury, Tweed,' he said. 'Tattersall, Throttlebottom, Twist.'

'Listen, maestro! If you're going into the House of Lords, many congratulations –'

'*Congratulations?*' roared H.M. 'The blighters have been tryin' to do it for years, to get me off the active list. And now the treacherous skunks have done it. They're goin' to stick me in the House of Lords in the next honours list.'

'But,' I said, 'just what is all this glorified train-calling you've been doing for half the evening?'

H.M. wagged his head.

'I got to think of a title,' he explained querulously. 'I got to tell 'em what title I want . . . *want! Phooey!* . . . so they can make out letters-patent. Do you like any of 'em?'

'Lord Ticklebury,' Molly repeated. 'No, I don't think I should like that.'

'Neither do I,' said H.M. 'I'm just tryin' to think of something that's not goin' to make me writhe. Gimme my bedroom-candle. I'm goin' to turn in.'

I handed it to him, lighting it in a less spectacular manner than with the flaming brand. The candlelight shone up on his face. He seemed to be held by some curious emotion we could not understand.

'But you wait!' he suddenly roared out. He pointed a malignant finger at me. 'I'm goin' to be some use to this ruddy country yet. Just you wait and see!'

Then he coughed, and peered at us suspiciously, and held the candle-flame away from his face. We could still hear him muttering names as he lumbered off down the hall to his room.